The
CROWDED
BED

Other titles published by transita

A Proper Family Christmas by Jane Gordon-Cumming
Coast to Coast by Jan Minshull
Dangerous Sports Euthanasia Society by Christine Coleman
Emotional Geology by Linda Gillard
Gang of Four by Liz Byrski
Neptune's Daughter by Beryl Kingston
Pond Lane and Paris by Susie Vereker
Slippery When Wet by Martin Goodman
The Jigsaw Maker by Adrienne Dines
The Scent of Water by Alison Hoblyn
The Sorrow of Sisters by Wendy K Harris
Toppling Miss April by Adrienne Dines
Tuesday Night at the Kasbah by Patricia Kitchin
Widow on the World by Pamela Fudge

transita

To find out more about transita, our books and our authors
visit **www.transita.co.uk**

The
CROWDED
BED

MARY CAVANAGH

transita

Published by Transita
Spring Hill House, Spring Hill Road, Begbroke,
Oxford OX5 1RX. United Kingdom.
Tel: (01865) 375794. Fax: (01865) 379162.
email: info@transita.co.uk
http://www.transita.co.uk

British Library Cataloguing in Publication Data
A catalogue record for this book is available from the British Library

ISBN 978 1 905175 31 4

Cover design by Mousemat Design Ltd.
Produced for Transita by Deer Park Productions, Tavistock
Typeset by PDQ Typesetting, Newcastle-under-Lyme
Printed and bound by Bookmarque, Croydon

ABOUT THE AUTHOR

Mary Cavanagh spent her childhood in the leafy climes of beautiful North Oxford. Amusing memories abound of eccentric academic neighbours and gentile snobs, most of whom were struggling to make ends meet on 1950's austerity. Being a pupil at St Barnabas Junior school in Jericho was a privilege and a delight; an experience she feels honoured to have shared with such friendly and unpretentious classmates. Milham Ford Girls Grammar was another story. Being lazy and academically challenged she was grateful to show a clean pair of heels. A hedonistic working life of sorts followed as a hairdresser, office clerk, graphic artist, barmaid, au pair, lab assistant and various other forgotten nightmares, none of which she took at all seriously. She married Bill, and had two sons, Alastair and Rory.

It was only as a mature lady of 35 that she pulled her act together and became a student at Westminster Teacher Training College. Whilst always being a voracious reader it was her English course that evoked the joy of creative writing. Wisely, or not, she chose not to teach and spent the next twenty years being completely fulfilled in medical management and administration.

The Crowded Bed is her first published novel, born out of her two fascinations. The strange and secret life that is lived within the mind, and the myriad of changes in social and moral behaviour over the last fifty years. Her favourite authors and influences are George Orwell, Daphne du Maurier, Ian McEwan and the Bennett boys, Alan and Arnold.

Although she's the proud grandmother of Ella Sophie and Daniel she refuses to give in to the march of time (poor sad old bat) and still wants to experience life as if she's twenty-five.

ACKNOWLEDGEMENTS

This must sound like an Oscar winner's speech, but I don't care. The raft of people who have supported me over my long struggling years of writing have to be thanked from the bottom of my heart.

Deborah Terry, my first critic and rock of encouragement when I was lashed by an endless barrage of rejection slips. Ruth Dowley for her valuable creative writing course at the OUDCE, and the class of '99. Christopher Gilmore who called me his *Avis Rara* and had faith in me, Peter Mole who pointed me in a very fortuitous direction, and Linora Lawrence (she knows why). Jane Gordon-Cumming, Edwin Osborn and Margaret Pelling, together with all the other supremely talented members of The Oxford Writers Group. Viv Hogg, Joan Godwin, Pauline Brown, and Audrey Low who read all my work-in-progress and cheered me on regardless. Lastly, but with a huge amount of grateful thanks, to Nikki Read and Giles Lewis from Transita for giving me the fantastic opportunity of publication. I love you all.

'Mary Cavanagh handles themes of murder, rape, anti-Semitism, adultery, alcoholism and physical abuse with unexpectedly deft wit to create a complex and satisfying drama.... entertaining, cleverly constructed and an impressive achievement. A dark and demanding read.'

Abingdon Park Readers group

Thus spake the Israelite:

'If you wrong us shall we not seek revenge?'

William Shakespeare,
The Merchant of Venice, III. i 63

'Very few of us are unfortunate enough to be in a position where our professional mistakes kill people'

Nick Hornby

'Very few of us are fortunate enough to be in a position where our profession equips us to kill people'

Dr Joe Fortune

THE PROLOGUE

GOOD EVENING, DEAR FRIEND. I'm extremely pleased to see you, but I'm sure you'll understand why I can't give you my full attention. Joe Fortune is just about to kill his father-in-law, and I've no intention of missing this long awaited event. I won't ask you to go away, but please stand back in the shadows with me and keep a low profile.

With careful and artistic precision he arranges the tools of his trade (or what you may prefer to term the murder kit) on a solid silver bon-bon dish borrowed from the grand piano. One syringe, one needle, one dose of the lethal elixir and a pair of disposable rubber gloves. He has no nerves, or panic, or negative thoughts. In fact he feels a strange sense of ceremony; something akin to a religious ritual that involves a great deal of bobbing about and mumbling, but in truth it must be a glorious surge of adrenaline. His victim lies prostrate, breathing deeply in an induced sleep, his baggy face looking no different to that of any other cosseted octogenarian. Joe has things to say of course, but he won't be justifying or explaining his actions. He really couldn't care less what either of us thinks. He's had to live with the reality and we haven't, so please resist the urge to make moral judgements. He's just about to draw up the fatal shot so if you're squeamish look away now. If not, enjoy the moment with him.

Moonlight as bright as the sun illuminates the room, allowing him to see clearly. The injection site must be carefully selected, as it could easily be spotted by an astute mortician. The anus is always the safest, but although he's seen ten thousand anuses (or is it anusii?) in the course of his career, the sight of Gordon's would have him gagging for a bucket. He's thus decided to reuse the venous puncture site created this morning by the district nurse. He slides up the sleeve of the pyjama jacket to reveal the soft underside of the left elbow and locates the small, red point of entry. With a steady hand he inserts the needle and swiftly plunges with his thumb; an action as familiar to him as clearing his throat. Briefly the victim begins to murmur and moan, but within seconds he's clinically dead.

Joe's lost count of how many deaths he's witnessed. Some silent and unconscious, some choking with terror, some indicating peace and relief. Each one a lottery of fate, and professionally administered by his exemplary code of conduct. This expedited one's his first (and certainly his last) but the final breath sounds exactly the same; a low exhalation as the life force slips away. But tonight it's a thrilling departure. He smiles with relief and self-congratulations. Goodbye and good riddance to Gordon Morton Moore. A fitting end to a bastard of the first order, and there'll be no last rites.

Having completed his mission Joe places his used equipment in a thick plastic box and observes the body in the bed. (The body! Oh joy. The *corpus mortalis!*) 'The next time I see you Gordon,' he muses, 'I'll be wearing my swanky Savile Row pinstripe, jazzed up by a bold red waistcoat, and Patte's gold half-hunter hanging on my teddy bear tummy.

With all the verve and confidence of a theatre luvvy I'll sail into the front pew, flashing my haughty, handsome, Jewish profile, to comfort my beloved Anna, the daughter you never deserved.'

Joe leaves the room, quietly closes the door, and pads back along the corridor to find his bed. After dropping the evidence into his black medical case, he slips off his long, white Moroccan *thobe* and carefully gets into bed beside a deeply sedated Anna. He hunkers down to reflect on his sin, and yes, dear friend, he's fully aware that he's sinned. Whether he cares or not is another matter.

*   *   *

Everyone knows what Philip Larkin said. 'They fuck you up, your mum and dad.' Josiah Fortune's mum and dad certainly fucked him up, but what choice did they have? They were completely fucked-up themselves. A 1945 wedding snap shows them as Rose and Harvey, two shy, shivering teenagers, arm in arm on the patch of bare earth that was called the garden at Kitchener Street. The groom wears his demob suit and the flat disc of his *kippah*, the bride a traditional long white dress that had already graced twenty weddings in Peckham. They were two people Joe had never known, nor could he imagine them ever being. They're trying to look happy, despite the tragedy of their slaughtered millions casting its giant shadow. (There were no real figures, nor ever were. Just a disbelieving silence and the binding of an invisible, unifying cord.)

'It will never happen again,' said Patte. 'We are the victors and a strong, just nation. We will guide the world into

3

a future without prejudice and we will never have to look over our shoulders again. We are so lucky. We have each other, a good pitch on Rye Lane market, and we will buy a sign-written van on the never-never with Harvey and Harry's demob pay.'

Abraham Moisemann and Son
Purveyors of Fresh Fruit and Vegetables
Peckham Rye London SE15
Established 1903

Josiah Jacob Dov Fortune was born to Rose after five years of bloody miscarriages. A puking, mewling, premature baby, his welfare was immediately assumed by Mitte and Patte, his grandparents. They were older and wiser. They knew what was what. Joe was a miracle baby, a Jewish Prince, and deemed to be a genius. The doctor said that Rose's nerves had been shattered by the trauma and he was glad she had the close support of her family. He also said that more babies might kill her, so he explained to Harvey about restraint and the use of French letters.

Josiah Fortune was thus raised as an only, lonely child by a quartet, but he could never understand where he fitted in. There were four corners of the earth, four sides to a square, and four points on the compass. The quartet seemed to exist for themselves, around themselves, and in servitude to themselves. He felt as if he was just a dancing doll, programmed to entertain them; his strings pulled and manoeuvred to suit the needs of a permanent grinning audience who applauded their little prince whenever he walked, talked, spat out his food or filled his nappy. He was cocooned and protected with an intense, overpowering anxiety, but it was just the Jewish way. The 'one love'. The one God. The respect, love and care of the whole family. History in their bones and in their hearts. Prince Josiah. Heir to bugger all.

Yom Kippur 1955: Joe was five. The synagogue had been hot, airless, and full of emotion as the final prayers of the *Ne'ilah* rounded off the commitment to the Atonement. With the blast of the *shofar* ringing in his tired little ears Joe now stood with Patte and his father while they consulted Rabbi Greenberg.

'Now you are five, Josiah, you will go to *cheder* classes,' said Patte. 'You will learn to read the Torah in our glorious and ancient Hebrew. Our language is the most beautiful in the world, my son. It runs like a river, and swirls like the wind. Now, let's have a memory of this wonderful day. Come and sit on the rabbi's knee and have your picture taken.' Joe hid his face on his arm and started to cry.

'He's a bit shy,' apologised Harvey. 'Now come along, our Joe. That's no way to behave. What will the rabbi think of you?' Protesting noisily the reluctant child was lifted up and plonked onto the rabbi's corpulent lap. 'There's a good lad. Smile for the birdy. Say *cheder*.' Joe refused. The rabbi was old. He had a wet beard encrusted with stale food. He stank of time gone by, and tobacco, and pee-pee pants. As the deadly fumes of the rabbi filled his nostrils he passed out and slithered with high drama from the royal lap. Two bloodcurdling screams were then heard from the gallery where a mother and grandmother had witnessed the dramatic scene.

A few minutes later Joe groggily came round to find he was surrounded, not only by the anxious, tear-filled faces of the quartet, but by the whole congregation. As he opened his eyes there was a loud wailing of joy and a burst of applause. He was clasped with fierce, bone-breaking gratitude and suffocated with slobbery kisses. But then voices of judgement began to murmur until there was a nodding and mumbling consensus of criticism. One voice eventually spoke aloud. 'Surely the boy hasn't been fasted. At five years old? Whoever heard of such a thing? You should be ashamed of yourself, Rachel Moisemann.'

Mitte squared up boldly, faced the muttering crowd and delivered a loud matriarchal proclamation. 'I can assure you, Dora Gold, our precious boy has *not* been fasted. He ate a hearty breakfast, and a proper dinner, and he had a nice sardine sandwich for his tea.' With perfect timing, Joe rolled his eyes and confirmed that Mitte was indeed telling the truth.

*   *   *

The photographs in the Morton Moore albums make everything look quite normal, but looking in is never quite the same as looking out. Look closer. The eyes always tell the truth. They see through a distortion, like the shaky reflection on the surface of still water, the stretching and shimmering of old glass viewed from an angle, or the refraction of light through a prism.

The life that little Anna lived behind the eyes is shown in endless snaps, taken against the backdrop of The Old Vicarage. Edwardian ruby-hued bricks softened by meandering creepers and gnarled wisteria. Sweeping lawns, edged with shrubs, and long-shadowed by ancient hardwoods. A fish pool that flashed with the red and golden lights of koi carp. A ha-ha wall with bridges to a meadow, backed by a wide vista of the green-swarded Chilterns.

Her parents stand, with seeming unity, before the heavy oak front door. Gordon, the mature and imposing merchant banker, and Eugenie, his full-smocked French beauty. A new marriage and new lives within the bursting belly. Then proudly presenting the swaddled bundles of Hugo and Anastasia. 'Such lucky children,' the Monks Bottom village folk all said . . . *'Oh, your daddy's rich and your ma's good looking* . . .' The babies thriving to become two toothless cherubs at either end of a grand, full sprung pram, and fluffy-headed toddlers clinging to adult legs. Endless pages followed of the twins with Mummy and Papa as they traversed the years and the seasons. They are here, they are there; together and apart; muffled up for winter, or bare-limbed for the sun. But smiling. Always smiling. Were they as happy? Anna's eyes may tell you.

Christmas Day 1965: Anna was five. She was sitting at a long walnut table that seated fourteen. A white damask tablecloth, silver salvers, tureens with big, fluted lids and crackers from Fortnum's. Three sets of cutlery, too heavy for her little hands to hold, and far too big for her mouth. A party of foreign visitors was spending Christmas Day with them; some very important people who had some exciting business with Papa's bank. A tiny Japanese man called Mr Ito, a German couple called The Krugers, and an American called Mr Cicero. Papa was wearing a paper hat and posed with a kukri to carve the turkey while the assembled company held in static mode for the camera. But Anna had started to cry.

Papa sighed. 'Oh, Anna. What on earth's the matter now?'

'I don't feel well,' she said. Her mouth wobbled and tears spilled down her cheeks.

'She iz very pale, Gordon,' said Mummy. 'I am sure she iz not vell.'

'Nonsense, Eugenie. I think that half-eaten packet of Turkish Delight might be more to blame. Now behave yourself, Anna, and smile for the camera. You too, Hugo. Stop looking so sullen. Let's have a happy Christmas photograph. Come along everyone. Let's raise our glasses with a champagne toast to the prosperity of CIK Technology. Cheers.'

A flash photograph was taken by Mr Huckstep. Mr Huckstep was the nice man who tended their garden on Sundays. It was his one day off from the furniture factory in High Wycombe, sacrificed to sweep and mow and dig and prune for the sake of the odd little luxury, like a motorbike to get to work on. Blurred in the background, the rounded, aproned figure of his wife, commandeered to wait at table and wash up afterwards. Their own festivities with their large family delayed in favour of the pittance they'd earn for a few hours at double time. 'Let's have one more snap, Huckstep', said Papa. 'Then you can stack up some logs in the drawing room. Come along children. Jolly smiling faces, please.' The Morton Moore family, and their prestigious guests, dutifully stared again at the camera and mimed, 'Cheese.'

Anna was beginning to feel very hot and sweaty and she put up her hand. 'Papa, I feel sick.'

'Anna, I want no more of your nonsense. Now eat up your turkey like a good girl, otherwise our guests will think you're a big baby.'

The taste of the turkey was making her throat go woomp, woomp, woomp. It tasted like her fingers did when she'd been playing with pennies. She stuffed it all in her mouth and ran from the table mumbling, but when she returned to the table she found some more turkey had been put on her plate. 'Perhaps you can eat that, Anna,' said Papa, 'seeing as the last piece has just disappeared down the lavatory. Your ingratitude incenses me,' but Anna continued to cry and turned a begging face to her Mummy.

'Pliz, Gordon,' said Mummy. 'She really iz not vell.' Papa's eyes returned a fierce look that forbade further protest.

Anna slowly swallowed each tiny morsel, but her tummy was dancing up and down. She knew she had to be a good girl, and be smiling and pretty for the important guests, but a big tidal wave was rising up inside her. She swallowed and gagged, but she could do nothing to stop it coming up, so she picked up the hem of her pink satin party dress and decanted into her lap.

All conversation at the table stopped, and no one moved a muscle. Papa's face froze and Mummy's eyes moved from side to side, staring at him for permission to move. It was Mrs Huckstep who took full charge of the situation. 'S'all right, Mr Morton Moore,' she said, skilfully concealing the offence and lifting the crying child into her sturdy arms. 'No bones broke. I'll see to 'er.'

'Thank you, Mrs Huckstep,' said Papa. 'You'll excuse my wife of course. Mrs Kruger has no English and Eugenie's the only one who can speak any German.' He then turned back to his guests. 'Now everyone, I'm sure my daughter will be better after a little lie down. Let me fill your glasses.' As if a radio had been switched back on, the table re-commenced its happy seasonal banter.

An hour later, Anna collapsed unconscious into Mrs Huckstep's arms. She was rushed to hospital where a kidney infection was diagnosed.

*　　　*　　　*

So, dear friend, I now bid you farewell. They're all yours. Make of them what you will.

The story of The Crowded Bed takes place in
The Present and The Past

The Present, being six warm June days,
from Thursday to Tuesday, in the year 2006

'The past is another country'

L.P. Hartley

CHAPTER 1

Thursday

T HE FRONT DOOR HAS SLAMMED, and the twins have fled in a mad, crazed euphoria of end of A-level-itis. I think I heard some loud mumbling that inferred 'Goodbye,' but at least that means an evening of peace. Now there'll be no interruptions, no strop or sarcasm. No showing off or noisy banter, no appalling table manners, and no demands for money. No hard words that say 'you're a sad old has-been, so butt out, slap-head'. I smile at Anna. 'Looks like a quiet night,' I say.

She smiles back. 'It's going to be a quiet weekend as well, Joe. They're both going away. Destinations unknown of course, but when are we ever told anything?'

'Par for the course,' I say, 'but they're quite normal.'

'Just like us,' she laughs.

I laugh too. 'Yes. Just like us.'

Two knives, two forks, two leather tablemats, and two crystal wine glasses. Candles lit, a bottle of Pinot Noir, and Errol Garner plays *Misty* on the tinkly piano. Anna's hair hangs like a skein of silken barley around her chin, and she is, as usual, fragrant and quietly moving; her presence moulding and bending to my mood. We absorb each other in an easy, congenial silence as the clink of cutlery, and a rare childless quiet, threads us together. Pudding is served. A hot lemon meringue pie with thick cream, and I know I shouldn't have a second helping, but I do. What the hell. One extra slice won't make a ha'porth of difference to my middle-aged spread, will it?

I slump completely stuffed, but a stiff scotch will go down well. A spliff would also be very welcome, but rules are rules. My secret little friend only comes out to play at weekends, so I light a small Havana and ignore government health warnings. Soon Anna will join me, and from the corner of my drowsy eye I'll see her sun-freckled face and cornflower eyes. She'll ease affectionately beside me and press her breasts into my ribs. 'You look happy,' she'll say as I lie there, eyes shut and grinning, looking the perfect picture of the contented man. But I'm not. I have these bats, you see. Their rubbery, umbrella-spoke wings wrap tightly around their slippery bodies, hanging upside down in my brain like little black hand-grenades, waiting to explode. There's also the cursed black dog at my feet, thumping its tail as it settles down for the evening. Bloody hound. Why, I ask myself? Sin I suppose.

Sin. Always be aware of sin. Thou shalt not, and thou shalt never. Ten Commandments for the Christians, but over six hundred for us Jews. I've always wondered if there is any damn thing that I can do (apart from breathing in and breathing out) that isn't sinful. I laugh, I bluster, and I posture. I say, 'Who gives a toss?' but deep inside I know that sin is always just round the corner, waiting to trip me up. Tonight it's Exodus, chapter 20, verse 13, that's causing me some concern. Commandment number 6, *'Thou shalt not kill.'* Quite right. Never was a deadlier sin more deadly, but I'm determined to rephrase this particular little action. I'm planning an unrequested end to a life or, in other words, humane euthanasia. A blessed release for me and an early bath for him. Positive assistance to the Grim Reaper. An imposed and necessary goodbye . . . A dream nurtured for twenty years . . .

September 1979: Joe's battered Morris Minor Traveller drove slowly through the big iron gates that fronted the entrance to The Old Vicarage. Behind him, in the back seat, Daniel was wailing loudly. Fat tears fell from the child's puffed slitted eyes, his chest jerked for breath, and the bubbly contents of his nose were plastered over his cheeks. In the distance Joe could see a droop-shouldered old man sweeping leaves with a birch broom, dabbing dewdrops with mechanical regularity on the cuff of an old tweed jacket. At least seventy years separated the two nose problems.

As Joe pulled on the handbrake the man ambled up the drive, holding the broom across his chest as if it were a weapon. An attempt at military foreboding. Halt! Who goes there? Friend or foe? Joe turned off the engine, got out of the car, nodded and smiled warmly. A concerted attempt to play the game and observe the rules. Conciliatory. Wanting to be liked, even by this *Last of the Summer Wine* extra, who was wafting a strong smell of damp housing and fried food. 'I've come to see Anna Morton Moore,' Joe said.

A lively wind rustled through the silver birches, distant rooks chattered, and the sun dazzled his eyes. If Joe had been a happy man he'd have fallen on his knees in worship of an Oxfordshire autumn, but anxiety shortened his breath and trickles of perspiration ran down the small of his back. The old man moved back, still holding the broom like a protective sword, his lips slurping over chipped brown dentures. 'Guvnor's away. Be back tonight.'

'It's Anna I need to see.'

'Gorn. Left this morning. Seems she's got some sort of 'ealth problem. 'Er mother've taken 'er to Switzerland to get 'er sorted out.'

The gardener, knowing he was conveying bad news, looked sadistically triumphant. Joe's head swam with a thick blur of blue sky, dry leaves, birds' wings and bonfire smoke, but Daniel's grizzling snapped him back to reality. When he lifted him out of the car the child clung to him, as tight and frightened as a baby baboon, coughed, hiccupped and dribbled out a sour mouthful of milky Weetabix. 'I've got a letter for Anna,' Joe said. 'It's very important. I'll put it through the letterbox. Could you possibly ask her father to send it on to her in Switzerland for me?' He started to walk the hundred yards down the drive to the front door, but the old man shot in front of him to bar his way. 'No visi'ers past this point. Strict instructions from the guv'nor. Give it to me. I'll make sure 'e gets it.' Joe set Daniel down, produced a Biro and wrote on the envelope in scrawled letters, *Very urgent. Please can you forward to Anna? Thank you.* He then passed it over, knowing that his whole future life was contained within. A gnarled, blue-veined hand placed it inside a rancid wellington boot.

Daniel began to complain again, whining, writhing, and kicking Joe's shins. 'Need wee-wee, Daddy.'

15

'My son needs to go inside and use the cloakroom,' Joe said.

The old man moved close to him. Threateningly close. His mouth so close Joe could smell his fetid breath. 'Been inside 'ave you?'

Joe nodded. 'Yes, I have.'

'I'll bet you 'ave,' the old sweat smirked, trying to impart the innuendo of a third-rate music hall comedian. 'What was it old Doris Day used to sing? *'Once I 'ad a secret love'*, or perhaps in your case it's once I 'ad a secret wife and child as well.'

Joe felt like swinging a punch, but he struggled to maintain the good manners that were so much part of being a good Jewish boy. Violence wouldn't get his letter delivered. The sarky old sod had the upper hand, didn't he? He would be the bearer of dispatches to the general, but making sure he over-egged the pudding to include lashings of his own ingredients. The old man pointed to a large beech tree. 'Tree'll do.' Joe walked Daniel over to the tree, and pulled down his dungarees, but they were already sodden. 'Sorry, Daddy. Sorry, Daddy,' the child tried to say, his words obscured by gulping and swallowing.

'It's OK, it's OK,' Joe soothed.

After helping Daniel to step out of his wet items, he walked the child back to the car, slipped his lower half into an old sweater and guided him into the back seat. 'We're just going. Lie down and go to sleep.'

How would this part of the story be reported back? 'You should've seen the kid. 'E was filthy, and what a bad-tempered little sod 'e was. Yelled 'is 'ead off, and the bloke done nothing. The little blighter must've been at least four, and 'e pissed 'isself.'

The old boy was slowly creeping away. No doubt Anna's father called him by his surname, and referred to him as his gardener, but he was just a tired, pathetic old shuffler, used to a lifetime of subservience and doffing his cap. 'The letter,' Joe called, 'you won't forget will you?' but there was no response.

The sun suddenly disappeared behind a cloud, and the air became chill. Joe got into the car and turned the key. Daniel was already asleep with his thumb in his mouth. They would have to go home, because there was no other place to go. Back to the unbearable realness of their being.

Above their heads a privately chartered aircraft flew to Zurich. Anna was being flown away. Banished, hidden from view, parcelled up and posted, but it had all been her own fault. Such a stupid girl. But what was her fault? *Fault: A defect, an offence, an imperfection.* Yes, it was true. She was defective, and imperfect, and she'd offended, but perhaps the word sin would have been more apt. *Sin: The breaking of a religious or moral law.* Yes, she'd certainly sinned, but Christianity had nothing to do with it. The only God in the Morton Moore family was money. What about morality? *Morality: The degree of conformity of an idea, practice, etc., to moral principles.* That, perhaps, hit the nail on the head. She was expected to live according to the rites and moral laws of the upper middle classes. You can't have the perfect English rose getting covered in blackfly, can you? Can't have her tainted by breathing the common air of the common man. It would never do. Douse her in Flit and tie her legs together. All that money spent on her, and she still ends up a common whore. It was thus decided that the rose needed a short sharp shock in pure clean water, but it was too late. She'd already wilted and flopped on her stem. Her bloom had perished, and her leaves had fallen.

Anna ran her hands through her hair and her fingernails stopped to pick and scrape at the congealing scabs. A bruise to her temple was black, her eyes bloodshot, and her hidden body still blotched and swollen in the hues of purple through to green. She sat in silence on the aeroplane, drugged with misery. Her mother sat beside her, drinking gin from a silver flask, and slowly sinking into a moribund state. 'Anastasia,' she said, with a curled lip. 'Your Farzer iz a vanker.'

August 1987: In the eight years since those confused, miserable days the hoops and loops of two seemingly hopeless lives had turned full circle. All adversity had been conquered. The sad, scruffy man and the strangely injured young girl were reconciled. Their wedding was imminent, and the path of their lives lay before them, strewn with the diamonds and pearls of love and perpetuity.

When Joe arrived at Claridge's Hotel Gordon Morton Moore waved his pink *FT* enthusiastically. 'Ah, there you are, my boy. Sit down, sit down.' Gordon clicked his fingers and a young waiter sashayed over to the table with the shimmy of a Latin American dancer. 'A glass of Merlot for my friend, please, Gerard.' The waiter poured the wine and paso-dobled away. Gordon then came straight to the point with business-like efficiency, posturing with an arrogant 'heads I win, tails I don't lose' face. 'Can I suggest 50,000 quid to fuck off out of it?' Joe smiled good naturedly, innocently thinking a joke was being played, but Gordon's expression didn't change. 'That's fifty grand, chummy. More than you've ever seen in your life, or likely to.' Joe slowly rose to his feet, hurled his wine in Gordon's face, bowed theatrically and left with slow dignity. But he was far from finished with him.

From a hidden vantage point Joe watched as Gordon left and followed quietly into the gathering night, his desert boots creeping in stealth and purpose. The Bentley was parked near to New Bond Street, and as his prey stopped to fumble for the key, Joe moved with the pace of a rabid dog. He pounced and dragged Gordon into the blackness of a narrow ginnel, hidden alongside an Italian restaurant. Despite Joe's profession as a healer and a humanist he found Gordon repulsive to touch. The odour of cigars and wine mixed with the gingery aroma of expensive soap, and from somewhere in the depths came another strange whiff, not unlike warm wax. With nausea held in his throat Joe spun his quarry round and pinned him against the wall, knee in groin and hands around neck. There was no moon that night, but Joe could see his face, lit up eerily by the yellow glare of the city sky. The cold, reptilian eyes showed no fear. From the restaurant kitchen loud noises wove in and out, obscuring the permanent rumble of the city's traffic. Doors opened and shut and loud Romano voices dissented. Cutlery jingled, crockery clattered, a cat screamed and flew over a dustbin. 'Why?' Joe shouted, but he knew already. He'd been sussed. Tumbled. Rumbled.

'Eight years ago,' Gordon said. 'I get back from holiday to find my house empty and showing the evidence of Sodom and Gomorrah. Some fine orgy, I can tell you. Clearly my daughter had been playing the slut for someone. When she does turn up she looks like she's been sleeping on the streets. Then you arrive with a snot-nosed bawling kid. You brought a letter, didn't you? Very eloquent prose from what I remember. I saw it all, you see, from a CCTV system. Bet you never thought of that? I couldn't get the number of your car or I'd have finished you long before now. I've still got the film, actually, so remind me to show it to you some time. You've changed a bit since then. Put on a bit of weight and had your hair cut, but there's no doubt it's you. Your distinctive facial features, shall we say? A Jew boy without a pot to piss in. A low-life, fortune-hunting adulterer.'

'Gordon,' Joe said. 'It was nothing like you think. Believe me, you've got it all wrong,' but then he stopped. What was the point in relaying the truth of the whole sordid story, chapter and verse? He'd never be believed. Joe increased the power of his grip, and the smooth, expensive face contorted with pain. 'Yes, it *was* me,' Joe admitted, 'but I shall tell you once, and once only. I didn't hurt her. The only pain I caused her was a broken heart. I brought her a begging letter. My last desperate and humiliating attempt to get her back. A letter she never received. You opened it, and read it, and decided in your wisdom your precious daughter wasn't going to settle for a bit of rough trade like me. Admit it Gordon, or I'll kill you.'

With Joe's hand clamped around his throat Gordon's voice was constricted, but he still managed to spit out the words like prune stones. 'I admit it. I kept the letter from her. She knows nothing of it.'

'Gordon,' Joe said, 'as far as buying me off is concerned I thank you for your kind offer. The bread would be very useful, because, as you so rightly say, I haven't got a pot to piss in, but I won't be going anywhere. From this day on you can butt your ugly head out of our lives. Every breath you take, every move you make, I'll be watching you. Tonight we'll make a solemn and binding pact. Neither of us will make one second of misery for her. You'll never tell her that you know I existed in her past, and I'll never tell her that you offered me a small fortune tonight to dump her. Throughout our future life I'll remain affable and polite to you, and you'll remain affable and polite to me. Is that clear? Oh, and on the question of my despised religion, I'm proud to be a Jew, but I can assure you there's no talk of Anna's conversion. Any children born to us will be brought up in which ever way she chooses.'

The two enemies reluctantly shook hands, quickly, dismissively and without eye contact. Thus their corners had been allocated and the rules understood, but Gordon had further points to score. He began to stride off, but when he reached the end of the ginnel he turned round with a triumphant expression. 'By the way, old boy. Just one more thing. Are you aware of her abortion?'

21

Abortion! The word winded Joe like a boxing glove in the guts. 'What abortion? Don't be ridiculous.'

'Ah-ha. Have I got news for you? Something Anna just forgot to mention. Tut tut. She always did have a bad memory. Well, we can't have you living in blissful ignorance, can we? Yes, old son. Down the pan it went, and good riddance. The only tragedy is that you emerged out of the mire again, but as you so rightly say, perhaps my daughter has a weakness for rough trade.'

Gordon disappeared round the corner and Joe slumped against a wall. What was he saying? Abortion! No, it wasn't true. Their parting had been a terrible and dramatic tragedy. A foolish and unforgivable act, but there'd been no hint of pregnancy. *Surely she'd have told him!* Gordon had to be lying. He ran out after him into the brightness of the metropolis. 'No, you've got it all wrong,' he cried, his voice high and hysterical. 'She'd never get rid of our child . . .' but the handmade shoes were disappearing into the foot-well, the door slammed, and the arrogant profile settled down. As the car drew off with silent grace Gordon turned with a hideous smile, ran his forefinger in a sharp cutting movement across his throat, and laughed.

As the tail lights disappeared into the night Joe stood weakly, trying to focus. Their child. Aborted. Terminated. Chemically killed and flushed down the sluice in the same way as thousands of unwanted, inconvenient conceptions. All signed away by the likes of him, a professional medic with a license to kill and no conscience in the matter. But this was *his* child, and modern medical ethics didn't enter the argument. His child would now be a happy, laughing seven-year-old. He'd be throwing easy, under arm cricket balls for him, or holding her hands while she bounced on a trampoline. Pulling off T-shirts splodged with chocolate ice cream and despairing at the endless pairs of sturdy Clarks shoes he had to buy. Applying magic cream to bruises, snuggling a tired and sweet smelling child under the duvet, and reading bedtime stories. He could see this child. A boy with his own proud, biblical face and Anna's barley-blond hair. Perhaps Sam or Ben? Or a girl, fine-featured and lovely like her mother, with his own thick black curls. What would her name be? Perhaps Deborah, or Julia, or Sarah.

His head began to pound and his hands contracted into fists. Now he realised why she wouldn't talk to him about their past. They'd had eight long years apart, but the dramas and confusion of their parting had remained unvisited. There'd been a choice. Bring it all up to the surface and examine it with bravery, or leave it buried. He'd wanted the full post-mortem but she'd insisted it lay untouched. 'Please Joe, don't make me turn it all up. I can't. It hurts too much. Let's just be grateful for our future.'

He slowly ambled up the pavement, turned into a small mews and sat down on a low wall. Beneath the dim greenness of a Victorian streetlight he produced his old tobacco tin to seek help from his little friend. He packed and rolled with shaking hands, lit up and drew in, deeply and urgently, but that night there was no help to be found. His head remained alert and troubled, rising above his inner need for oblivion, his thoughts fragmenting into atoms. Two hours later he concluded that sitting on a wall all night wasn't going to improve his condition, so he stood up and strode out to find the tube station. His feet thumped with painful pulls to his calf and thigh muscles. His head buzzed and he was blind to danger. Traffic was forced to divide for him. Lights flashed, brakes squealed, and cockney cabbies cursed, but he needed this bold march. This urgent striding away from this night into whatever Joe and Anna Fortune's tomorrow was going to be.

When he got in she looked up smiling. 'Did he behave himself?' she asked merrily. 'He can be so pompous when he wants to be.'

'Fantastic night,' Joe replied. 'We got on well. I could really get used to dining at Claridge's.' She asked him where they'd sat, what he'd selected from the menu, and which wines had been chosen. She then ran through an amusing repertoire of Claridge's stories. The ancient waiter with the eye-patch and the limp. The shock of seeing one of their neighbours romantically entwined with another woman. The time Edward Heath came over and shook hands with Papa, and the best story of all . . . The time she'd found a fly in her cheese souffle. Her father had threatened the chef with The Health and Safety Act, and they'd ended up with the meal free, *and* a weekend in the penthouse suite, *and* best seats for *Jesus Christ, Superstar*. And the punch line! It was her brother Hugo who'd slipped the fly on the plate while her father tasted the wine, and they'd both just sat back and enjoyed the fireworks. It was the first time she'd ever divulged any details of her childhood. She'd always clammed up and looked away when he asked her questions, in the same way she'd refused to discuss the history of their own past. That night she bubbled over, but he knew it was just a relief for her anxiety. She then closed the book and he heard no more.

Later, as they lay sleepily in bed together, he rested the heel of his palm on her navel and splayed his fingers in protection of the secret life within her. Perhaps he should have flaunted Anna's new pregnancy that night as the ultimate trump card. He should have stood with his limbs in a star, his crutch proudly projected in the pose of the conceited stud and bragged his consistency. £50,000 to fuck off? He wouldn't have left her for the national debt. When Anna fell asleep he remained wide-awake, thinking of their lost child, but his thoughts weren't the shallow feelings of sentimentality or the deep grief for a death. It was something much more profound, and as he stared into the darkness he weighed up the case with a court room analysis. Think, Joe. Think. Separate the emotion from the facts.

Conception, he concluded, had been inevitable, so careless was their birth control. At the time of their severance Anna must have been pregnant, but she'd never even briefly mentioned any anxiety. So how far on was the pregnancy advanced? The horrible drama of their parting had forced her to run away from him. She was young, and frightened, and traumatised, and who could have blamed her for collapsing and revealing all to her parents. Gordon had obviously then forced her into the termination. But what about his letter? The letter he'd left at the house was a salve to all her misery and insecurity. It told of his deep love for her, that he would never let her down, and they would be married despite the minefield of obstacles that lay ahead. Clearly she'd been sent away to Switzerland to get the job done, but there would have been plenty of time for cancellation. In the days of 1979 termination wasn't the instant done-deal it became. Firstly a medical professional would have insisted on a slow, official lab-test confirmation of the pregnancy. Then another's approval would be sought. The procedure, even one privately arranged, would not have been carried out before counselling and a cooling off period. Thus, had his letter been sent on to her, it would have arrived well in time to stop her going ahead. Anna would have returned to him, and their child would have lived. Unequivocally.

Question: What did that make Gordon Morton Moore?

Answer: The murderer of his child.

He spoke silently to the cherished girl sleeping beside him. 'You'll never know of this, Anna, and there'll be no blame for you. Whatever you did was an answer to your suffering and the cruel circumstances of our parting. Nothing was your fault and I forgive you. All my pain will be contained within myself.'

That night his hurt buried itself deep inside him, bottled up like a noxious gas. One day there would be retribution for the death of his child. '*Let vengeance be mine*,' saith The Lord. 'Let vengeance be mine,' saith Joe Fortune. '*If you wrong us shall we not seek revenge?*'

One day, he vowed, he would kill Gordon Morton Moore.

CHAPTER TWO

Thursday, continued . . .

ANNA NOW SITS CLOSE UP BESIDE ME and looks kindly into my eyes. Don't look too hard, Anna. Don't peer too deeply.

There's a big rehearsal taking place in the Fortune Head Theatre tonight. Listen to this, Gordon. I'll hire an anonymous, dark-coloured saloon and stick on some false number plates. I'll drive down to Monks Bottom in the dead of night and park alongside the meadow where there are no houses or street lights. I'll climb over the old five-bar gate behind the blackberries, scurry down the long dark drag of the garden and let myself into the back lobby. Then up the sweeping staircase to find the master bedroom and there you'll be – lying on your back and snoring with the cadence of a traction engine. But before you have time to utter a scream of terror, I'll leap into action. I'll gag you. Then I'll blindfold you.

No I won't. I'll let you see everything and tell you in triplicate exactly what I'm going to do. I'll tie you to a chair while I leisurely drink a scotch and smoke a cigar. No, a joint. I'll smoke a big spliff and tell you that not only am I a fornicating, despised Jew I'm a drug addict as well. Just to rub it in, I think I'll make you watch a video of *Fiddler on the Roof*, while I sing all the songs to you. (I do a mean Topol impression guaranteed to make my children squirm with embarrassment.)

Once you're begging for mercy, I'll murder you. A quick hypodermic where the sun doesn't shine and curtains it will be. Oh, Gordon, I'll get such a thrill as I see your bleary old eyes close. Then straight back to the hired car and hot wheels to the M4. Your body will only be discovered next morning when Queenie Croften, your loyal old drudge, totters in with the breakfast tray.

By that time the substance will be completely undetectable and there'll be no suspicion of foul play. The perfect crime. I have the means, I have the technology, I have the skill. Oh, Captain Fortune, what a clever chap you are. All I need now is the opportunity (and the guts).

I'm jolted out of my reverie by the urgent jarring of the telephone in the hall. It pulls, it sucks, it impels you to answer in case it's important, but it rarely is. Anna answers and I can tell by her resigned and patient tones it's only her father. It usually is at this time of night. Funny, I was only just thinking of him. What will it be tonight? He's lost the top to the toothpaste? He's got his slippers on the wrong feet and can't understand why his toes are turning out at ten to two? She returns with a bemused expression, and I raise my eyebrows in polite enquiry.

'The silly old buffoon wanted to know if I could remember when his subscription to *Punch* is due, and he thinks the front door could do with a coat of varnish.' Patient smiles are exchanged. Ah, les viels hommes!

Every road to sleep should be like the opening shots to *The Shining*. Do you know what I mean? Mile upon mile of virgin snow and green fir trees. A clear blue sky and a holy silence. The peace that leads us to a trouble-free slumber. Anna and I slip into our cloud-soft kingsize to seek oblivion. The gorilla and the fawn embrace beneath the duvet, blindly finding lips, and mumbling the usual terms of endearment, knowing with telepathy that tonight is one of our 'I love you, but I'm too knackered,' nights. We shuffle, exhale and wearily arrange our bones for sleep.

My road to sleep hangs cruel. Hogarthian toothless crones and mocking imbeciles stick out their legs to trip me up. I jerk and flutter. The bats mock, the dog's tongue lolls wet and foamy, and the whole cast of actors in my play jostles for attention. It's just a normal night for me in The Crowded Bed.

I wake at 2.00 a.m. with a severe attack of indigestion. It must be the revenge of the lemon meringue pie. Or is it the revenge of The Crowded Bed?

Joe has woken Anna. The red LED shows 2.00 a.m. He's thrashed and battled to retain his sleep but he's lost the fight. He sighs, stretches and scratches his balls. He groans and rubs his chest. He plumps his pillow and turns over, sighing deeply. Anna's wide awake and troubled too. The dark so empty, the night so long. The vicious tongues of night convey the fear that isn't there by day. Time is supposed to be a healer but time has never healed her. She's trapped inside herself and there's no escape. She pushes the pendulum of time away with fierce resolution, but it always returns to smack her on the back of her head.

She keeps getting his little phone calls. 'I've had a really bad day. I'm very weary. It took me an hour to dress this morning. Ten minutes to put on my shoes. Mrs Croften made me a lovely egg custard and I just couldn't face it, etc, etc.'

She keeps getting little phone calls from Queenie Croften too. 'Anna, dear. I'm ever so worried about yer Pa. 'E gets these dizzy spells and 'e goes all vacant. 'E gets right grumpy sometimes but I'm sure 'e don't mean it. It's not like 'im, is it?' (Isn't it?)

'Why, oh why?' Anna pleads to the horned screamers of the night, 'Why can't these dizzy spells carry him off? Die, you bastard. Die, so all my chains and padlocks can fall like cobwebs to the ground.'

The sulphured London air wafts gently in through the bedroom window and she inhales gratefully. The perfume of Arabia. It's the sweet smell of the place her love has brought her to and not the place she comes from. Joe's still shifting and restless and she thinks he's in pain. 'What's the matter?' she mumbles.

'Shush,' he says. 'I only need some bi-carb. Go back to sleep,' but she knows she won't. The bed's far too crowded.

1968: Anna was eight. Hugo had just returned home from a music lesson. He'd walked all the way from the bus stop in pouring rain and he was soaking wet. He stood in the kitchen while Mummy towel dried his hair, but he was crying because he'd lost his violin. He thought he might have left it on the bus, or in the bus shelter, or in the sweet shop in Henley. Papa came in, and grabbed Hugo, and pulled his trousers down. Whack, whack, whack. He told him he had to go back and retrace his steps, and he wasn't to come home until he'd found it. Mummy put on her Burberry, and reached for the keys to her Mini, but Papa jerked her back by an epaulette. 'For God's sake, Eugenie. Stop mollycoddling the stupid boy. What he needs is a bit of character building.' Mummy was made to stand aside while Hugo walked out alone into the gathering autumn darkness.

Anna threw on her gaberdine mac. 'I'll come with you,' she shouted after him.

'You'll do no such thing,' said Papa, but Anna was already out of the door and running down the drive. 'I'll teach you to defy me, Anna,' he bellowed. He caught up with her and hauled her up by the belt of her mac, so she was dangling. He smacked her hard on the legs. Whack, whack, whack.

Ten minutes later a van drew up. It was Mr Greene from the local paper shop. 'Your lad left his violin in my shop, Mr Morton Moore.'

Largesse from Papa and the offer of a drink. 'We're so grateful, Mr Greene. Actually Hugo's just popped back to Henley to look for the very article . . . Perhaps you ought to whizz out Eugenie, and see if you can catch him before the bus comes.'

Mr Greene declined Papa's offer. He had his evening papers to mark up. Mummy drove out and found Hugo sobbing in the bus shelter.

1958: Joe was eight. No one had asked him if he wanted to learn to play the violin, but being a genius the quartet expected him to be outstanding at everything he touched. He was just told, 'If you can play the violin, Josiah, you will always be invited to weddings and *bar mitzvah*s.'

One cold winter afternoon, Mitte took him to his regular violin lesson at Grove Park, but he was coughing so much it had to be abandoned. She told him he was going straight home to bed, but he was delighted. Even being a captured victim of her over zealous pampering was a delight, compared to scratching and scraping his way through 'Three Blind Mice' for the nine hundredth time. She pulled down his bobble hat until it covered his eyes, and garrotted him with his scarf. 'Try not to breathe,' she said. 'There's a smog coming down.' He was then marched onto the tram. 'Now,' she said. 'I'm getting off at Prior Street, and going to the chemist to get some Friar's Balsam for your chest. You're to go straight home to your Mum, and sit by the fire until I get back.'

The tram conductor was given strict instructions to make sure he got off at Kitchener Street. 'There you go, sonny,' he said, helping the ailing child down the step. But in a rare moment of unsupervised freedom Joe took his chance. He ran, puffing and choking, up to the old bomb site round the corner, where the blackened ruin of a church still sat like a decayed old tooth stump. The hated violin flew from his hands, and as it disappeared into a stony cavernous crater, Joe clapped. Oh, joy! His musical career was over.

Once at home, he hurled himself into his mother's arms. He wailed and cried with crocodile tears pouring down his face. He was *so terribly sorry* but he'd left his violin on the tram. He was beside himself with sorrow because he loved his violin so much. When Mitte arrived ten minutes later he went through the whole charade again. 'Never mind, ducky,' she said. 'We'll find it, don't you worry,' and she pulled him so tightly onto her knee the hard metal of her suspender dug into his thigh.

When his father and Patte got home from their normal twelve-hour day selling fruit and veg from their pitch in the market, they were immediately ordered back out by the matriarch to go to the tram station on the other side of New Cross. 'Don't worry, our Joe,' said Patte patiently. 'Someone will have handed it in.' But they got home two hours later, shrugging and bewildered. They sat the sad-faced child down and told him, with great kindness and regret, that they couldn't afford to buy him another one. 'The van's clapped out,' Patte explained. 'We've got to have a new one and it'll take every penny we've got for the deposit. We just don't have the money.'

'I promise I'll save up all my pocket money and buy myself another one,' Joe replied, nodding vigorously, but he already knew that at sixpence a week it would take him four years and he thanked God for making violins so expensive. It never occurred to the quartet that he wasn't telling the truth, but he was given two hours of ear slamming about the dishonesty of people who find violins on trams.

1969: Anna was nine. She was a Brownie. A seconder in the Fairy Pack. Brownies was the bestest thing she did. Hugo was a Cub. It was their turn to go to the church hall to help serve teas to the old age pensioners, but Papa had given them strict instructions to come straight home afterwards. They weren't allowed to go to Cow Lane. Papa said it was a filthy place where all the common people lived, and if they went down there they'd catch head lice, or polio, or start dropping their aitches. But that afternoon they dawdled down to Cow Lane with Ronny Huckstep. 'Come in, dears,' said Mrs Huckstep. They had a lovely time with Ronny, and Trevor, and Dennis, and Malcolm, and Linda, and Tracey and baby Hayley. They played Happy Families, and Grandmother's Footsteps and they were asked if they'd like to stay to tea. 'Yes please,' they said.

They had fish fingers, beans, and chips, and a raspberry jelly for pudding. They ate at a Formica table in the kitchen, and it didn't matter if they talked with their mouths full, or spilled things. When Mr Huckstep got in from work he walked them home because it was getting dark. 'Here's your two angels, Mrs Morton Moore,' he said. 'It's been a pleasure to entertain them,' but Papa stepped out of the shadows.

'Thank you, Huckstep,' said Papa, 'but I think in future we can provide all the entertaining they need.'

Papa shouted that they were disgraceful and disobedient. He said that from now on they were confined to barracks. They were sent to bed without any dinner, but later on Papa came into Anna's bedroom and took away her Brownie uniform. 'The Monks Bottom Brownie pack will

34

have to manage without you in future, and I've decided it's high time you left that sub standard little village school. You'll both be going to The Unicorn School in Oxford as soon as I can make arrangements. You'll also be taking elocution and deportment classes.' Hugo's uniform was also removed, and he was given a good hiding for taking his sister into the den of iniquity. As Anna lay in bed she could hear Hugo crying, and downstairs Papa was shouting at Mummy. There was a muffled scuffling, and the sound of breaking glass, as an empty gin bottle landed on the lawn. Then the sound of Mummy crying.

1959: Joe was nine. Since music left his life his only social activity was his weekly *cheder* class with the rabbi. Rabbi Greenberg was now even fatter and smellier, but the quartet thought he was God's deputy on earth and hints were made that Joe might grow up to be a Rabbi too. But for Joe, being Jewish was beginning to seem like a terrible plot that stopped him from doing all the fun and happy things that Christian children did. He wanted to join the wonderful world of enjoying himself at the Wolf Cubs, the ABC Minors, and the public swimming baths, so he went round every member of the quartet in turn, hoping to divide and rule, but Mitte said, 'ask Patte', and his mother said, 'ask Patte', and his father said, 'ask Patte'.

'Wolf Cubs!' expounded Patte. 'Rules and uniforms! All that marching and saluting. Remember the Hitler youth. No, you cannot go.'

'Patte, please can I go to ABC Minors?'

'ABC Minors! All that jostling, and cat calling, and bad manners. No, you cannot go.'

'Patte, please can I go to the public swimming baths, then?'

'Public swimming baths! Covering yourself with other people's dirty water that's been pee-peed in. You'll catch all sorts of things. No, you cannot go. Now stop all this naughtiness and be a good boy. You must go to your lesson with the rabbi, and afterwards a little bird tells me your cousins are coming to tea.' Felix, Jack, and Melvin came to tea every Sunday afternoon, so what was new? Their lives were every bit as boring as his, except that Felix had some secret postcards of naked ladies, and Melvin had some secret postcards of naked men.

1970: Anna was ten. Papa wanted to find out the times of the cricket on the television, but the *Radio Times* was missing. He marched up and down the drawing room shouting that he wished that he could put something down and come back ten minutes later and find it was still there. 'Good God,' he shouted. 'Does it have legs? Has it walked out of the room all by itself?' Anna and Hugo and Mummy were in a blind panic. They rushed around and bumped into each other, looking under cushions and behind curtains. Their faces were creased with worried and puzzled expressions. They got down on their hands and knees and peered under furniture. Papa said the twins would have to pay the whole of the paper bill out of their pocket money if it wasn't found, but then Mummy stealthily removed Anna from the room.

'Kvick,' she said. 'Pedal down to ze paper shop and buy anuzzer vun. If Mr Greene 'asn't got vun left ask if ve can borrow his vun please.' Fortunately Mr Greene had one left.

Once reunited with the precious *Radio Times*, Papa demanded a pot of tea, and tea was always made to the strict rules laid down by his colonial Indian childhood. Four heaped caddy spoons placed in a warmed Wedgewood teapot. Bubbling boiling water poured on, stirred rapidly with a small hardwood stick, and a three minute infusion with a folded linen cloth over the pot. Then stirred again gently and allowed to stand for a further sixty seconds. Finally, poured carefully through a silver tea strainer into a fine porcelain teacup and served with thin slices of lemon. But Mummy suddenly remembered she had to pick up some dry cleaning from the post office before it shut. 'Right,' she said. 'You both know exactly vat to do,' and she rushed out.

When the kettle had boiled Hugo began to pour the boiling water onto the tea leaves, but then he stopped and laughed. 'Today, ladies and gentlemen, I think a little extra tang will be in order.' He then peed into the teapot, but not just a few drops. A whole ten-year-old willy full.

Papa sipped his cup with his eyes fixed firmly on the television screen as leather smacked willow. 'Was it all right, Papa?' they asked.

'Acceptable,' he said. 'This Nilgiri has a particularly piquant flavour.'

They curled up together on Hugo's bed, silently laughing. 'Next time I'll piddle in his suit pockets,' said Hugo. They laughed and laughed until tears ran down their faces. Hugo was so happy he wanted to play film stars. He wanted to kiss Anna all close up and twisty on the mouth like the film stars did, so she let him.

The next day Mrs Huckstep found the *Radio Times* folded up inside Papa's *Daily Telegraph*.

1960: Joe was ten. He still crept around like a little SAS soldier trying to trick his way into an expansion of his social life, but to no avail. The only constant was the dreaded *cheder* classes, and the quartet's continual mutterings about his future life as a rabbi was beginning to terrify him. Thus, he made as much attempt as possible to expose the impossible hocus-pocus of the Bible. By adopting a serious face, and feigning academic interest, he managed to tie Patte up in knots. 'Who wrote the Torah, Patte?'

'God of course.'

'I didn't think God was a real person on earth.'

'Well, God told the scribes what to write down.'

'But Patte, the scribes were the only ones who could read and write, so how do we know what they wrote down was the truth?'

'Oh Josiah! Questions, questions. Our story is a history and an exciting adventure. Tales born on the wind, and handed down through the long line of our forefathers leading back to Israel. Now will you stop all these questions and be a good boy.'

But Joe didn't ever want to be a good Jewish boy. He still wanted to be a Christian because at school all the Christian children went into morning assembly and it all sounded so happy. The Jewish children weren't allowed to go in. They had to do work that stinky Rabbi Greenberg gave them instead, but he never ever gave them anything to do. He came in about once a fortnight, lit up a Capstan Full Strength, and read the racing pages. When he left he always said the same thing. 'Next time I come I want to hear all about Jonah and the Whale.' The rabbi never did get round to finding out what they knew about Jonah, but they all knew which horse was likely to win the 2.30 at Epsom.

Joe would stand most mornings at the classroom door listening to the sound of singing coming from the hall.

> *'All things bright and beautiful,*
> *All creatures great and small,*
> *All things wise and wonderful,*
> *The Lord God made them all.'*

Well, Joe reasoned, if the Lord God made everything, he made the Jews as well, didn't he?

> *'Glad that I live am I, that the sky is blue.*
> *Glad for the country lanes, and the fall of dew.*
> *After the sun the rain, after the rain the sun.*
> *This is the way of God, since the world begun.'*

How happy, how fresh, how real. How unlike the Torah and the Talmud and all the wailing and bobbing of the synagogue.

'Patte, why can't I go into morning assembly?'

'Because I said so.'

'But Patte, Alfred Black and his brothers go into assembly.'

'That is because they are not Jews.'

'But Patte, Alfred's father and his grandfather go to the synagogue.'

'But Alfred is *not* a Jew, Josiah. His mother is a *shikse*.'

'What is a *shikse*?'

'A temptress.'

'What is a temptress?'

'Oh, Josiah. Questions, questions. Marriage for our people is a precious virtue, but Alfred's father was foolish. He should have chosen a good Jewish girl, but he cast his eye in the forbidden city. Mrs Black spread her net and he was blindly captured. I'm sure he bitterly regrets it.' Joe found it difficult to understand why Mr Black should regret it. All the popular songs were about falling in love and Alfred's parents looked as if they were in love. They held hands all the time and kissed in the street. Mrs Black had a fat belly and Alfred said she was having a baby. Alfred also told him how they made the baby. Joe knew he was lying. Yuck! The quartet could never do anything so disgusting, but he thought he'd better ask his cousins their opinion. They studied the postcards, thought about it, and decided they were all adopted.

1971: Anna was eleven. She and Hugo had been chosen to play Mary and Joseph in The Unicorn School nativity play, but on the morning of the performance they had a dress rehearsal and Hugo got his lines all muddled up. He snatched the tea cloth off his head, and burst into tears. Anna put her arm around him. 'Don't worry,' she said. 'It's going to be all right. I'll tell you what to say,' but he just kept crying and his nose ran snot all over his top lip. Mr Bolton tried to be kind, but there wasn't time to be kind. He had a play to produce, and the male lead was hiding in the art cupboard. He had to recruit Jeremy LeProvost (who was a king from Orientare) to play Joseph, and Seraphina Heppenstal had to be a king instead of a cow.

When Anna and Seraphina tiptoed onto the stage to peep through the curtains Mummy and Papa were just taking their front-row seats, nodding and smiling to the other parents. Mummy wore a mink coat, and high heels, and her hair was swirled up on her head like a woven basket. Seraphina said she was by far the prettiest mummy. Papa wore a dark pinstriped suit, and a red polka dot bow tie. He got out a large cigar clicked the lion's head on his gold lighter, and rolled the end in the flame. Seraphina said he looked like her grandad.

Mr Bolton suddenly flapped his hands. 'Places, children, places.' The lights were lowered, the curtains swept back and as Mr Burgess on the piano bonged out the opening bars of 'Away in a Manger', Jeremy LeProvost carefully helped the virgin off the donkey. But this was a unique production. Mr Bolton, disguised as a goat, had to follow him on hands and knees to whisper his words when he dried up. At the end, when the cast lined up and bowed, Papa didn't clap. He marched round to the back of the stage and the audience could hear every word as Mr Bolton was asked to kindly explain himself. 'Hugo was word-perfect yesterday, Mr Bolton. I rehearsed him myself. You've handled the situation very badly. Very badly indeed.'

'Mr Morton Moore,' he stuttered. 'Would it not be a good idea to ask Hugo to play the piano instead? He really is outstandingly gifted for his age.'

Hugo was found, still curled up with the sugar paper and poster paint. 'Fetch your music, Hugo!' demanded Papa. Hugo played the 'Dolly Suite', and then accompanied the whole school as they sang 'The Twelve Days of Christmas '. Everyone clapped hard and Hugo took three bows all on his own. But Papa wasn't proud of him. When they got home he took him upstairs and hit him with a belt that had a big brass buckle, and his bottom bled all over his white pants.

1961: Joe was eleven. 'Hands up who'd like to play Joseph?' said Miss Whinny, trawling the top juniors for budding actors one dark November day. Joe was on his feet like a shot. 'Me! Me!' he pleaded.

'Well, Joe, you certainly look the part,' she said. 'You'd make an excellent Joseph, but I don't think your Patte would approve.' Miss Whinny wrote a note for him to take home, and of course Patte forbade the role immediately. Joe wailed and sobbed and threw himself on the kitchen floor, kicking his heels hard on the quarry tiles in an explosive fury. His mother and Mitte danced anxiously around him, worried that he might have a fit, and offering him all sorts of compensations, but he refused to be appeased. Common sense intervened in the shape of his Uncle Harry, who informed Patte he'd already agreed that Joe's three cousins could play minor roles. Felix was a shepherd, Jack a lamb, and Melvin an angel. 'See reason, Dad,' he said. 'Christians are always welcomed into the synagogue as our guests, so why can't the boys make guest appearances in a Christian play? Can't see much harm done.'

So Joe got the starring role in the nativity, but that was secondary to his real objectives. He'd fallen in love with the Virgin Mary. Louise Stephens was the school beauty, with big blue eyes, long blonde hair, and a nice line in hand holding. She was the first girl he'd ever thought about kissing and he was besotted. At the end of the performance they were alone in the changing room. 'This bloody zip itches,' the little cockney Madonna complained, roughly pulling off her blue dress and trampling it on the floor. Joe saw the erogenous zone of an armpit, a swathe of flaxen hair against a smooth white shoulder, and a breathtaking glimpse of two pink nipples through a lacy topped petticoat. He caught her hand, stabbed his puckered lips against her cheek and had his first erection. 'Gerroff,' she said, wrinkling her face in genuine protest, but he wasn't deterred. He fell deeply in love with Louise and followed her around in slavish devotion, yearning to kiss her again, but he was rejected without tenderness. 'I don't love you, Joe Fortune,' she said, with a wild head toss. 'I love Adam Faith.'

1972: Anna was twelve. She was under the blankets with her little tranny listening to Stuart Henry on Radio Luxembourg.

Papa burst through her bedroom door, threw back the bedclothes, pulled up her nightdress and smacked her hard on her bare bottom with a riding whip. 'Can I remind you, young lady, that The Unicorn School costs a fortune,' he bawled, 'and if you think you're going to listen to trash all night and go to school tired out you've got another think coming.' He then started to stamp her tranny under his foot. Hugo rushed into the room, swinging a golf club, shouting at Papa that he was a cruel bastard. Papa grabbed Hugo by his hair, pulled him out onto the landing and pushed him back into his own bedroom. Hugo was screaming. Anna called for Mummy but she didn't come, so she ran downstairs to find her. She was in the drawing room, with a glass in her hand, looking out of the window. 'Do you know, Anastasia,' she said. 'I can't see ze church clock. I sink I need glasses now. Vill you find out ze time for me?'

Hugo was beaten with the golf club. He lay in bed, traumatised into silence. His face was the colour of skimmed milk, and he was sick all over his pillow. The next day he fainted down the stairs, banged his head, and started slurring his words so the doctor had to be called. 'Bad day at rugby yesterday,' Papa said to the doctor, 'but you know what these young lads are like. Far too exuberant. Throw themselves around like young puppies.'

Hugo had to go to casualty. He had concussion, and two broken ribs, and he was told he had to stay in bed for a week. Mummy wandered in occasionally, but she stood at the end of his bed sniffing, and making little mewing noises, and didn't seem to know what she was supposed to do. Mrs

Huckstep took hold of her shoulders and led her out. 'I'll see to 'im,' she said. 'Strikes me 'e's not the only one round 'ere needing the quack.'

That night Anna crept into Hugo's room and thanked him for trying to save her. Hugo lay too weak to move, but he was defiant and angry through the haze of his pain. 'I tried to help you, Anna. I had to do something. I'm nearly as tall as he is. I shall get bigger and stronger, and one day I'll win. One day I'm going to kill him, Anna. I promise you faithfully, one day I really am going to kill him.'

1963: Joe was thirteen. He'd just won an open scholarship to The Apprentices Hall, the most prestigious and ancient public school in London, and what swank there was on the day he was offered his place. A couple of years before the family were bursting with pride when Felix had got into the local grammar, but Joe's achievement was the *victor ludorum*'s crown. Suddenly the Fortune/Moisemann's were the royalty of Kitchener Street and Mitte went round and knocked on every door. 'Just thought you'd like to know,' she boasted 'Our Joe's won a place to The Apprentices Hall. He's one of the cleverest boys in England, you know. There were only three scholarships for the likes of him in the whole of the country. The uniform alone's going to set us back fifty quid, and what with tennis racquets, and satchels, and season tickets, and all the orders, we're going to have to tighten our belts. But he'll want for nothing.'

All the neighbours came round and admired the child prodigy, to pat him on the back, and give him half-a-crown.

They talked about 'The Little Professor', or 'The Future Prime Minister', but Patte rubbed his hands together and looked at Joe with adoration. 'I think it'll be Rabbi Fortune if I'm not mistaken, eh, Joe?'

'But Patte, I don't want to be a rabbi,' pleaded Joe. 'I want to be a doctor.'

The quartet were silenced. A doctor! A doctor! Our son, the doctor! Equal to (perhaps even higher than) a rabbi. One above a dentist, two above a lawyer, three above an accountant. Four pairs of hands clasped with joy. Four faces beamed with delight. Four pairs of brown eyes filled with tears of pride. 'Dr Fortune,' they sighed. 'Dr Josiah Fortune.'

CHAPTER THREE

Thursday, continued . . .

M Y INDIGESTION'S GRIPPING ME LIKE A VICE, so I pull on my *thobe* and pad down to the kitchen to mix some bi-carb. All's quiet apart from the hum of the fridge. My deep night thoughts have, as usual, been those of nostalgia mixed with nausea. My life as a child. Running, always running, to keep ahead of the game and avoid capture, but my feet treading the treacle of intense solicitude. I swig the bismuth and sit down at the kitchen table, waiting for my colic to ease, but my peace is shattered by a scuffling and giggling. My errant twins have returned, their youthful happiness mixed with alcohol and (most probably) inhaled narcotics. Maybe they're trying not to wake their sleeping parents but they're failing with spectacular selfishness. The door opens and Sophie is silhouetted; tall, beautiful and with a wild madness of Cimmerian hair. 'What's up, doc?' she stage whispers, wavering for support against the even taller frame of Josh.

'Guts ache,' I say. 'One piece of lemon meringue pie too many, I guess. Did you both have a good night?' They exchange wry, wicked glances. It could mean a lot, it could mean nothing. Josh goes to the fridge, removes and cracks opens two bottles of Becks and passes one to his sister. The twins slurp from the neck and slump down on chairs to talk to me, but their version of talk isn't the purest form known to man. They only address each other, asking questions but not looking for answers, softly mocking their patient, tolerating parent. I'm tired and the solitude suited me. I love them but I wish they'd go away and leave me alone. This is the price I pay for ensuring their mental and physical freedom. For providing a life of love and openness. They are the products of a happy marriage, a tolerant, egalitarian society and political correctness.

Anna enters the room wearing a blue oyster-satin wrap, her eyes blinking in the glare of the kitchen fluorescent. She stands behind me, slips her hand over my shoulder and gently rubs my chest. 'Poor love,' she says. Josh and Sophie exchange pathetic glances at our geriatric affection.

'Been talking to this old barmaid at the Dun Cow tonight, Dad,' says Josh. 'She knew you from Kitchener Street. Joanie someone. Fat blonde. Right old slapper.'

'Ah, that would be Joanie Bayliss,' I say, ruefully. 'You wouldn't believe what a stunner she was at sixteen.'

'She says you were a cracker as well. Can't imagine what happened. Too many large dollops of pudding, I suppose. She said all the girls were after you, but no one ever caught you.'

'S'rite, Josh. Mitte would have floored any *shikse* with a frying pan that set their cap at me. Had to save myself, you see, for the Jewish Princess.'

'Surely Dan's dog-faced old mother wasn't your first and only. Did you and Joanie have a thing going?'

I find his eye and smile ruefully. Although I've provided them with birth control and the full safe-sex spiel they assume that I'm impotent and their mother is grateful.

'That's for me to know, and you to find out, my son. Anyway, do you think I'd embarrass your mother by boasting of my conquests.'

The twins, being loose-tongued and deliriously happy, attempt to grab a rare opportunity to nose into the taboo of our pre-married life. They look at their mother with wide-eyed wonder. 'In your dreams, Dad,' says Sophie, 'but I bet you've got something to brag about, Mum. Uncle Felix told me you were the most beautiful girl he'd ever seen. Did you have a huge queue to the door at Monkey Bum?'

Anna lowers her head modestly. 'No chance. Grandpapa had a huge frying pan too, and Hugo guarded me like a soldier.'

The mention of Hugo shuts everyone up with a respectful silence, but just at the right moment I release a loud burp, my dyspepsia resolves, and everyone laughs with relief. I look at my watch and stand up. 'Don't you two be much longer, and don't forget to turn out the lights, oh, and I hear you're both going away for the weekend. Take good care of yourselves – you know exactly what I mean – and take your mobiles. Remember, we're always here if you need us.'

Anna blows them a kiss and circles her arm around my expanded waist. We climb the stairs together like two arthritic cripples, lurch into our bedroom and crawl back into our marital bed. We kiss, mumble syllables of affection, and turn our backs, desperate to recapture what's left of a night's sleep. But with the touch of the pillow on my cheek I know that sleep will evade me.

1963–1964: How Joe loved The Apprentices Hall. He was called Fortune, not Mr Fortune like his dad, just Fortune. A boy like any other with no condescension concerning his scholarship status and no prejudice of his religious definition. He even found that he was allowed to go into assembly. Well, at least no one stopped him, and Patte never found out. Life at Kitchener Street still endured with the same gentle tones of conversation saying the same familiar things. 'He said, she said, yes please, no thank you, pass the, it cost, I know, hurry up, eat up, keep warm, be careful, get up, go to bed, be a good boy.' Oh yes, be a good boy. He was still expected to be a good Jewish boy.

Every day started with the flurry of Mitte and his mother getting him off to school. At thirteen-years-old he already towered over them both, but they danced about him like two sweet thrushes would a cuckoo. A good breakfast and a clean hanky. Satchel loaded, and its weight commented on daily. His sports equipment, ironed and spotless, in a separate drawstring bag. His season ticket located, and then an anxious waving off as he sallied forth into the perils of the straphanging rush hour. At 4.00p.m. his journey was reversed, in less frantic mode, back to Kitchener Street. Arriving home tired, inky fingered, and stinking of London Transport. A stodgy high tea, and two hours hard graft with his homework. Lights out and too exhausted for carnal thoughts.

1965: By the age of fifteen the good boy had been kicked well into touch, and on Saturday afternoons he'd invented an escape route. 'Just going to the library,' he would shout, and Mitte and his mother would rush out from the kitchen, bustling with concern. They checked the time and the weather and looked at him with worried bird-like eyes. They always tried to persuade him that it wasn't worth going but, being obviously out-gunned, they told him what time he had to be back, to be careful crossing the road, and not to talk to strangers.

He never went near the library. He would go to the local fleapit, and absorb himself with the celluloid world of romance and adventure, sinking into raptures over Grace Kelly, Marilyn Monroe, Brigit Bardot and Julie Christie. Of an early evening he would group with a crowd of other bored and seeking teenagers in the park on Peckham Rye, smoking and telling dirty jokes. Girls, shy and giggly, were grouped on the roundabout with their backs turned. Boys, gruff and mouthy, lounged on the swings. 'Make a circuit, girls,' shouted the boys, and the girls slowly shuffled their feet on the tarmac until they came face to face with each other, and neither party could think of a single thing to say.

But soon shuffling little girls on roundabouts weren't enough for Joe. He fell in love with Joanie Bayliss. Joanie had long, bleached-blonde hair, the face of a film star, and he thought she was the most wonderful girl in the world. It wasn't real love of course, but he didn't know it at the time. He was really in love with the mystery of what was under her clothes and the coat-peg in his pants.

1966: Joe and Joanie were standing under a tree behind the public conveniences in the park, trying to look like Diana Dors and Rock Hudson. It was the witching hour, the time between light and dark, and Joanie was bewitching him. Behind them, a few defiant, sooty trees stood like dark hands, and at their feet some bad tempered sparrows were suppering on a squashed chip. Inside the echoing lavatories a chain was pulled, and the sound of running water gushed. He and Joanie pushed together like two cows in a byre. 'You smell nice,' he said.

'Evening in Paris,' she replied, in her best mid-Atlantic accent.

'Fancy an evening up the allotments?' he asked her. 'My grandad's got a nice warm little toolshed we could go to.' She giggled, but he smothered her mouth with his lips. He put his left hand round her waist, and his right hand crept up inside her tight jumper, but she removed his hand with an indignant hiss, and pulled away.

'We're not really allowed to do this, are we?' she said.

'Bullshit,' he said, pulling her back towards him. 'Let me, Joanie.' He nuzzled against her, and blew in her ear, trying to manoeuvre his hand up her jumper again. 'Please, Joanie.'

A Victorian lamppost suddenly flashed on, causing Joanie to turn a luminous green. She softened in his arms and he seized the moment, fumbling blindly with a hard, conical undergarment. At last her warm, heavy breast fell into his cupped hand. His ankle linked around hers, he pressed himself closer and began to move her in an amateur version of the rumba. But then she started to sniff. 'I really want to, Joe, but I'm too scared 'cause you're not allowed.' He ignored her and began to scrabble up her skirt with his free hand, but she pulled away again and shoved her breast away.

'We can't, Joe. You're only allowed to go out with Jewish girls. You'll get into trouble, and then I'll get into trouble.'

'Don't be daft. I can do what I like. My cousin Felix is seeing that Irene from the baker's. She's a *shikse*.'

'A what?'

'A *shikse*. You know, not Jewish. We can do what we like, Felix said so.'

'The hell you can. We've all been warned off you. That little granny of yours makes sure we all know you're more precious than Prince fucking Charles. Oh, I can't do this, Joe.' He heard the clack of her slingbacks as she ran away from him without looking back.

But he soon found out Joanie was right. He wasn't allowed. A week later he and cousin Jack were sitting on a park bench. They'd laughed so much their faces were wet, their ribs ached, and their foreheads were resting on their knees with exhaustion. Felix had been caught in the front parlour with smiling Irene, the fat and jolly girl from the baker's. Uncle Harry and Auntie Hilda had gone to The King George as usual on Sunday night, and you could normally set your watch by them. Eight o'clock out of the door, a few Double Diamonds with the quartet, a rousing chorus of 'Now is the Hour,' and tucked up in bed by ten thirty. But that night Auntie Hilda tripped up the step going into the pub, and banged her head on a door handle. Solly the bookmaker said she looked a bit dicky, and thought she might need a little lie down, so they accepted a lift home in his car. Being somewhat noisily absorbed, Felix didn't hear the silent purring of Solly's Daimler, or expect the front door to open. The near naked Irene was hurled out into the street, followed by red faces all round. Felix was propelled up to his room by a wild and fuming Uncle Harry, and although Jack had his ear pressed hard against the wall the only words he heard were 'sin' and '*shikse*'.

When the laughing stopped the harsh demands of their people filtered down. 'Thou shalt not fornicate out of wedlock,' and 'Thou shalt only lay thine eyes on nice Jewish girls.'

'Trouble is, Jack,' said Joe, 'I just don't fancy our girls.'

'What! Like Melvin? Good God, not you as well.'

'No. I am *not* like Melvin. I love girls, but I just don't fancy *our* girls.'

He reached into his trouser pocket and withdrew a dog-eared postcard he'd bought on a school visit to a museum. A perfect woman's body stood skewered and naked in a shell. Botticelli's Venus. The perfection of the Aryan woman. But it wasn't just her body that spoke to him. It was her expression. A five-hundred-year-old face of perfect peace and serenity. Her placid eyes stared without seeing, and her mind was lost in thoughts only of him.

'That's for me, Jack. I don't give a monkey's nut for all their rules and regulations. That's what I want, and that's what I'm going to have.'

CHAPTER FOUR

Friday

WELCOME TO RAVENSWOOD HEALTH CENTRE; a shining example of what the National Health Service can provide if they come up with the money. Rebuilt fifteen years ago from my crumbling, single-handed practice, it serves the heaving populous of Ravens Hill; a less than salubrious area of cosmopolitan south London. I'm now the senior partner of seven general practitioners, with a full compliment of attendant staff. It may not seem like a madhouse, but settle back, open the popcorn, and experience the crazy, death defying world of the family doctor.

The door opens and the maladies stagger in. Maladies, no doubt, bequeathed by poverty, Dickensian housing (re-invented as high rise flats), and polluted suburban air. They sit, I ask, they answer. I touch, I listen, and I peer. I give my verdict and act upon it, be it a prescription, or referral, or sod-all as the case may be. They smile, they thank me and retreat. The door closes and the door opens again for an action replay. Day-in day-out my head is filled with the cacophony of the soft machine, as bones grind against sinews, pumps fill sumps and lungs wheeze compressed air.

'Tis now five o'clock. I clear my in tray, make a dozen phone calls, sign my repeat prescriptions, and anything else that needs my cross. I throw down my pen and sigh. That's it, Joe. You're off the hook until Monday morning, but all the same I examine my hand-held gizmo for news of impending disappointment:

Saturday: An empty page. Hooray.

Sunday: Mum's 80th birthday. 1.00 p.m. Lunch and tea.

Fuck! My heart sinks. Can't get out of that one. Do I hear a big black paw scraping at the door? 'Get back to your basket,' I shout silently, 'and don't even think about putting in a guest appearance over my precious long weekend.' I get up, and leave my consulting room. Time to go home. 'Good night everyone,' I say. 'See you on Monday morning.'

Home. Sunny Lea, 14 Ravens Hill Rise. A double-fronted detached villa, built in 1865 for a manufacturer of wax candles, Mr Bertram Spiller. Situated far away from the stink, noise and congestion of both traffic and railway line, it sits high up on the hill where ravens ruled before nineteenth-century expansion queered their pitch. A summit where, on a clear day (with the aid of a fifty foot scaffold tower and a periscope), you can see St Paul's Cathedral. I turn the key in the front door, and, out of habit and respect to my forefathers, I touch the doorpost. Like Eleanor Rigby, I remove my Dr Fortune face and place it in a jar by the door. Instantly I become Joe, devoted and loyal husband, fond and caring father, and (as you well know) would-be murderer of one detested father-in-law. I slip into the old moccasins that I very happily walk in, and head for the kitchen.

Anna, having left her geriatric social worker's face in the jar by the door, has her feet up on a chair, and a large G and T in her hand. 'Good day?' I say, not really expecting her to go into elaborate detail.

'No. The usual awful day, but nothing that a child-free weekend with you won't fix.' She gets up to embrace me, and as I take her in my arms I challenge and defy any ghosts or spirits to invade and spoil this rare nirvana. I've thought about her and wanted her all day. I've imagined her smell, the softness of her skin, the sound of her voice being nice to me, and her enthusiasm for my body. My head drops forward and my face nuzzles deep into the soft cushions of her breasts. She sighs and presses her fingers into my buttocks. This should be my cue to be a confident, caveman lover, and throw her over my shoulder, but ten hours on the hoof have rendered me as fragrant as a zoo and my lady deserves better.

I throw off my shiny-arsed suit that has absorbed my patient's blood, sweat, tears and leaky Pampers all week, and hurl the rest into the laundry basket. I enter the shower cubicle, throw my head under the gushing spray, and open my mouth. The hot water is a sensual and divine pleasure as it beats on my bare crown, most of my hair being sadly absent these days. When I retire I will grow what little is left and get a pony-tail going again. That's the real me. The old me. No, the young me. The me I used to be.

I start to lather my furry body aggressively, but I have to be very careful I don't drop the soap or I'll never find it. It's not just bad eyesight. An alien larger creature has invaded my body and my bulk won't lend itself to doubling up in the confines of the shower cubicle. Not that I'm a fat slob. I just have a very expanded waistline. Anna's face calls it my lovely teddy bear tummy. My children call it my disgusting gut. I know I should loose some weight, but what the hell! I spend my life doling out advice to my punters concerning alcohol abuse, and healthy eating, and blood pressure, and the perils of tobacco. I just don't want it to apply to me. Leave me alone, Dr Killjoy. I'm in a very good mood. You'll have gathered that I'm feeling very relaxed and happy. Enjoy this time with me. It's all too rare these days.

I now sit upstairs in my study, cleansed, refreshed and wearing a clean white Moroccan *thobe*, a loose, full-length garment I wear with great affection to parade my biblical roots. I sink down in my old armchair, stretch and sigh, pour a glass of red and roll up from my old tin:

J & F Bell
Three Nuns Tobacco
Empire Blend
Glasgow
Tobacco of Curious Cut

And curious it certainly is. I flatten my lips and draw in. First blow since Sunday, and it tastes like paradise. I hold the delicious smoke in my mouth and swallow, yearning for the kick that will release the coiled spring. I look out of the window to contemplate the peace of an early summer evening. In a hazy dip on the far horizon the city of London shimmers, and below in the garden our bad tempered tom cat, Me-Toom-Tum, hunts stealthily under the ancient apple tree. I give thanks for my home, which I'm proud to say was bought and paid for by me, Joe Fortune, the Jewboy without a pot to piss in. Well, these days, not only do I have a pot to piss in, the pot is full to overflowing.

In the middle of the 1960s my cousin Jack joined the family green grocery business straight from school, and Patte took on a second stall. By the end of the decade he had five, all trading from street markets south of the river. Gradually there was more expansion and now, thanks to Jack's brilliant business acumen, Moisemann's has become the largest commercial supplier of fruit and veg in the capital. I'm a director without portfolio, but being a major shareholder I do very nicely, thank you.

So. Time for my daily dream. The old bastard has to be bumped off urgently. I'm unable to allow his advancement into dependent old age, and dying by natural causes (no matter how miserably) is far too good for him. My bitterness remains for which he is responsible. Every single day of my life my unborn child is still loved and remembered. No doubt loved and remembered by its mother as well. The pact I made with Gordon all those years ago has held firm. We still hate each other's guts. With military cunning we move like creeping silent enemies, battle lines drawn and parallels respected. With the good manners of the officer classes, we each hide behind our own particular version of past events, but the pain still attacks me. Sometimes sweeping in with a full battle cry, sometimes just the barely audible sound of distant firing. But the time has come, Gordon. Your days are numbered. Now what if I pushed you down the stairs? How does a broken neck appeal to you?

My mobile suddenly erupts into life. 'Hallo monkey-man,' purrs a familiar voice. I can smell the Osca de la Renta. I can see the lip-glossed and seeking mouth. I can hear the fizzling remnants of an old flame. It's Nola.

'Joe,' she says. 'About the family bash on Sunday. Just to say my rotten sod of husband has buggered off sailing and ...' There now follows a very complex story on why she and Felix might be late. Of course it's all a load of eyewash. She's lonely, and she wants to talk to me. She knows exactly where Felix is, and so do I. Sailing up a terraced side-street in Broadstairs, with a fat and jolly legal secretary, manipulating copious mounds of flesh and laughing like a drain. I feel sorry for her so I'm a bit naughty. I flirt a bit, and try to cheer her up, but in truth we know the score. Joe Fortune and Nola Moisemann may have had a colourful theatrical past, but she's been firmly off-stage for twenty odd years.

'Bye, love,' I say. 'See you Sunday.'

Now perhaps a little music to unwind to, and I slot in a shmaltzy compilation CD. Dusty Springfield sees the look of love in my eyes, Carly Simon assures me that nobody does it better, and Toni Teniel begs me to do it to her one more time. Keep it up girls, but I can feel my tired old eyes starting to close ... just a catnap ... just forty winks ... just a little time to ponder my first, sweet taste of honey ...

1966: Joe was sixteen and the loneliness of the long distance adolescent was playing at The Odeon. The gang from the playground in the park had all become absorbed with more interesting means of entertainment, such as courting, and football, and hippy hippy shaking at the Hammersmith Palais. Felix was in his first year up at Oxford, Jack was in fine voice selling his wares on the market stall, and Melvin had fallen madly in love with his maths master. For Joe the routine at Kitchener Street still persisted with the same dull, plodding regularity. Every day he went to school, he worked hard, he came home, he did his homework and he went to bed. He passed eight O levels at 'A' grade, and won the fifth form biology prize; a book token for five shillings. As a serious student of biology, and taking his responsibilities very seriously, he bought a copy of Henry Miller's *Tropic of Capricorn*.

Then, as soon as school broke up, it was off to Westgate-on-Sea, near Margate, for a jolly fortnight of sun, sea and sandy sandwiches. In the 1960s things were on the up for everyone and the Fortune/Moisemann family had acquired a second hand holiday caravan. Joe hadn't wanted to go of course, but being the trapped man-child that sixteen-year-old boys (especially Jewish boys) were in 1966, he had no choice. Every morning he escaped alone for a long walk; head down and round-shouldered, suffering the nausea of being banged up, cheek by jowl, with the quartet. He was unable to rise above himself, feeling like a balloon, pumped to bursting but unable to soar. A leaden-footed clumsy oaf. A sweating clod living in a world of restraint and temperance. He tramped furiously for miles along the coastline, wishing he could find another world where he could be the person he wanted to be, and not the person they expected him to be, or thought he was.

The mysteries of the female flesh still evaded him, but he fantasised. One minute believing that every girl who saw him would faint with lust; another knowing that his ugliness would make them clutch each other with hysterics. He was a mess of the first order. He would dump himself down on the sand, tight-chested and angry, trying to pluck up the courage to end it all. Such was the pain of adolescence, but it was a pain that the quartet seemed to know nothing about.

1967: Joe was seventeen and still a lumbering man-child. Still suffering intense loneliness and frustration, and still a clumsy virgin. His cousins, however, had fared rather better. Felix was devouring the multifarious fruits of Oxford, and Melvin (to the silent shame of his parents) had taken up with a Bond Street hairdresser and declared himself to be madly, madly gay. Jack had a regular slot in Patte's toolshed up at the allotments with the ever-obliging Irene (Felix's ex from the Bakers), and although she'd made it quite clear to Joe she'd make room for him too he just wasn't interested. Ever the perfectionist he still wanted a milk-skinned, quiet beauty who stood in a shell. But who? When? How? He didn't intend to be greedy, or expect it to happen very often, but he just wanted to cross the great divide. A wry secret he could withhold from the quartet, and he dreamed wickedly of shocking them.

'Come on our Joe, eat up, there's a good boy.'

'Sorry Mitte, I'm not hungry. My appetite has been gratified. The young stag has held fast onto King Solomon's hem, and feasted on dates and apples and pomegranates, and chased the little foxes through the vineyards. In other words, I've fucked. Did you hear me, Mitte, or perhaps you've no idea what that means. Trying to imagine anyone in this house indulging in passionate activity strains my imagination beyond belief.' Well, that was the pipe dream. The reality was much too clandestine to reveal.

He'd always noticed Kit because she was so different. Everyone on the street market talked about her as 'That Kit. That mad redhead. That weird Irish woman,' but to Joe, Katherine Kennedy was a gift from the gods. She shone as if the sun had come out at midnight; a bright star in the drab, monochrome sky of Kitchener Street's suffocation. In a bold statement of defiance and freedom, exotic creatures like Kit had burst out of the sterile ground with the advent of the swinging sixties, but she was certainly no slave to the fashion dictats of the time. Long, flowing velvet dresses of emerald green and peacock blue hung on her lean goddess's body, and her honey coloured pre-Raphaelite curls either blew wildly in the wind, or were restrained beneath a sequined gypsy scarf. Her face wore a constant expression; an inanimate gentle mask of black eyelashes, low-hooded purple lids, a complexion of palest ivory and dark plum lips. She was the Venus of his dreams. She was desire, she was freedom and she was nearly as old as his mother.

She ran a small shop on Rye Lane, fronting the thoroughfare of the street market. Today it would be called antiques and ephemera, but in those days it was just junk. On Saturdays he started to give her a hand, to move things and tidy up for her. It became a regular routine, but it didn't go unnoticed by Jack, working the stall on the other side of the road. 'She fancies you,' he said.

'No chance,' Joe replied. 'She's batty. It's only my Saturday job to earn bit of pocket money.'

Patte was also keeping a cynical eye on him. 'You watch that one,' he said. 'She's a spider. A right rum 'un and a dolly mixture short of a quarter. When you've finished at the end of the day you're to come straight home in case she starts taking her boots off.' Was Joe supposed to know what that meant? No one had ever talked to him of such things, and even the Felix and Irene incident hadn't been mentioned in his presence. He did know of course. There were always whispers about someone up the street or round the corner who couldn't keep their boots on. But Patte was right. Kit eventually removed her boots.

It was at the end of a long cold day. There hadn't been much trade and she'd stood around with her hands dug deep into the pockets of an old fur coat. 'Let's pack it in,' she said. 'Come upstairs and have a glass of port. Warms you up much better than cocoa on a day like this.' She walked up the stairs, and he followed. 'Throw some coal on the fire, there's a dear. I'll just get the bottle.' He dropped a few pieces of cold, shiny coal onto the mound of glowing embers, and as he agitated with the poker the new flames leapt up, casting a warm light in the gathering darkness. He didn't hear her come up behind him, but he knew she was there. He could feel her eyes burning on the back of his neck, an invisible tentacle reached out and he was caught in the web. He waited, as still as a statue, holding his breath and knowing that the time had come. She pulled his shoulder and turned him round. She still wore the fur coat, but she took his hand, placed his palm onto the warmth of her naked breast, and let the coat fall. Her pale, posing body was a shock to the innocent daydreamer – a mixture of horror and delight in equal portions. He recoiled, afraid and flustered, but she fixed him with the look of a sphinx. 'It's what you want as well, isn't it?' she said. 'Don't waste time denying it.'

'But I don't know what to do,' he mumbled, gripped with a sudden desperation to run away.

'Oh, I think you do, Joe. I think you know exactly what to do.'

Kit received him at his own pace. He tried to be slow, but he instantly found a black empty place where there was him, and no one else but him, and he was flying blindly out of the world with the speed of a comet. His arc of release was a shock but such an explosion of fulfilment he thought he might lose consciousness. He fell back to earth as if he was being sucked into a vortex, his head faint and his whole body singing with primaeval gratification. Afterwards he cried. A real childish sobbing and messy distress. 'I hurt you,' he wept. 'I'm so sorry.'

'No, my love,' she said gently, 'that was my pleasure.'

'But you screamed,' he said.

'Yes,' she said, smiling softly into his watery eyes. '*That* was my pleasure.'

It was with Kit that he at last grew up. He burst from his chains, and his reach and touch stretched to the outer edges of the universe. She was never the older woman and he was never the schoolboy. They were lovers. Equals in a strange and secret union that he kept wholly to himself. She took him into a new stratosphere of wonder, delight, and discovery that superseded the schoolroom, filling his head with music and poetry, literature and astrology, alternative religions and fine art. She had a way of telling him things that made him think he'd worked out the answers for himself. Patient reasoning, questions answered with questions, the pavement philosophy of the Socratic world. Kit's bed was a magic nest hidden in a misty tree. As he lay with her he picked the stars from the sky, and planted them in her hair, while she threw her six legs around his naked body.

1968: Joe was eighteen. He was now a man of six feet three, with a broad, muscular chest span, a body covered in dark silk and long hair drawn into a thick pony-tail. He was an accomplished and eager lover, skilled in every contortion known to man, and vain in the knowledge that he fulfilled every pleasure Kit sought. He was now able to discuss theoretical and scholarly concepts with wit and irony, and could offer opinions on the diversities of life, the universe, and any other goddamn thing he was supposed to have an opinion about. But this adult expansion had somehow not conveyed itself to Kitchener Street, despite the fact that he'd won a place at Oxford University. To the quartet he was still the schoolboy, and never more demonstrated than the day they all accompanied him to the Oriel College Open Day.

The breathtaking beauty of Oriel stood in her midsummer loveliness. The sun-kissed mullions, and green-grassed quadrangles, linked and twisted with a mediaeval magic that proclaimed hallowed ground – something he couldn't believe was going to be his future. He understood how the quartet gooed and gaahed, because he was swallowing with awe himself, but that day he prayed for the sudden death of one of them – any one of them – to deflect from his squirming discomfort. Every tutor, fellow, visiting parent, waitress, gardener and general odd-bod was nobbled and forced to hear his full biographical profile, his list of outstanding academic achievements, and how proud they were of him.

A college scout, a quiet, polite man called Bransby, took them up a narrow stone staircase to show them the undergraduates' rooms. He too was subjected to their set piece. 'He got eight 'A' grade O levels, and four 'A' grade A levels,' his mother boasted. Patte fixed Bransby's eye, pointed at Joe, and whispered 'Apprentices Hall' with a proud nod. His father, who couldn't really think of anything profound to say, enquired of Bransby what his overtime prospects were like, and Mitte wanted to see the exact room reserved for Mr Josiah Fortune.

'I'm so sorry,' Bransby said. 'Mr Fortune's room isn't allocated yet.'

'Well, this room looks very nice,' said Mitte. 'Not too far from the bathroom and there's a nice view over the cobbles. Perhaps, Mr Bransby, you can see to it that our Josiah gets this room.' She then started grappling in her handbag, and Joe's stomach lurched, thinking that green-folding was going to be proffered by way of a bribe, but she was just searching for Felix's photograph.

'Do you know my other grandson, Mr Bransby?' she said, shoving Felix's ancient *bar mitzvah* photograph under his nose. 'Felix Moisemann. He goes to Queen's College, and he's learning the law.' 'Oh, Mitte,' Joe wanted to shout. 'You're supposed to say that Felix is up at Queen's reading jurisprudence,' but Bransby, being a discreet and professional college servant, was impeccably polite. No, he was afraid he didn't know Mr Moisemann, but he'd keep his eye open for him.

Patte then began to mutter and fuss about the location of the synagogue. Bransby had to admit he no idea where it was, but was dispatched to find out, which took ten minutes of foot-hopping and whispering, to the tone of 'well, you'd have thought he'd have known, wouldn't you?' On returning with the information he stood respectfully with them, while they studied maps, and asked about bus routes. 'I think it would be prudent to say that Jericho is within walking distance,' Bransby contributed.

Joe stood, flushed with a deep, bubbling shame and humiliation, but he knew that Bransby must have seen it all before. 'Goodbye, sir,' he said, shaking him warmly by the hand, and choosing his words with the skill of a natural psychologist. 'It's been a pleasure meeting you, and I'm sure you'll settle in very well at Oriel. I don't think you'll be homesick. We're one big happy family here.' He gave him a brief salute, and a kind smile.

'We're off to the Cadena Café now, Mr Bransby,' beamed Mitte. 'Afternoon tea and all the trimmings. It's not every day we get a chance to hob nob so we're all having menu C.'

Menu C presented a confusing array of options, and a patient waitress, dressed as a Victorian parlourmaid, stood with her pencil poised. The Earl Grey and Lapsang Souchong were quickly dismissed. 'Nothing like a good old pot of Typhoo,' Mitte declared, but the sandwich fillings took several minutes of consultation and lip sucking. At last a consensus was reached; bloater paste and cucumber, cream cheese and cress, and beef and horseradish. The choosing of jam and cream scones versus toasted teacakes took up nearly the same length of time, but mercifully there were no options on the gateaux. The decision had already been made by Menu C. It was chocolate éclairs, or chocolate éclairs. One each. But then Felix arrived, and the bonhomie of the occasion suddenly collapsed. He'd brought his girlfriend, and being a strictly family occasion, strangers were unwelcome.

Christa was a Danish laundry maid at Queen's, with breasts and buttocks like four competing beach balls; the usual stereotype adored by Felix, and she definitely wasn't of the family faith. Before she'd even sat down the atmosphere turned chilly, but the quartet were fully frozen into silence at the besotted couple's erotic performance. They ruminated their sandwiches with leering, bovine motion; they parted the scones and licked out the jam with stiff tongues, and in eating the éclairs parodied fellatio. Even drinking their tea, they giggled and poked their fingers suggestively in and out of the fancy cup handles.

With the afternoon ruined, a second pot of tea was not required, and as they all rose to leave Felix winked at Joe and jerked his head towards the gents. 'What do you think of my Danish pastry?' he asked, as they stood to pee together. 'Shags like a trampoline.'

'Felix, you're nuts. You did it on purpose, didn't you?'

'Well spotted, Sherlock. This is 1968 and I'm twenty years old. Things are changing for young Jews. The world's changing and there's new thinking. The sooner they get that in their thick skulls the better. We can, and we will, do exactly as we like.'

Going home on the coach the quartet grouped tribally together, their mouths rotating with clockwork intensity. The appalling scene was played over and over again. Their minds were firmly made up that 'things were going to have to be said', because Felix 'was at it again', but Joe wasn't included in this intense family pow-wow. He sat alone, reading *The Ballad of the Sad Café*.

Three months later it was cold and raining as another autumn crept in like a cat burglar. He and Kit had indulged their usual hard passion; her elbows spread wide, her breasts swinging loose, her face hard-pressed and suffocating on the pillow. He'd lain his cheek on the hard protrusions of her spine, idly murmuring his usual acceptance speech of enjoyment and gratitude. The darkness of six o'clock was unexpected and blasts of rain smacked against the window-panes like hurled nails. Below them the busy pedestrian street life of Rye Lane began to vanish as the people fled to find shelter. 'These are my people,' Joe thought, 'leading good and simple lives, but soon this life will no longer be mine. I've been selected for escape. Tomorrow night I'll be at Oriel College and my new life stretches ahead of me like a shimmering jewel on the horizon.'

He leaned back on a mound of pillows, posing with parted knees and knowing that he was a beautiful boy. Kit sat beside him, leaning her cheek on his shoulder, idly fingering the inside of his wrist. He suddenly had a desire to kiss her. His lips sought hers and he felt a rising up within himself of something that he thought must have been a moment of deep and genuine love. Whatever it was, it was to be their goodbye kiss. They both knew their affair was over. It had been a grand passion but the two planets, drawn together by gravity and momentum, were now destined, by the same forces, to move apart. 'I'll come back and see you,' he said.

'No you won't,' she replied. 'This time tomorrow you'll be somebody else. Go, with my blessing, and my memory.'

When he left her the rain was still falling fast, but he pulled up his collar, opened his mouth to the heavens and dawdled home. How he loved moving slowly in the rain that night and being the only idiot on the street. Joe Fortune. Free spirit. But as soon as he walked into Kitchener Street he had a feeling of foreboding; as if something had gone in before him. It had stopped, turned, and put a warning hand up to his chest. Nothing looked different, but a smoke of strangeness hung like the fug of burnt toast.

The usual scene presented when he walked into the back room. The firelight threw a darting brilliance over the faces of the quartet, and the table lamps cast soft shadows onto the aged, foxed wallpaper. The comfortable tones of *Down Your*

Way emitted from the old Bakelite wireless. His mother was knitting a dishcloth. His father was sitting at the table, polishing the family's shoes on the *Daily Mirror*, and giving a little 'har' on the toes as he rubbed. Patte was reading the *Jewish Chronicle*, muttering under his breath in Hebrew, and Mitte was sewing name-tapes onto his new Oxford clothes. After every article was completed she exclaimed, 'There! That's for Mr Josiah Fortune of Oriel College, Oxford.' His freshman's scarf and tie had been laid out, with religious precision, on a tray, waiting to be shown to any relative, or neighbour, or insurance man, or even the milkman.

He was made to go upstairs straight away to change out of his wet clothes or he'd be bound to catch his death, but that evening joining the queue to the Jewish 'special place' was a very attractive option compared to their endless fussing. He refused food and there was a full five minutes of clucking from the caterers, and being told he'd be dead (again) by tomorrow if he didn't have a plate of the dog sick they called goulash. He won in the end but he had a manic desire to grab the Oriel scarf and strangle them both. All he really wanted to do was to go to his bedroom, to be on his own and dream, but tomorrow he would fly away to freedom and he was duty bound to join them.

A play by J.B Priestley started on the wireless, something that Joe would have liked to have listened to, but Patte waved his hand in the air with authority, indicating that it be turned off. 'We don't want that tripe on. I can't abide those whiny northerners.' Joe thus sat down on the hearthrug in front of the fire, enjoying the warmth, but feeling every bit like the

72

little boy who'd played at their feet with his toys. He quietly opened his book, *Bonjour Tristesse*. The quartet was impressed; they thought he was reading in French. 'You read so much you'll wear your eyes out,' Mitte complained. 'You've been in the library all day. Can't you give it a rest?'

'What would you suggest, Mitte?' he replied. 'Perhaps I could take up knitting?' Patte told him not to be so cheeky.

Gradually, as bedtime approached, the usual routines were followed. On the stroke of ten Patte declared, as he did every night, 'Ah, well. Time for the wooden hill.' He and Mitte fussed and muttered and went up to bed. His parents usually followed some ten minutes later, after going out the back and preparing the morning tea tray, but that night something was afoot. They began silently mouthing to each other and there was some head jerking. His mother at last kissed him goodnight, dabbed her eyes and muttered about missing him. 'Ah, well. Make sure you phone us up every Sunday night. You'll be allowed home for the odd weekend, won't you, and we can always get down to see you on a day return. Try keeping us away. Nighty night.'

His father carefully cleared the shoe-cleaning paper from the table and placed the shiny shoes on the hearth to warm for the morning. 'What have you been reading in the library today?' he asked, absently, rubbing his hands together.

'Poetry,' Joe replied politely.

'Ah!' his father said, holding up one finger, and turning his head like a Victorian actor. 'She took me to her elfin grot. The lady of Shalot.'

With patronising superiority Joe breathed out. 'I think you're getting your Keats and your Tennyson mixed up, Dad.'

'Well, there you go,' his father replied. 'I haven't had your learning, son. Stands to reason. I was never much good at school but I liked a bit of poetry. 'The boy stood on the burning deck' and all that stuff. Anyway, you've had the education for it and we're right proud of you. Did you know that you and Felix are the only boys from round here that ever got to go to any university, let alone Oxford? Two in one family, eh? That says something, doesn't it, but you must get your brains from the Moisemanns. My old grey matter's nothing to write home about.' He laughed. Joe laughed too. 'Son, can we have a talk?'

Harvey drew out a chair, and sat down at the table. Joe knew what was coming. A father and son chat of course. The standard man-to-man warning procedure that parents thought of as their duty in those days. 'Son.' He cleared his throat. 'Son.' He swallowed hard. 'Son, what I'm trying to say ...' He was trying, he was really trying. Sweat had broken out on his brow and he flustered like a dislodged chicken. 'What I'm really trying to say is . . .' He ran out of words again, but bravely stumbled on. 'Your mother and me. We really wanted brothers and sisters for you but . . . ' he held up his hand, 'it was not to be. All we've ever had is the precious gift of you. You're all we've got and we want so much for you. We want you to be happy, but we want you to have the life we never had. A good career, money, a nice home and a big family. Tomorrow you'll be off. Of course we want you to go, and we're bursting with pride, but we're sick with worry. Jack and Felix are going wild.

They're breaking our hearts with their loose and unsuitable women. I may sound like a stuffed shirt but we don't want you to go the same way. Somewhere in the future there's a perfect Jewish girl waiting for you. Will you keep yourself just for her?'

Joe stared ahead, looking at the wall but seeing nothing. He could hear his father's anxious breathing, the tick of the clock, a tap dripping in the scullery and the occasional faint squeak of a floorboard above his head. Did his father know about Kit? Was this his way of telling him he knew? 'Dad,' he replied gently, 'Felix says that's all out the window. It's 1968. These days things are changing and there's new thinking. Our religion's unfair. If the synagogue accepts the children of Jewish women to be Jews, no matter what religion the fathers are, why not the reverse? It's going to happen soon, Dad. Felix said so.'

His father groaned. 'That boy's going to be the ruin of our family. He's talking through his hat as usual. He's supposed to be learning the law but he doesn't half come out with a load of old baloney. No, son. Nothing's going to change. Your children will only be Jews if you marry a Jew. Maybe things aren't fair in your eyes, but it's the way things are, and the way things are going to stay. Joe, we really are the chosen ones, you know. Sometimes I wonder if we haven't been chosen to suffer, but we're so lucky. We have each other, we have God and we have the 'one love'. Can you imagine looking over your shoulder and seeing the long line of our forefathers going back to Abraham? See how tall they stand. How valiant, how courageous, how proud. We don't talk much of our sadnesses but can you see the millions of our people – yes, Joe, millions – who've died in pain just for being and we must honour them.'

Had Joe been standing his knees would have buckled beneath him. His father's simple words struck like bullets to his heart, his sins stung like angry bees, and his ears burned with shame. His body had sinned. He'd sucked, and slobbered, and clawed, and clasped, thrusting for the selfish peak of release. His soul had sinned. He'd been a rebel, a traitor, a defector, a turncoat. How could he have thought of leaving them behind? How could he have forgotten the suffering of his forefathers?

For the first time in his life he saw his father as a good man. A simple man. A kind and patient man. Yes, all these things irritated him to the point of madness, but that night he was gripped with an overpowering love for him. He looked over his shoulder. He saw his father and Patte leading the long line of his forefathers, and his head sang. Suddenly he wanted to be a good boy, a precious son and a devout Jew. To be part of this tight knot they all belonged to. He was a Jew! Being Jewish was something he couldn't buy, or win or educate himself into. He just *was*, and his body heaved with the power and strength of his lineage. Now he wanted to save himself, in purity, for the unknown Jewish wife who was waiting for him somewhere out there in the future. One day his children would look behind them, and there'd be a gnarled old Joe Fortune at the head of the long and winding line, leading back into the mists of biblical times. The privilege of his birthright reached out and touched him.

'Oh, Dad,' he promised, 'I won't let you down.' A smile of utter contentment covered his father's face. They stood up, kissed each other twice on the lips, and clasped their arms around each other. They both breathed out with the love of their God melting over them like warm honey.

Joe entered his cold, bare little bedroom and undressed, rejoicing in the sight of his dark, hirsute body; the body of a true Israelite. He held his precious Orthodox penis in his hand like a cherished pet; the cut of the true Jewish man. For years he'd slept naked but tonight he needed the chastity of pyjamas. He slowly slipped them on, tying the cord round his waist, and buttoning the jacket up to the neck. He searched under his pillow for the old crumpled postcard of Botticelli's Venus, held her in his hands one last time, and tore her into small pieces. Had the child become a man, or had the man become a child?

1968–1974: Joe's time at Oxford University encompassed six long years of medical training, but only a few short paragraphs can vouch for it. His night of enlightenment in the back room at Kitchener Street hadn't actually affected his life as magically as he'd envisaged. On the one hand he knew and accepted his fate; on the other hand he had no desire to meet it head on. Patte had written a letter to the rabbi in Jericho, introducing Joe as a keen new member of the congregation, and soon after he arrived in Oxford there was an eager visitation. 'Hallo, Joe. I'm Rabbi Weisenbluth,' followed by enthusiastic hand shaking and smiling, but the synagogue held no more enchantment than before. Yes, he was an intensely proud Jew, but he found no impetus to go out and seek fellow Jews, or even more to the point, Jewish girls.

Felix came to see him in his first week, brought him a three-pack of condoms, and told him all the best places to look for birds. After the Christa incident Felix had bravely confronted the major family row, which ended with him shouting obscenities and walking out. Both his parents had cried for days, but could he care? Could he bananas. 'The old fogies can get stuffed,' he said. 'I'm going to lead the life I want, and I strongly advise you to do the same, Joe. Your time here will go like shit off a shovel and you don't get another chance. Then it's the hard slog of work for forty years and – God forbid – marriage! Yuck!'

'But what about *Shabbat*?' Joe said. 'It'll seem so strange not to have it any more. Do you think you could come round on Friday nights? Just to light a candle and mumble a bit.' Felix looked at him if he was mad.

'The Sabbath may rise at sunset, but so do I, sunshine. You can stick your candle up your arse. Love and peace.' After that he didn't see much of Felix. He was in his final year, and having spent the first two feeding his face on the Danish pastry he had a lot of catching up to do.

For Joe, the concept of time was metaphysical. It must have moved but it hung heavy on his hands. Apart from his lectures and seminars he had no other life, and his room in college became a bolt-hole from society. A cell where the prisoner imposed his own exile. His door was always shut and nobody ever knocked, but his window was always open.

As he sat, poring intently over his textbooks, the sounds of Oxford life filtered in. The laughing babble of snatched conversations, the cacophony of birdsong that flew from nearby Christchurch meadows, and the clatter of bicycles rattling on the cobbles in Merton Street. Autumn – winter – spring – summer and round again. Joe's Oxford years were filled with loneliness, and the swinging sixties swung into the seventies without him. All around him his peers were learning how to philosophise and argue, and discover all the wonders he'd found with Kit. Becoming lefties, or agnostics, or dropping drunk on a Saturday night, but most of all they had an undefinable thing called fun. Becoming intrinsic members of a naturally occurring club; its manifesto woven on the loom of youth and its membership binding for a lifetime. It's doubtful if anyone remembered sanctimonious, boring Joe Fortune, who crept about like an outsize Jewish nun. He kept his head down and devoted himself to his studies. He got a congratulatory first class honours degree in physiology, and continued his further years of medical training, but all he really did was to wait for the little spectre in the corner to introduce herself.

She did of course.

CHAPTER FIVE

Friday, continued . . .

'JOE,' ANNA WHISPERS, shaking my shoulder to wake me. The lady who loves to be called my shikse slides onto my lap and nuzzles my face. Our kiss is long and so tender it could be our first. I brush her hair away from her face and look at her with familiar longing. There's a small red scar on her eyelid and another on her temple. My lips brush them over like a butterfly's wings on a flower; a silent acknowledgment of our unspoken history. 'Come, my love,' she says, pulling me to my feet, and leading me by the hand to our bed. I pull my *thobe* over my head and her satin dressing gown falls to the floor. The moves, sighs, and perfect timing of the seasoned pros begin.

My Venus is glorious in her nakedness. She's still the perfect goddess who stepped out of the shell, and came to me in bold adultery one summer's morning so many years ago. Her limbs are long, smooth and creamy; her breasts heavy and firm. Her jaw unsagged, her face unwrinkled. I run my hands gently down over the rounded arcs of her pelvic bones, my fingertips pausing to acknowledge her only flaws; the war wounds of our fertility. I am *not* glorious in my nakedness. I'm ashamed that mother nature has kidnapped my young lover's body and replaced it with one several sizes too big, but despite my imperfections she still adores me. I'm clasped and caressed and moaned over. Small clever fingers knead, massage and urge me on. As usual, she tells me what she wants and how she wants it. As usual, I acquiesce, knowing that whatever she wants, I want it too.

I leave my body, and float gently up to the ceiling to watch the performance, a skill known only to a fortunate few, courtesy of *cannabis indica*, but it's hardly a spectator sport. There's no soft focus and trick shots about us, I'm afraid. Down there I'm turning and diving with the skill of a dolphin, but from up here I've got all the grace of a JCB digger. Another sort of earth moving, I suppose. Down there she's elegant and lithe, slithering around me like a sea snake, but from up here she's slung round my neck like a furious clockwork frog. I try not to leave her. I always try to stay on earth, but I can feel myself leaving for the black, empty place where there's no one but me, and all the pleasure is for me, and I love only me, and I'm flying and flying out of the world . . . but she's flying with me. Two voices sing out loudly and we free wheel back to earth on a downward thermal.

I thank Anna, with overflowing gratitude, for a fabulous fuck. I also thank my children for not being here, for without them I am spared the squeak on the stair and muffled voices which guarantee to immediately let the tyres down. Last, but not least, I thank my heart, lungs and knees for acting as support staff, without which I would be a floundering old jellyfish.

Through her tousled head I can see our bored observer slumped drunkenly on the windowsill; a wrinkled, faded, brown velvet monkey. He's seen more of us, and knows more about us, than we ever will. On her bedside table stands a photograph of me in 1979, shaking hands with the queen.

The married man, the father of a three-year old child, whose skin, under the crisp white coat, was sweat-soaked and salty after an illicit lunch-hour making love with the perfection of nurse Anna Morton Moore.

She rises to her knees. Slowly, she licks the shape of a kiss to the top of my bald head and leaves to prepare my *Shabbat*.

December 1974: Joe's finals were only three months away, and the Hippocratic Oath loomed. He was revising hard in the Cairns library, but convinced (as one always is) that he was bound to fail. He was suffering from study overload; his brain stuffed like a cushion with intricate facts, while his memory seemed unable to trot out the simple skill of tying a sling. As he tried to concentrate on the complexities of the human eye he could hear a strange crunching sound. It was Ursula Liebermann, rubbing the roots of her wiry black hair. In the silence of the library the sound enlarged to an industrial roar and he began to seethe with irritation. He leaned over towards her. 'Headache?' he enquired. She didn't answer. She got up, gathered her books and walked out with tears running down her cheeks. He followed. He hardly knew her and didn't particularly want to get to know her any better. She'd just always been around. Part of his student set, and a fellow Jew, but she might as well have been a Cocker spaniel for all he cared. After finals they would pose for a group photograph, shake hands, go their separate ways and instantly forget each other.

She was sitting on some stone steps when he found her. Spits of sharp rain, and winter's fingers, were lifting up her hair, but she didn't seem bothered. 'What's the matter?' he asked. She shook her left hand like a fan, but Joe looked blank. 'It's all off,' she said. 'My fiancé's dumped me. Finals coming up. Brilliant timing wouldn't you say?'

As if by autopilot Joe put his arm tenderly around her shoulders. Perhaps it was relief from the intensity of studying, perhaps it was the force of fate. He'd never know what was directing him that night, but he felt a strange sympathy for her. She slumped against him and began to sob again, interspersed with obscure, vitriolic outbursts babbled in between gulping snorts. Endless Kleenexes were soaked and discarded, but eventually she blew her nose like a trombone, and sniffed loudly. He gave her time and then placed his hand under her elbow, helping her up with the tenderness afforded to a frail patient. 'Come on,' he said. 'Let's go over to the Royal Oak. I'll buy you a drink.'

He bought her a large vodka and lime and himself a pint of beer. The fruit machine clattered, shouts went up to drown out the noise of falling coins, and the barmaid's laughter carried high and astringent. The till pinged musically, glasses clinked, pints slopped, and in the background Rod Stewart's gravelly throat bemoaned the imperfections of poor old Maggie. Joe suddenly realised he'd become strangely happy. He felt a dreamy sort of relaxation in his gut and a warmness flooded his limbs. He patted her hand. 'I'm sorry for your troubles,' he said. 'Look, there's some half decent cheese and tomato rolls on the counter. Do you fancy breaking bread?'

'You're very kind,' she replied.

They munched noisily, talking earnestly of their ambitions in a fast flow of comfortable conversation. She wanted a career in anaesthetics. He wanted oncology. They nodded sagely and discussed the merits, drawbacks, research and career prospects of both areas. Two mature and nearly doctors, poised to leap into the huge, frightening place called the rest of their lives. Time passed easily and Joe began to enjoy the rare sensation of one-to-one conversation, and although he knew that no male/female agenda existed between them it was very welcome to be in close proximity to a woman. By the end of the evening he'd asked her if she'd like to come with him to Jack's wedding the following weekend. His mother had been badgering him to 'bring his girlfriend', and he thought if he turned up with someone it might at least shut her up. 'It'll be the usual bun-fight,' he said. 'Serious hats and gold and the full clown slap. Think you can stand it?'

'Thank you, Joe,' she said. 'I'd love to come.'

They didn't make the wedding ceremony, due to missing a coach and slow winter weather, but the instant Joe walked into the reception with her the quartet pounced. Patte, who was the lead fiddle-player in the entertainment section, stopped the proceedings to welcome 'Joe's young lady' with a flowery little speech and a round of applause. Mitte took her arm, and dragged her round the room for intense introductions to each member of the family, accompanied by muddled explanations as to their exact positions on the family tree. Then his father settled her comfortably in a chair, and presented her with a toppling pile of food, a knife and fork, and encouragement to 'dig in'. His mother sat close up beside her, gleefully regurgitating her vast repertoire of anecdotes about little Josiah, the epitome of perfection and entertainment her only child had been.

At first he despaired for the day to be over, but as the familiarity of his people wrapped around him like a warm shawl he longed for his own fulfilment. Jack had found his bride, Naomi, a traditional choice and, as history would prove, his soul mate. After a ten-day honeymoon in Cyprus (courtesy of a potato exporter who was grateful to be contracted to Moisemann's) they would settle down to begin a lifetime of contentment. Joe was suddenly gripped with an intense jealousy he had no explanation for. He looked up. Urshie had her head bent, and was smiling politely, as his mother filled her ear with a story involving much laughter; an oft-told comedy tale of himself at the age of five, standing on a stool and decapitating a cuckoo with a poker as it burst out of a clock. Urshie just happened to look up too, and they exchanged a conciliatory smile. 'Parents, huh. Everyone of us a Jewish Prince or Princess.'

His body became as soft as soap. There was a warm invasive tingle in his crutch that began to turn into an unmistakable erection, but he couldn't understand why this was happening. It wasn't Ursula Liebermann he wanted. He was back in his bedroom at Kitchener Street, with a dog-eared postcard in his hands. Sliding his inky schoolboy's fingers down the perfect contours of Botticelli's Venus, and drowning in the thoughts behind her gentle eyes. Urshie was the antithesis of his dreaming, but as the day wore on something began to draw him strongly towards her.

But Felix certainly wasn't impressed, and he sidled up, giggling drunkenly. 'Which lamppost did you find *that* tied up to?' The happy, heaving throng of the wedding party didn't notice Joe propelling his cousin outside to wrench his arm up behind his back. The cold air smacked them both like stones in a sock, and frost sparkled in the gathering gloom. They'd never even exchanged as much as a cross word before.

'If you don't apologise, you smarmy bastard, I'll break your jaw,' Joe threatened, holding up a bunched fist.

'Hey man, only kidding,' Felix blustered.

'You'd better be,' snapped Joe, pushing him hard over a low slippery wall, and striding back inside.

Later that night the quartet accompanied he and Urshie to Victoria coach station. 'Look after each other,' Mitte instructed 'and come back and see us soon.'

'You make a lovely couple,' his mother gushed. 'I've never seen our Joe look so happy.' As the coach moved off everyone waved like lunatics.

'I think they liked you,' Joe said.

'I liked them too,' she replied, but the question they never asked themselves that night, was whether or not they really liked each other.

The bright lights and crawling traffic of Bayswater and Notting Hill gradually gave way to the shadowy darkness of the A40. Having spent the afternoon indulging in the rich food of a traditional Jewish feast the overpowering warmth of the coach lulled them into drowsiness. Gradually their heads lolled together, their cheeks touched, she turned her head and they kissed. His hand reached out, their fingers linked and Joe asked the inevitably loaded question, 'Would you like to come back to my room for a coffee?' But strangely, as the words slipped out, the bewildering range of emotions he'd felt in both his heart and his genitals suddenly evaporated.

'Yes, I suppose so,' she replied.

They alighted at the Gloucester Green terminus and walked the short distance to his cold bedsitter in Walton Street. A monk's cell that reflected his detachment – indeed his absence – from something called life. There were no garish pop posters on the walls, no heaps of dirty clothes, no hurriedly-kicked-under-the bed girlie magazines. No dirty dishes, or empty beer cans, or half-eaten packets of chocolate digestives. The single bed was made, the sheets were clean, and his minimal clothing was hung out of sight in a small oak wardrobe. His study table was neatly stacked with textbooks, A4 pads, and a complex card-index revising system.

They sipped the obligatory Nescafé hunched over a small electric fire; an ambience as romantic as an igloo and as congenial as a funeral. She looked at her watch. 'I've missed the last bus home,' she said. Oakthorpe Road wasn't that far. He could have offered to walk her home, but he didn't. She could have asked him to walk her home, but she didn't. On that cold December night, the brainwashed, frustrated idiot and the sad girl on the rebound became just two suitable Jews together, members of the same club, feeling neither love nor affection for each other, but knowing that would be of little consequence in the face of fate. Shivering profusely, they began to undress.

Despite his long years of self-imposed celibacy Joe was comprehensively familiar with the many variances of the human female form. He'd peered and poked and probed at its diversities in a wide range of ages, shapes and degrees of morbidity for the last three years – but that was his medical student life. They were the punters, his trade, the daily duties; the fastidiously non-sexual side of his profession. Now, with the prospect of physical union, he longed for the sweetly remembered leap of passion to invade him, but, as Ursula began to disclose her naked body, the roaring desperation he'd felt with Kit failed to materialise. He just didn't like what he saw. Her body was muscular, squat, and virtually waistless. Her breasts were small and flat, curiously blue veined, and tipped with wrinkled nipples as huge and dark as organ stops. Her legs were short and thick with buttocks as flat as a navvy's shovel, and her profuse black bush could only remind him of his own maleness. He turned out the light with a silent sigh, knowing he was required to get on with it.

'Haven't you forgotten something?' she asked. Had he? It appeared he'd forgotten something very important, but where were they? The light went on. After an embarrassing and clumsy search Felix's original starter-pack of condoms turned up in a brown paper bag at the back of the wardrobe. The light went off again, but despite Joe's intense and frequent couplings with Kit, he'd never used one before. In the darkness there was a great deal of tearing, and fumbling, and indecision, until Urshie eventually puffed out noisily. 'Oh, come here!' she snapped, grabbing it impatiently, and dressing his half-hearted dimension with the same brisk action Mitte had used when she rammed a bobble hat down on his head. He emptied his mind and filled it with Marianne Faithful.

A brief sneeze later he realised that he wasn't just an incompetent lover, he was a magician as well. The condom had completely disappeared. Urshie got out of bed, wrapped herself in an old paisley eiderdown, and departed to the bathroom, returning with the limp, offending article in her hand. She looked at it with disgust, wrapped it tightly in the paper bag, and bombed it into the wastepaper basket.

'Joe. You've never . . . have you. . .? It was your first time, wasn't it?'

After his lack lustre performance Joe had no intention of revealing the fulfilment of his past experiences. If he had, it would have been something on the lines of 'cometh the woman, cometh the man '. 'It'll get better,' he said, with little conviction.

A few weeks later, after numerous silent-and-eyes-shut attempts at improvement, it became obvious that they were (as the agony aunts termed it) incompatible. They were just on the point of parting with an, 'Ah well, no bones broken,' when Urshie discovered she was pregnant. Like a rat in a trap, she spat her hatred at Joe. 'There'll be no shot-gun job for us, you bungling idiot. You're not ruining my life. I know exactly where I can get an abortion, and I'm having one.'

Most men, faced with an accidental, loveless pregnancy, would be pleased of the offer to rid them of all their responsibilities, but Joe found himself in an intense mental despair. All he could see was the small life he'd unwittingly created. The tiny limbless, swimming tadpole that held the genes of his lineage. The first child to be conceived as the next generation of the Fortune/Moisemann family. It was safe and warm, and there was a large, loving family waiting for it to become part of them. He was already in love with his unborn child. 'Please,' he begged her. 'Please, Urshie, don't kill our child. Think of the long line of our forefathers. Surely we must have some love for this child we've created. I know we're not in love, but I promise I'll be a good father. Perhaps we'll grow to love each other as well.'

They verbally fought. Urshie curled her lip and venomously expressed her humiliation and disgust with Joe. Hard and harsh words were used like weapons in a yelling and screaming match that had the rest of the house banging on the door, and telling them to put a sock in it. They physically fought. Joe shook her by the shoulders, and begged her to see reason. Urshie retaliated, with hard punches to his chest and shoulders, smacking him hard round the head, and telling him he was a self-centred, spoiled sod. They soul-searched until they both lay exhausted on the floor of Joe's room. 'Please, Urshie. You didn't *have* to tell me, did you? You could have finished with me, and gone off and had it done and I'd have known nothing about it. But you chose to tell me. Surely that shows you've got mixed feelings. Surely you didn't just want to rub my nose in the dirt to hurt me. You don't hate me that much do you?'

She stared into space for days like a convicted prisoner, contemplating the choice of walking the plank, or being electrocuted, but she finally relented in the face of his persistent pleadings. 'OK,' she snapped. 'I'll have the baby, but don't think for a minute I'm sacrificing my career for it. And don't think for a minute that we're going to fall madly in love either. If I've got to put up with you, then you'll just have to put up with me.' Joe took her in his arms, and enfolded her as gently, and as sweetly, as he dared. 'Thank you, Urshie'. He lowered his hand and circled his palm on her belly, in what he thought was a gesture of unity, but she kicked his shin.

'Fuck off,' she shouted. 'Just leave me alone.'

The quartet was humiliated. It was shameful. 'You've let the family down, Joe,' and then embarrassed silence. Yes, he'd let them down, but they'd got what they wanted, hadn't they? A good Jewish daughter-in-law, and the prospect of a sweet little grandchild to cluck over.

Six weeks later there was a sad little ceremony in a miserable Oxford register office. No serious hats, or gold, or clown make-up. No violins and singing and dancing. Just the quartet, and Urshie's parents, meeting for the first time on a bitter February day, trying to pretend it was a time of joy and celebration. A set meal in The Golden Cross, the bride and groom with eyes cast away from each other, and their mouths aching with false smiles for the benefit of their respective loved ones. Their disappointed loved ones, whose over-zealous conversation and false gaiety attempted to disguise what was obvious to all: that the happy couple couldn't think of a single thing to say to each other, or be happy for. 'Don't mention the baby,' was the order of the day, but Joe yearned to jump on his chair, and shout, 'A toast to our baby! Your grandchild. The honoured guest'.

The day was thankfully brought to a close after the Black Forest gateau had been forced down. Nobody wanted coffee. It was getting dark. The Liebermann's back to their sub post office in Birmingham, the quartet back to Peckham, and the newly weds back to the freezing, vacuous bedsit in Walton Street.

But the reluctant bride and groom had lives to lead and exams to take. They both passed their finals, with distinction and honour, as the two top students of their set, and attempted some sort of united celebration with them all. Champagne corks popped, and glasses were raised to Dr Joe and Dr Urshie. 'The Fortunes.' The golden couple.

But sadly, no bubbles last for long, and domestically things were far from golden. They moved from the bedsit, to an equally soulless flat on the Cowley Road, and it soon became clear that Urshie, having been coerced, was now determined to revel in her misery. She had no time for Joe; no conversation, no news, and no enthusiasm for the coming child. She would sit with her head in a textbook, her ears closed to his attempts at conversation, uninterested in his day, and unforthcoming about hers. In the absence of genuine need or desire for each other, they dropped into a routine of occasional robotic, silent unions. The new husband seeking a spark of affection, the new wife obliging with her contracted duty, and gratefully tearing up the contract as soon as the blossoming child came between them.

The baby became a huge stretching mound of pushing elbows and knees and Joe begged Urshie to let him touch the seeking, round protrusions. He put his ear to her navel, trying to envisage the apple head and the tiny, curled body inside her, but he could tell she was holding her breath, silently begging him to stop. In spite of this, he tried so hard to maintain his side of the bargain in every way. Cooking simple meals, telling her she looked pretty when she clearly didn't, making sure she ate and slept properly, and whispering words of sympathy when she suffered from heartburn and the throb of varicosed veins. Nothing produced a spark of gratitude, so after weeks of humiliating rejection Joe realised that his efforts were never going to change their hopeless situation. The final admission that their marriage just lacked love, be it romantic love, common love, or the one love: the main ingredient they had both acknowledged as missing from the start.

Thus, in seeking oblivion, he transferred his affections, and *cannabis indica* became his sweet, faithful companion. In every hour of darkness, his little friend came to the rescue, and gave him the courage to seek another forbidden pleasure; Exodus chapter 20, verse 14, *'thou shalt not commit adultery'*, known more colloquially as 'a bit on the side'. *'Thou shalt not'*, God always declared, loud and clear. Well, Joe reasoned, he'd sat about for six long celibate years waiting for the queen of all queens to arrive. Now she was here, nothing had changed.

August 1975: Joe and Urshie had nearly completed their obligatory time rotating the wards, and they'd both got the career choices they wanted. She had an anaesthetics appointment that she would take up after the baby was born, and he was appointed as junior houseman on Professor Alton's oncology firm. He knew he'd landed a plum, and was dizzy with success, but Urshie had to spoil his euphoria. 'If you went into geriatrics you'd be promoted into space within three years,' she bawled. 'Oncology only offers dead men's shoes, Joe, and you'll be nearly dead yourself by the time any shoes fall vacant.' Was there a word to describe what life was like for him at that time? 'Shite' was about all he came up with, but following his appointment, things lurched in a much sweeter smelling direction.

Dr and Mrs Fortune were invited to a 'meet the minions' soirée; a regular feature extended by the flamboyant and patronising Professor Alton for his kow-towing staff.

Marcus and Carina Alton are At Home on
27th August 1975 from 7.00 pm–9.00 pm
and Request the Pleasure of the Company of
Dr and Mrs Josiah Fortune
Dress Informal

'Bloody cheek,' Urshie exploded. 'Mrs Josiah Fortune! They know sodding well I'm Dr Ursula Liebermann. The only use they've got for me is your appendage – the adoring little woman on your arm. Well, I'm not traipsing around after you like Olive Oyl!'

'Well, do you want to come or not?' Joe enquired indifferently. 'I'm not bothered either way. I'm actually not that keen on going myself, the man's such a pain in the arse, but it's a three-line whip to show my face. I'll make your excuses with pleasure.' After much posturing, and indecision, Urshie agreed to attend.

The great prof held court wearing a yellow bow tie and tartan waistcoat, his big, corporate belly protruding as extensive and firm as Urshie's. The sycophantic gathering stood in audience before him, their heads cocked and forced to listen to his tedious stories of life as a medical student in the postwar years. He was a bore to trump all bores, but he was a bore Joe had to tolerate for his career's sake.

Mrs Alton's reputation as a serious *femme fatale* had already reached him by the grapevine, but she wasn't the voluptuous, buxom siren he imagined. Of medium height and as slender as a reed, she dipped and swayed like a swan around her guests, confident in her classy looks and her status as the trophy wife of a very prestigious man. With her honey blonde hair swirled up in a royal chignon, and wearing a short, black dress and high heels, she oozed a quality that made all men lustful, and all women jealous. She handed out canapés, dispensed drinks, meeted, greeted, and united the party.

'Hello, Joe,' she gushed, shaking his hand and smiling, 'and you must be Ursula. Now, my dear, we mustn't tire you out. Let me find you a nice armchair.' She grabbed Urshie by the hand, and directed her with a firm, positive instruction that left no room for objection, or manoeuvre. 'Let me introduce you to Alison? She had a lovely baby girl a few weeks ago, and I'm sure you two have lots and lots in common.' Urshie had nothing in common with Alison McLean, who'd been a florist before her marriage to a laboratory technician, but she found herself obliged to pal up with a complete stranger for a blow by blow account of childbirth and breast-feeding.

As more guests arrived, Joe began to get pushed to the back of the room, but then he heard Mrs Alton's commanding, cultured voice calling to him from the doorway. 'Joe, sweetheart. I wonder if you could do me a favour?' He carried six cases of wine from the back of her car to the utility room behind the kitchen, after which the favour was required of him. As he put the last box down she shimmied towards him. 'You know, Joe,' she said, 'I've been watching you, and I think you've been watching me.' He dropped his eyes like Bambi. 'Come on lovely, look at me. I think we're both suffering from the same complaint, don't you?'

'And would that be Portnoy's Complaint, Mrs Alton?' He was self-impressed with his quick and witty answer, and was equally impressed with her reply.

'Only to the circumcised, Joe, but I think that was poor old Portnoy's main problem wasn't it?'

The room was an unpretentious jumble of laundry baskets, shoe polish, vegetables in racks, strings of onions, tins of cat food, a Hoover, and old hats and macs. Behind the door hung the daily help's floral overall, and on the floor her worn out bunion-shaped shoes. He breathed in a sharp, pungent mingling of soap powder, paraffin and firelighters; the smell of an old fashioned ironmonger's shop, and forever after a sensorial memory of that day. She dropped the Chubb lock on the door and reached out both her arms to him.

Clothes were quickly rearranged to accommodate a primitive, but very urgent connection up against the Hoover Keymatic. She used his body only as a means to her own needs, seeming not to notice his important part in the proceedings. For Joe she aroused such instant passion that he didn't notice or care either. Ninety seconds later she swung on his neck, as light as a lace-winged moth, her feet coming to rest on top of his shoes. 'No complaints, Portnoy,' she said. 'Now kiss me.' He wanted to kiss her too. Grinding congress was one thing, and he was happy to oblige, but sweet affection, no matter how phoney, had to be part of the deal.

But part of the deal as well was the business-like terms and conditions she laid down. There would be absolutely no emotional ties. They would meet as often as they could arrange but would be wholly discreet and respectful towards each other's partners. 'We've both got too much to lose for it to be otherwise,' she said. 'Marcus and I had a wonderful love affair that lasted years, but when his children grew up and he finally left his wife for me all his passion just seemed to fizzle out. I'm not in love with him any more but I've no intention of losing the lifestyle he provides for me.'

'I'm just about to become a father,' Joe said, 'and I take the responsibility very seriously. But I'm not in love either, so our little arrangement will be perfect.' They then remembered to disengage themselves. Once their clothes were reassembled they arranged their next date – a roadhouse motel near Banbury on the following Wednesday afternoon. She straightened up and breathed in deeply. 'Back to the fray then.' She walked out ahead of him with a straight back and elegant poise. He followed her, knowing she'd used him, but knowing that her cool confidence was a smokescreen for a tearing sadness and loneliness as deep as his own. It wasn't sin. It was social work.

As they entered the room again all eyes turned to greet the stunning and glimmer-eyed Mrs Alton. She walked up to her husband and affectionately slipped her arm around his vast circumference. 'Can I get you a drink, darling?' Urshie, sitting po-faced and captive, hadn't even noticed Joe had been missing.

When they left that night Carina fussed around Urshie as she settled herself into the old Morris Minor Traveller they'd just acquired. 'It's been lovely to meet you both,' she said. 'It's so nice for me to get to know all the members of Marcus's team. Thank you so much for coming, Joe.' She turned on her heels, but then changed her mind, walked back, and leaned her head through the car window. 'How long before the baby's due, Ursula?'

'Two weeks,' Urshie answered, trying hard to sound bright and friendly.

'Well, if there's anything I can do for you, please shout,' she said. 'I really mean it. I've got loads of time on my hands.' Urshie smiled politely and wound up the window. She was spoiling for a major row, having spent the whole evening hearing tales, not of clamping gums and projectile vomiting, but the versatility of oasis foam and the scourge of the chrysanthemum fly.

'Well, that smarmy cow can butt out,' she said. 'What a slag. Did you see her in there? Eyes popping out of her head, and wiggling her silly little arse at all the men. She must be nearly forty for God's sake. Pathetic bitch.'

'No Urshie, I didn't notice,' Joe sighed. 'I was too busy looking at you.'

September 1975: On the night of Daniel's birth Joe tried so hard to fall in love with his wife. During the last few days of her pregnancy they'd had no rows or upsets; in fact they'd become strangely comfortable with each other. She didn't sleep well and he'd rise in the middle of the night to make her a pot of tea and to massage the hard, solid mound of the baby. Strangely, that night she pulled her own hand over his and held it still on her navel. 'It's all become real, hasn't it?' she said. 'We're going to be parents. Thanks for being so patient with me, but it all scares me to death. Not the actual birth but what comes after. I can't help being the way I am but I'll try to do my best.'

Labour started gently, and as the pains peaked she retreated into herself. The first deep contraction showed as a sharp suck of breath and a startled expression. It was time to get to the hospital. Joe picked up her small packed suitcase, took her hand, and guided her to the car.

In full labour she was stoical and brave. She gritted her teeth and pushed her back into the bed. She endured the pain in a brave, solitary silence, her eyes telling a story of being lost inside high tabernacles of endurance, known only to the female of the species. Towards the end it became an agony. She grasped his forearms with an overpowering strength, nails making small half moons in his flesh. She panted and pushed and strained, her cries guttural and primaeval, trying to will her body to release the baby. He encouraged her. He panted with her. He sweated with her. He felt a desperate pity for her as he stood, pain-free and guilt-ridden; a mere spectator to the genesis of his child. Slowly the small dark ellipse grew and grew, and to an intense shout of joy from them both, the waxy head emerged into the world. 'Let it be me,' Joe said to the midwife. With the next contraction there was a rush of slopping water, and a purple, downy baby slid into his welcoming arms.

He'd sworn to himself that he wouldn't be predictable and he'd carefully rehearsed the words, 'Urshie, we have a fine son,' or 'We have a beautiful daughter,' but of course he shouted out like every other excited father, 'It's a boy!' A surge of choking tears precluded any more words. He cut the umbilical cord and Daniel Fortune snuffled his first breath.

Joe and Urshie sat in the usual head-of-the-bed-and faces-together pose, admiring their production. The baby's beautiful wizened face contorted and squirmed, and his tiny stick-like limbs stretched and struggled. The wonder that came over Joe at that moment overshadowed all the inadequacies of their relationship. In years to come he'd reminisce that at that moment, and only at that moment, he and Urshie really loved each other. 'He's perfect,' he said. 'Urshie, we have a perfect child. Thank you so much.'

Was this exquisite child really the product of that sad, cold, loveless night? The sad night suddenly became a joyous celebration and a song and dance of gratitude.

'He looks like you, Joe. He's got your brow and chin.'

'Ah, but he's got your mouth, and perhaps your eyes.'

'Maybe he's got my father's nose.'

'Just as long as he hasn't got my Patte's eagle beak.'

They sought each other's lips with genuine emotion. They smiled into each other's eyes, and sank their grateful heads together, while Daniel wound his tiny flower like hand around Joe's thumb, gripping with a powerful strength that denied his weak, dependent status. That night Joe knew there must be a God for giving him a son. Here he was. His heir. The reason for his being. When he grew up Daniel Elijah Dov would turn his head and see the long line of his forefathers, with himself, an old, geriatric Joe Fortune at the head, preceding his father, and Patte, and Urshie's father, and grandfather, and all the unknown dead spirits that had made him what he was. He would remember and respect the slaughtered millions, and he would carry the houses of

Fortune and Moisemann and Liebermann into the twenty-first century.

Joe lifted the baby from Urshie's arms and moved to the window where a full moon hung, illuminating the sky. 'Daniel,' he said. 'I'm your father. I will always love you and I thank you for coming into my life. Can you see the moon? Our God made the moon, for all his people, and here's your first line from the Torah. Genesis chapter 1, verse 16, *'the lesser light to rule the night.'* May the light of night keep you safe and protect you in your bed for all of your life.'

Urshie's breast had never been the firm, round globe Joe desired in his hand, but as Daniel slowly sucked, it became a wonder of nourishment and comfort. Maybe, now, there could be a new beginning with Urshie. Perhaps not deep love, but enough love to hold them all together. He felt something so hopeful, so all consuming, and so precious it was like the first warm spring day after a hard winter. You forget every sort of coldness, and discomfort, and weariness, and all you have inside your head is the warmth of the sun, the stillness of the air, and the lifting of your spirits. You fool yourself into feeling that hereafter life will always be like this, and the cold won't come back.

Sadly it was a myth perpetuated on a dream, or a dream perpetrated on a myth. Either way it was a dead duck.

CHAPTER SIX

Friday, continued . . .

ANNA HAS CALLED TO ME THAT OUR SUPPER IS READY. I slip on my *thobe* and descend the stairs. Time to celebrate *Shabbat*.

Come, my friend, to meet the Bride, let us receive the Sabbath.
From the '*Lekha Dodi*' – Solomon Alkabetz, 1540

All over the world my people are gathering in a genial celebration of the Sabbath, but it's always been a very lukewarm event at Sunny Lea. As you're already aware, due to the discriminatory rules of my faith, my twins are not Jewish, and the two stroppy rebels decided, at the age of twelve, that they had no interest in seeing their father ponced up as Bible Man, and wailing out of tune. They firmly announced UDI and joined a martial arts club on a Friday night. Thus, while I celebrate whenever I can with Daniel and my family, my only company is usually a polite, agnostic Christian who adores me dressing up as her beautiful Israeli. I light a candle and mutter some Hebrew, but our meal is non-kosher. Tonight it's a cold onion tart, couscous, a tossed salad, strawberries and cream and a particularly ripe Brie. We happily munch, and quaff a cold sparkling white, but just as we're relaxing in the perfection of our own company there's the shrill sound of the bloody doorbell. Standing on the doorstep is Dan with an overnight case in his hand. 'Dad,' he says. 'Mum died this afternoon.'

I take him up to my study, and pour us both a brandy. At her home in South Africa Urshie had suffered a fatal stroke. Being widowed two years ago, and otherwise childless, Dan is her only family and he will fly over to arrange her immediate funeral.

What does one say, how does one act, when ones detested ex-wife dies? A death is always a shock, but in reality for me it's no more than a shrug of the shoulders and a truthful declaration of indifference? Why should I have to drag false sorrow out of the bag? I've always nurtured a deep hatred for her, but what is hate? Is it the emotion we invent when we want to retrieve lost love and the love has irretrievably gone? In that case, it isn't hate I feel, because I'd never loved her. But did I ever wish her dead? Yes, many times I'd wished her dead, but now she is, in a strange sort of way, I *am* sorry. I think what I feel is an intense compassion for Dan, and gratitude for his life.

My son is now thirty and tonight his face shows both the fresh bloom of youth and the grey pallor of an old man. I notice for the first time the start of crow's feet etching round his eyes, and an emerging heaviness of his jowls, but to me he'll always be the newborn baby, zonked drunkenly at Urshie's breast, or wetting his pants on the day I passed a letter to a vile old gardener.

I hand him the glass and he sips slowly, staring into the carpet. 'The truth is, she was a lousy mother and we both know it. Dad, what *was* her problem?'

The misery of your children is always much greater than your own, isn't it? Their pain hurls itself at you. You have to catch it, whether you want it or not, and you can't throw it back. I choose my words slowly and carefully. 'Dan, when your mother and I parted I made a right balls up of everything. I tried so hard not to use you as a channel for our poison, but because of that I couldn't talk to you, or explain what the issues were. I've never asked you this, but did she ever say much about what happened?'

'Only the usual diatribes. You were a dirty two-timing bastard.'

'Par for the course. I was. We both know chapter and verse what she thought of me, but I just wondered if she said much about Anna?'

'The only thing I ever heard her say about Anna was catty. When I showed her your wedding photo, she said, 'Ah, Tinkerbell. The little bimbo.' I remember that because I thought it was an odd thing to say, and I'd never heard the word 'bimbo' before.'

'Is that all? About Anna, I mean.'

'When the twins were born she said she hoped Tinkerbell's body was messed up by stretch marks and she got fat. More claws.'

'Dan, your mother was a bitch of the highest order. She certainly gave both of us a hard time, but she did one good thing. She gave birth to you. That's never going to be a waste, is it? Let's give thanks for her life and yours.'

Dan suddenly begins to shift around and clear his throat, but he looks up and smiles. 'Well, Dad, that's my perfect cue.

You might say that with every death comes a life. We were going to tell you all on Sunday, at Mitte's party, but Graznya and I . . . You're going to be a Patte.' He slides his eyes away from mine and rubs his face, his evening shadow rasping over his broad palms like sandpaper. 'I don't suppose the old forefathers will think much of me, will they, but it's been OK for Josh and Sophie hasn't it? They're fabulous kids and the family worships them. Things'll be fine for my kid too. We've got to think global village these days, haven't we? Tell me you're pleased.'

My whole body contracts and my heart turns over with grief. My son is in love with a beautiful Polish Catholic, a fellow architect, and now she's to have his child. This is a time for celebration and congratulations, but Dan and I both know of the hidden agenda. On the night Anna and I told him he was going to have a baby sister or brother he'd put his ear down to Anna's belly, willing the tiny foetus to kick him. 'Danny, you know the baby won't be Jewish like us?' I'd said 'but he or she will be just as loved and cherished, within our family.' Anything I say now will be hypocritical. Sauce for goose and gander. Glass houses and throwing stones.

I wave my hand absently in the air, like a ham actor dismissing a triviality. 'I'm thrilled for you both,' I say, but of course I'm lying. I'm destroyed, but all the old rhetoric in the world could never decimate the love I have for him and there'll be no bad blood between us. 'Me a Patte,' I say, smiling, and wiping a tear from my eye. 'I like the sound of that.'

Dan beams. 'Thanks, Dad. I knew you'd be OK about it.'

The plane to Johannesburg leaves at midnight so he has to go. 'Would you like me to come with you?' I ask. 'I can drop everything. Honestly. I'd be honoured to be a bag carrier,' but he shakes his head.

'I'll be fine. Tell Mitte I'm sorry we can't make her birthday party but we'll take her out to tea at the Ritz to make up.'

I kiss him on both cheeks and hug him compassionately. He finds Anna and she holds him too, long and hard, with the genuine love she's always had for her stepson. As we stand on the forecourt, watching him drive away, I feel my body shrinking and losing height. As if I'm slipping away into insignificance and reducing to a person of no consequence or purpose. I need time to adjust, but there's nowhere to hide and no one I can confide in, least of all my gentile wife who knows nothing of the turmoil in my head, nor ever will. 'Need a bit of air, hon,' I say.

I go into the garden and lean on the diseased old apple tree. A full, glistening moon hangs high above my head; the same moon I showed to Daniel on the night he was born. *'The lesser light to rule the night.'* The moon that has watched him safely survive all the hideous snakes and dangerous ladders his mother and I thrust upon him. I reach out to an atrophied branch and trace patterns in the hard, desiccated wrinkles, searching within myself for a thread that will haul me into acceptance. Of course I know I won't find one. My only solution will be to keep my sorrows inside my head, but why is my head filled with Jerzy? I haven't thought about him for years, but strangely it's Jerzy Pomananski who creeps out to find me.

When I was a little boy Jerzy worked in the kosher deli and he was always so nice to everyone. He lived in a room over the shop and he never married. Summer and winter he always had his sleeves rolled up, and on his forearm a number was tattooed. I was always a cheeky boy and I asked him once, 'Jerzy, why have you got a number on your arm?'

'Because I am very, very lucky,' he replied.

'Then when I grow up I shall have a number tattooed on my arm and I'll be lucky too.'

'I hope to God you'll never be as lucky as me.'

In 1980, when the area was redeveloped, the deli was pulled down and Jerzy committed suicide. Does that make things easier to understand?

Melancholy invades me. I think of Auschwitz, and Belsen, and Dachau, and the millions of my people who were lost in those shameful, man-made murder factories. I think of the burning books, and bayoneted babies, and the fragility of Israel. OK, OK, I know what you're thinking. Why should it still matter so much to me? Those that live by the sword should die by the sword, and you can't have it both ways. All I know is that I want it both ways.

I hear a twig crack behind me, and Anna is standing there. 'Are you all right, my love?'

'Sure,' I say, 'but two shocks in one night rather throws one. I can't pretend to care about Urshie's death, but I have to be grateful to her for Dan's being. The other news must be the best ever, though. Can you imagine it? Me, a Patte? I'll have to grow a beard down to my knees.'

'Come on in,' she says. 'Let's open a bottle of champagne and celebrate. After all, I'm going to be a grandmother. I do think of myself as Dan's real mother, you know, and I love him just as much as Josh.' Why do her words make me want to burst into tears? The first time I made love to her I promised her that Judaism would never come between us, and it never has. In our marriage my own wishy-washy version of my religion has always been just my thing, and of no consequence to us as a loving and devoted couple, so how could I now sit her down and explain it all.

We slump together on the sofa, sipping our bubbles of celebration, but it's Urshie's death that looms up and takes precedence. 'Are you glad Urshie's dead?' I ask her.

'I'm sorry,' she says. 'I'm truly sorry. She was so clever, and so successful, but I doubt she was ever happy.'

Talking about Urshie is rare and dangerous territory for us both. 'How can you be so nice about her?' I say. 'Don't you even hold the smallest grudge? Now she's dead it's such a good time to talk about that horrible violent night and everything that came after. There are still so many things left unsaid. Everything's a closed book with you, isn't it?'

She fails to answer, and the unsaid words will remain thus. She settles the small of her back comfortably into my body, but faces away from me, denying eye contact or closer scrutiny. I can tell she's disappeared into a world that doesn't include either me or the present. 'I swallowed my stethoscope this afternoon,' I say. She nods. 'I think André Agassi's so goddamn beautiful I'd like to fuck him.' No response at all. Where has her mind gone? What black hole has she slipped in to? She eventually gets up, flashes me a small apologetic smile, and pretends to be busy. She plumps up cushions, picks up the champagne flutes and shoos Me-Toom-Tum out of the room. 'Time for bed, Dougall said,' she says.

3.00 a.m. and Anna emerges into darkness. Oh, those vicious tongues! She can tell he's awake. He lies inert, flat on his back, but his breathing is tense and he sucks his teeth. What does he want from her? What does he know? What does he suspect? He frightens her. Tonight the past has been brought alive – so alive her memories are like a full colour cinema show. The pictures go round and round before her eyes, in a dervish whirl of dread. Before they married she made him promise that they would never dredge up the past. They never have done and it's never mattered. Well, it's always mattered to her, of course, but it wasn't for sharing. How can she ever forget the hurt? She still feels the pain. It's there, all day and every day. Get a grip, Anna! Hold yourself together. You are woman. You are strong. There can be no tired talking in the dark. No confessionals, no revelations. Let this time pass, as it surely will. Nurture him with calmness and love, as you always have. He can never know the secrets of The Crowded Bed, because if he did she knew he wouldn't love her any more.

3.00 a.m. and I emerge into darkness. I can tell she's awake. Scratchy dry sounds of her limbs sear against the sheets, as if she's shifting on straw. Crunchy rasps of her hair on the pillow and the odd loud sigh. The searching for comfort and the uneven breathing. What are her stories? What are her secrets? With Urshie's death the things so carefully buried are creeping up to the surface with mole-like stealth. The ground moves and this muddy, blind creature sniffs the air, seeking to dredge up the past. As we lie silently together our conscious presence hangs in the night. We're both trapped and paralysed by The Crowded Bed. Sliding doors fly open and all the baggage of bats, and black dogs, and ghosts, and hang-ups, and neuroses, that we've brought with us into our marriage shoot out. We're invaded by our inner selves; squeezed, crushed, cramped, chock-full to bursting and pegged down like Gulliver. Cold swords and spikes shoot up between us, dividing us to separateness.

Words form in my head. I rehearse inwardly. I clear my throat, my lips move but my voice is silenced. Can she hear my ribs knotting and my throat swelling? I try to stem the flow of tears. My fingertips clutch the sheet. My back arches. I sob once, but try to make it sound like a nasal problem. I lie there in anguish as the twin scenarios do battle in my head. The thing I've never been able to confront. Ursula, the woman I never loved, and who never loved me, had my child, but you, Anna, whom I did love, and still love, with every tiny fibre of my heart and soul had . . . I cannot form the word. Anna, I should rise from my bleariness, and put on the light, and make you tell me. I should fire a gun and clear the bed. I should roar and scream and chase the mob away. I want to hold you, and tell you that there'll never be blame,

111

but I still want to hear the story. You ran away and left me. I never knew about our first child, but *he* knew, didn't he? Your bastard father knew. *How could you have told him and not me?* Was he cruel and threatening? Did he make you ashamed of me? Did he say you were carrying the spawn of the devil or the web-footed beast? I came with a letter telling you how much I loved you and how much I wanted you back, but the arse-hole kept it from you. Anna, if you'd got the letter our child would have lived. It would have, wouldn't it?

A warm hand reaches out and touches me. 'Go to sleep, my love.'

July 1979: Joe wanted to go back to a sound, untroubled sleep, or he wanted to wake up. But he could do neither. He was completely paralysed. He couldn't open his eyes, and he had no idea where he was. If he was at home he'd hear the early morning traffic on the Cowley Road. If he was in his on-call room at the hospital he'd hear loud, quarrelling voices and the clunking of breakfast trolleys being trundled to the wards across concrete. Where the hell was he? A smooth, female body pressed against his back, and he felt sweet kisses on his shoulders, so he definitely wasn't at home. 'What's the time?' he mumbled.

'Twenty past five,' she replied.

He stretched out his leg, trying to find a cool spot in the upper reaches of the single bed, enjoying a tight, sinewy pull to his muscles. Was he gorgeous, or was he gorgeous? Michelangelo would have crawled on his hands and knees to sculpt his male perfection. Carina began to mew urgently, slid her hand to his crotch and began her usual skilled encouragement. She had to leave, and she wasn't going before her pound of flesh had obliged. 'Give me a minute, Carrie,' he mumbled. He didn't want Carina. He wanted his fantasy.

A huge oyster shell was coming up out of the blue Aegean. The sun was shining and sea birds were calling. Very slowly it started to open until the perfect Venus body of student nurse Anna Morton Moore stood before him. Her pearly limbs were glowing and radiating desire for him. Her long blonde hair was distressed and overflowing. She was walking out of the shell, with her arms outstretched towards him, and she was saying, 'Please, Joe. Please make love to me.' He turned his attention urgently to the business in hand.

When he got back from the shower Carina had gone. Out the side door like lightning in head scarf and dark glasses. Down the fire escape and off through the empty streets to hotfoot it home before her husband's 'Good morning, darling,' call from Edinburgh. It was rare for Joe to spend whole nights with Carina. Their clandestine affair had been conducted, with great discretion, in a variety of venues. Motel rooms at her expense, in houses borrowed from discreet friends, carefully plotted sessions in her own marital bed, or (if things were desperate) in the back of Joe's Morris Minor Traveller. Last night had been a rare treat; an opportunity seized while her husband was away and Joe was on-call. They were long past the stage of kissing goodbye, and there were never any fond declarations of love, or emotional drains, to spoil things; just business partners satisfying a mutual need that neither could find within their marriage vows. The brief moment of unity and optimism he'd felt with Urshie on the night of Daniel's birth hadn't lasted. His marriage was a sham. A withered branch on a blighted vine with the only green sap being his son.

Daniel was now three years old; an angel of a child and Joe's only true happiness. How he treasured him. How he loved the sight of him in his stripey OshKosh dungarees as he laughed, and jumped up and down, and clapped his hands. How he loved his sturdy little body. His smooth warm skin. His bonny rounded limbs. His dark, curly hair that grew in a woolly line down his back, exactly like his own. 'Please, Daddy, read *Billy Goats Gruff*', he demanded, pushing a dirty, dog-eared, Ladybird book in his face, and Joe would take him on his knee, and read the same old words again, and again. '*Click-clack, click-clack, over the rickety bridge.*' They made all the sounds and did all the actions together. They squirmed and shivered with fear when the troll made an appearance, and then Joe would grab him, and tickle him, and pretend to be fierce, and blow a loud raspberry into his tummy. He loved him wholly and completely, and although he never regretted his birth for a minute, he disappointed his wife on all counts.

Despite her maternity leave, Urshie had forged ahead of him in the career stakes, and was by far the most successful graduate in their set. She'd now been appointed as registrar in anaesthetics, and would return from work with a hard-edged confidence and a supercilious expression. Joe, although now the senior house officer on oncology, was lower ranking and although he was completely fulfilled by his work Urshie continued to badger him to seek promotion in less competitive areas of medicine. When he refused she accused him of being lazy and unambitious.

'Lazy,' he shouted back. 'That's rich coming from you. Who the bloody hell goes to Sainsbury's and makes sure our child has clean clothes? Me, Urshie. We're supposed to share everything down the middle, and by God, I do far more than my half. You're much too important these days for domestic duties.'

Usually their rows would end up with screamed abuse and hurled objects, but lately the division of labour battle had collapsed into apathy and things were sliding into squalor. Washing-up was piled in the sink and the bathroom floor was covered with heaps of dirty washing. Even the washed washing, that no one was going to iron, sat in damp piles for so long it started to stink, and he had to go to the laundrette on cold nights, with a sleeping Daniel in his arms, to watch their clothes going round and round. Just like his life. Going round and round in an ever-increasing spiral of misery and concession. He and Urshie were still unable to find the slightest shred of affection or common ground, and their occasional marital union was a dark and mechanical obligation, usually in response to a ferocious row; a blind mime that bluffed the admission of complete incompatibility and failure. Now the dancing shadow of Anna Morton Moore had fallen over Joe's peculiar status quo. For the first time in his life, he had truly fallen in love.

He knew he was in love because he felt ill. How could he be so changed? He'd lost charge of himself and was happily hurtling out of control. A body steeped in the excitement of hoping that something was going to happen, and knowing he wanted it to happen, but dreading the consequences of either her acceptance or rejection. Love had reduced his brain to a snail's pace as he immersed himself in constant reveries about her. She woke him from a troubled sleep, she stopped him from following the word on a page, and she lodged, as a fantasy, during every jerk and shimmy of his convoluted sex life.

Despite seeing her, and speaking to her in his professional capacity every day on his ward, Anna remained a fantasy. But her adored her. He was compelled towards her like wasp in summer to a jar of jam, but he felt no sweetness from the jam. There'd been no eyes meeting over a crowded ward and no flirting. In fact she'd given him no sign that she regarded him as anything more than a colleague. She emanated a contained coolness and wore an air of disinterest like a flack jacket. She spoke when she was spoken to, she answered fully and intelligently, but never volunteered more. Her voice was formed of perfect vowels and resonance; words spoken with a quiet, imperturbable refinement, by a girl who had nothing to prove, and sought neither attention nor admiration. The young rogue males called her The Ice Maiden from Hell. The also-ran female pack called her The Snotty Cow. Joe called her exquisite.

Before he came on duty that night he and Urshie had had a blazing row over which one of them had forgotten to buy milk, and the next thing he knew he was being viciously smashed over the head with a tin tray. 'You're a vain, idle bastard,' she yelled at him. 'It's a pity you don't spend as much time thinking about your career as you do looking in the mirror.' He swung round to defend himself, but she grabbed his pony-tail. 'I think we'd better have a little talk about you and oncology anyway, Joe,' she yelled, 'because if the rumours I'm hearing about you and that Alton bitch are true, you and oncolgy might just part company.' Joe, shocked with terror, emphatically denied the charge, but added venomously that Carina Alton looked as if she'd be much better in the sack than she was. But inside he felt a huge, nauseous wave of guilt and fear. How could rumours about him and Carina have surfaced after nearly four years of fastidious discretion? He was suitably scared. House officers caught having affairs with their professors' wives were likely to end up seeking work in Alaska or Christmas Island.

Urshie suddenly went for him again, flailing at his chest and hurling abuse, until Daniel ran into a corner, crying loudly. The bewildered child threw himself on the floor, curled up in a ball and put his hands over his ears. 'Daniel, don't cry,' Joe pleaded, picking him up and whispering comforting noises. 'Let Daddy give you a hug and a kiss. Mummy and Daddy don't mean it. Come and play horses.' Joe knelt down so Daniel could climb onto his back. He then bounced him up and down in the usual game of bucking broncos that gave the child such fun, but as he thrashed about with mock hilarity his heart ached. What were they inflicting on this poor child? How much worse could things get before he was psychologically damaged?

Urshie had retreated into a sullen silence so Joe made Daniel's tea. Tinned spaghetti on toast, a KitKat and a banana. He washed him, helped him into his pyjamas and laid him down in his cot. His sweet-smelling, sweet-natured child reached out his arms and twisted them around Joe's neck with a strangling strength. 'Night night, Daddy.' Urshie sat with her nose in a textbook, seemingly oblivious of her son's need for a goodnight kiss. Joe walked over to her, and put his mouth up to her ear. 'You . . . are . . . an . . . evil . . . bitch,' he said slowly and acidly.

'And you're a fucking waste of space,' she snapped, without looking up.

Hospital wards take on a unique atmosphere in the evenings. There's an exodus; a contracting of time and space; a wrapping round of the familiar, the gentle and the kind. The staff are sparse and slip into the roles of mothers putting their children to bed. Lamps are lit, soft shadows fall and the smell of an institution evaporates. With all the clank and cackle of the day wound down, a comfortable in-for-the-evening feel takes over, even on a cancer ward.

Joe was now casually sprawled behind the nurse's station, pretending to read a set of case notes, and watching the breathtaking Anna as she assisted the bed-ridden with their bedtime drinks. She was easing her arm around Mr Briggs, a desiccated terminal case, who was too old and ill to realise what delights of cherry pie was holding him. Her long slender fingers eased the spout of a drinking vessel into his wizened mouth, and, as she spoke kindly into the stone-deaf ears, Joe looked at her with longing. After weeks of indifference she looked up, found his eyes, smiled, and held his gaze for several long seconds. As if she was saying, 'take your time. Just fill your head with me, and take me inside yourself.' An invasion of senses rushed into him like a desert wind. He became weak, confused, and childlike. A hot flush appeared over his collar and rose up the back of his neck. His body turned tricks; heart thumping, lungs hyperventilating and loins congesting.

It was getting dark, and with little left to do the ward settled down for the night. Joe's normal routine would have been to waste time in the hospital canteen, or read a book in his on-call room, but he found he was unable to leave. The skeleton staff became bored. Books and knitting were produced. Crosswords puzzled over. 'Dr Fortune, would you like a cup of tea?' Anna asked him, with refined courtesy. He nodded, and followed her into the ward kitchen which, like most of the domestic rooms in the old hospital, smelled of gas, rancid dishcloths and Jeyes fluid. As she made the tea she casually told him her grandfather had been a High Commissioner in Darjeeling during the time of the British raj, and her father had taught her how to make a perfect cup of tea.

'Do you take sugar, Dr Fortune?'
'Call me Joe.'
'Do you take sugar, Joe?'

Joe wanted to flirt, to be lively, witty and amusing, but to his fury he only found a tongue-tied silence. She stood eighteen inches away from him, sipping her tea and looking out of a window that faced a disorder of rusty drainpipes and ventilation shafts. He could see her blurred, double-edged reflection in the dirty, age-stained glass, framed against a sunless dusk. Her expression was fixed and she seemed to be oblivious to his presence. He searched madly for an opening gambit and was just about to ask her if she'd been away on holiday yet when the staff nurse appeared at the door. 'Mr Briggs is *in extremis*, nurse. No doubt if you'd been busy being a nurse, and not idling your time away making pots of tea, you might have noticed. And perhaps Dr Fortune, you might be so kind as to offer your professional services as well.'

Mr Briggs was wheeled into a side room. Obligingly he took several hours to pass away and Joe and Anna became four soothing hands on the dying body. They discovered a fluid and easy harmony, with no silences or struggling effort. They discussed the meaning of life and what they each felt was the meaning of death. Where, they wondered, did the life-force go? Joe talked of his God and the special place the Jews go to. Anna told him of being a child brought up in an old country vicarage, and although her father could trace their Anglican genealogy back to the seventeenth century, she'd never absorbed Christianity into her life, nor had any belief in a place called heaven.

Mr Briggs' life-force departed just after 2.00 a.m. leaving behind his earthly face, as hollow-cheeked and gnarled as a garden gnome. Together they laid the body out with respect.

'Life can be really awful,' she said, 'but death's even worse, isn't it?'

After Joe had completed the death certificate his protocol should have sent him firmly back to his on-call room, but, overcome with exhaustion, he laid his head on the desk in the ward office and fell asleep. He awoke as the early morning light was edging through the windows, and as he opened his eyes he saw Anna's blue eyes in line with his. She'd been asleep too. He slowly stretched out his arm towards her, but she was too far away to touch. She stood up and hung towards him over the desk, took his hand, placed his palm over her breast and covered it tightly with her own. As Humbert said of Lolita, *'It was she, dear readers . . . It was she who seduced me.'* They were completely alone and the ward stood still. No crashes, or clunks, or cries for help. No sudden dramas, or bad dreams, or vomiting, or incontinence. Illness was held suspended in reverence to Joe and Anna's new found love.

They came off duty and emerged into a clear, warm July morning. 'Best not to be seen together, I suppose,' she said, so he walked twenty yards behind, following her black stockings and chaste sturdy shoes. Her raffia shopping bag hung loosely over her shoulder and bobbed against her thigh. She walked north up the Woodstock Road, turned into Tackley Place and went into a large, four storey house. When Joe entered he heard her voice calling his name. He looked up through a spiral of banisters to see she was standing thirty feet above him.

Her tiny, eaved kitchen became a womb. The gas hissed under the kettle and the rising sun glinted off a mirror behind her head. They sat on small white-painted chairs at a small table covered with a red check tablecloth. She released her hair. It fell heavily down her back and she rubbed her tired head. As they sat with mugs of brewed Arabica he gently pushed wisps out of her eyes. 'Anna,' he said. 'This isn't a game for me. I've really fallen in love with you. I've never said those words before in my life, but we don't have to make love if you don't want to. I can wait for the time to be right.'

She lifted her head regally and stared at him, unsmiling. A look of mature confidence that told him she was in complete control. A look that made him realise that this was to be something far removed from a lusty tumble with a giggling teenager. 'The time *is* right,' she said, 'and it's not a game for me either. I've been in love with you for a long time. Can I make you happy, because I know you're unhappy? Everyone says the Fortunes fight like cat and dog. Sometimes you look so worn out. So sad. So absolutely finished.'

'I've never loved my wife,' he said, 'but being Jewish just got in the way.'

'Does it matter that I'm not a Jew?'

'Oh, my love, I don't care if you're a Buddhist, or a Sikh, or even a bloody Druid. Many things may come between us but I promise you it'll never be Judaism.' Then he laughed. 'But my mother would call you my *shikse*. It's our word for a non-Jewish girl.'

122

'Shikse,' she said. 'I love the sound of the word. It excites me. Say it again.'

'My shikse. My shikse. My shikse.'

'I've only ever had one other lover,' she said, 'but I never want to discuss our pasts. Do you promise me, Joe? Our pasts are in the past, and there they'll stay.' He nodded. He agreed. He promised her.

'Did you love him, though?' he asked. She gave him a look that spoke of disappointment already, her face cast down with an expression that said, 'Is this man stupid? I've just told him that we won't talk of it and already he wants to.'

'I'm sorry,' he said. 'I know exactly what you mean. We'll never talk of it.'

She drew the bedroom curtains against the strong sunlight, and the room became peachy and tent-like. He moved forward to take her clothes off, as he thought he'd be expected to, but she stood back and shook her head. They moved apart. Slowly and separately they undressed. She even took the time to hang up her nurse's dress and put her underwear in the laundry basket. Then the perfect Aryan woman, whom Joe had loved for so long, stood in the shell. She stood confidently, posing in a tableau of display and extreme vanity. Long limbs, heavy breasts, the dip and curve of waist to thigh and her face affecting a mask of peace. He knew she was controlling him, as if she was saying, 'This is me, and I know I'm beautiful. I give myself to you, completely to you, but you play by my rules.' As he moved towards her he felt ungainly, ugly and male. A shuffling primate with an erection. She remained serene and composed. She picked up his hands, pulled his arms wide apart, and held them horizontally. She then slowly ran her lips from wrist to wrist, turning her face and brushing her cheeks against his skin, as if she was enjoying the sensuous feel of velvet fabric.

Her bed linen was cold and clean and smelling of her perfume. He sank his head deeply into the pillow and filled his lungs. Only three other bodies had moved beneath him. Kit (his teacher), Urshie (his life's mistake), and Carina (his compromise). Anna Morton Moore would be his fourth, and last, and his life's love.

She lay quietly beside him, turning to rest her hand against his thigh, but he was suddenly diffident and indecisive, not knowing how to start and terrified of being inept. It all had to be completely right – flawless in fact – but the flow of natural rhythm that had passed between them so far was in danger of faltering and failing. But he was rescued. She rose to her knees, straddled over him and stared at him. 'Let me make love to you. It's been a long time for me, so please be patient if I'm less than perfect.'

Anna was a skilled but simple lover. She used no tricks, or aggression, or the power of the jungle. Just gentleness and the careful caresses of a deep and precious intent. She guided him in equal proportions to her own pleasure, and, with perfect timing, elected the moment of their union. With the precision of Victorian engineering she fitted as close and as comfortable to him as his own shadow. Each cog and wheel found a place in the free flow of their perpetual motion, seeming to rise and fall in time to the hiss and suck of an alternating steam engine. Joe's ears were gradually filled with her undecipherable mumbling. She anxiously exhaled. Fingernails dug sharply into his shoulders. A heel kicked his calf, her teeth grazed his cheek and as she called his name he released himself into the dark and empty place, where before there'd been him and only him, and all the pleasure was for him, but on that morning he felt a magnet of love and desire that took her with him. With perfect co-ordination they rushed and pulsed into the comfort of the angels.

As he lay back, burned out and dribbling, he opened his eyes and saw Daniel playing at the side of the bed with what he called his Bizzy Box. Lego bricks, a pile of scruffy Ladybird books, a bendy Rupert, some plastic cups and saucers, and a scruffy, hand knitted golliwog. The child stared at him, in a puzzled questioning sort of way, but Joe ruffled his hair and he went back to his toys. Ursula Fortune also made a shadowy appearance. All he ever got were her barbed words of criticism. The knife she turned so frequently. He was a failure. A snail. She poisoned everything. He kicked hard and pushed her away with his bare foot.

Joe awoke to discover they'd slept contentedly for six hours. The sunshine had left the room, but he could tell the day still hung with a sizzling heat. He turned towards Anna, and gently kissed her shoulder, but she sprang completely awake, and laughed and grabbed him, and they blazed again, crying out like wild geese. 'Anna,' he whispered. 'Tell me. What are the things you most love about me.' She said it was his Jewishness. He was an Israeli. A beautiful Israeli. It was all the things he was that didn't say middle-class, Home Counties England. She didn't tell him that he was forbidden fruit.

'What are the things you most love about me?' she asked. He said it was something about Venus. Her eyes and her Aryan beauty. It was all the things about her that didn't say Jewish. He didn't mention forbidden fruit either.

Joe rose reluctantly and dressed to go. 'I'm on duty again on Saturday night,' he said. 'Will you come to my on-call room? We can have a take-away, and a bottle of wine. You can even stay all night. There's honour among thieves that we turn a blind eye to . . .'

She finished his sentence for him. 'You were going to say adultery, weren't you?'

'I was, but it's not our word, is it?'

'No. It's got to be love.'

'It is, Anna. I promise you it is, so will you come?'

She shook her head. 'I want to but I can't. I have to go home. It's my nineteenth birthday on Saturday and my father's organised a party for me. The whole thing's going to be an endurance. I don't want to be there, but I have to be.'

Joe was disappointed, but this wasn't the time to search for any sort of damper to the perfection of the day. In any case, his other life demanded him, but first he had an urgent errand. He drove to Broad Street and went to the toy section of Boswell's department store. Not to buy a conscience gift for his child, but to buy a birthday present for his beloved. He chose something he couldn't really afford; a nightdress case disguised as a brown velvet monkey. In a hastily chosen card he wrote:

> *To Anna Morton Moore who is nineteen on Saturday.*
> *Anna, I love you with every cell of my body, and every atom of my soul. This monkey is to remind you of this special day, and perhaps to remind you of me.*
> *Joe*

He drove back to her flat, rushed up the stairs, dropped the carrier bag outside her door, rang the bell and ran away.

Doreen, the baby-minder, lived at Risinghurst and he was already over half an hour late. A traffic jam on the London Road delayed him further, and by the time he arrived he found that Daniel's long wait had forced the child to curl up and go to sleep. He'd woken up, red-cheeked and grumpy, and he grizzled and kicked as Joe tried to strap him into the child seat in the car. But Joe's usual patience was missing. He shouted with irritation, firmly telling him that he was a naughty boy and Daddy was very cross. Joe was perhaps less cross than worried. He had to finish his affair with Carina, and he wasn't looking forward to dumping the lady so swiftly and callously, but then it suddenly struck him that he now had the classic excuse. Last night Urshie had smacked him over the head with a tin tray and accused him of an affair. He'd phone Carina, tell her he'd got the wind up and they had to cool it for a while, but of course it would be finished and there'd be no further confrontation or upset.

Just a gradual realisation, on her part, that he wasn't coming back.

He looked at his watch. Professor Alton would still be doing his Friday afternoon ward round, so he stopped at a phone box in Morrel Avenue. 'Hi Carrie. It's me. Listen . . .' but before he could say another word she interrupted him.

'Thank Christ you called. I've had a letter. I suppose you could say it's a poison pen letter. It's about us!'

Carina had received a typed note through the post.

Dear Mrs Alton
We know all about you and the Fortunate young man.
Would your husband like to know?
A wellwisher

'Joe, you're going to have to keep your head down for a while. Jeez, we've always been so careful. Seriously, love. No contact. OK? God, I'm going to miss you,' and she put the phone down. So that was Carina sorted. What luck! But it didn't solve the question why someone was being so vicious as to send poison pen letters. Was that how Urshie had found out? Did someone send her a letter too? He wasn't going to ask. Dead and buried. Each day it would retreat further and further into the background, and eventually disappear.

With his numerous delays Joe was very late getting home to the cramped flat that fronted the traffic-congested Cowley Road. Carrying a still miserable Daniel in his arms, he dragged his feet down the steps to the tenebrous desolation of the semi-basement. Fleshy, mossy growths poked out from between crumbling green bricks and the void smelled moist and stale. As he pushed the door open he heard the merry sound of music. Urshie was home, and busy in the kitchen, which was most unusual. After yesterday's vitriolic row he was expecting her to be sullen and tight-lipped, but he wanted her to be that way. He wanted her to be in the worst mood possible so he could invite further conflict and throw in a hand grenade about separating. No mention of Anna; just the first bombshell to test the temperature. Cards on the table. It'd all been a sad mistake and they had to stop pretending etc, but it wasn't going to be like that. She appeared smiling. 'Oh, you look so tired,' she said, with genuine concern. 'Poor you. Did you have a bad night?'

'A long death,' he mumbled. 'Didn't get a wink. I crashed out in my room. Sorry I'm late. Overslept.'

Normally he'd have got a screaming earful for picking Daniel up so late, but her sudden change of behaviour could only mean one thing. She was about to announce something that would seriously inconvenience him, followed by a couple of bottles of beer and an early night to further impose her power. She was cooking fish. They ate the fish. They both looked aghast at the washing up, but she touched his shoulder with an heroic gesture. 'Go and sit down, I'll do it.' Joe sat down. No need to be told twice. It was the first domestic work she'd done in over a fortnight. She then revealed the inevitable inconvenience he knew was coming. 'I've been invited to go on a course in October,' she said. 'To Isaiah Goodman's cardiac unit in London. They're using some amazing new anaesthetic techniques. It's a fantastic career chance for me, but it means I'll be away for two weeks. I can't turn it down, Joe.' Of course he raised no objection. He congratulated her. It was no skin off his nose. He'd have left her by then.

That night a rare happy atmosphere was created as they played with Daniel. They played Snap, and let him win all the time. 'Isn't Daddy silly?' Joe said with wide, surprised eyes. 'He can't even tell Noddy and Noddy and Mummy can't even tell Big Ears and Big Ears. But Daniel can. Daniel's ever such a clever boy,' and the excited little child, revelling in the rare attention of united parents, jumped up and down and clapped his hands with a surge of joy spreading over his face.

'I winned,' he shouted. 'I winned.'

Joe then read *The Three Billy Goats Gruff* yet again, until the small curly head flopped forward with exhaustion and he was carefully put to bed.

As he'd predicted Urshie then produced two bottles of beer. All evening Joe had inwardly rehearsed the careful words he wanted to say. To make the bombshell sound like the whispering fall of a dandelion puff. He'd try to make his voice soft and gentle, be nice to her, just tell her slowly and sweetly, with a sad and sorry look on his face, that he wanted to leave her. Perhaps squat down at her side and take her hand. 'I'm sorry, Urshie. I'm really sorry, but it'll be for the best in the long run . . .' but his mouth froze and somehow the intended words failed to fall out. Instead it was Urshie who brought up an on-going problem: their need for a bigger flat. Daniel was nearly four and far too old for the cot at the end of their bed. He needed his own room and a proper divan. 'The flat. Yes, the flat,' Joe said, trying to sound interested. 'We must get out of here. Look, Colin from A and E's got a new post in Swindon. I'll have a word about his house off St Clements. It's got two bedrooms and a little garden.'

At ten o'clock Urshie yawned to indicate that an early night was required. Joe wasted time for as long as he could ironing a shirt for the morning, hoping she'd fall asleep, but he couldn't delay getting into bed for ever. That morning his lungs had been filled with the gasp of Anna's perfume, but his marital bedroom was rank with old urine saturations of Daniel's mattress, and their own stale sheets. Outside, the never-ending car flow of the Cowley Road swished by. The pubs were kicking out, and fuddled voices shouted drunken goodbyes or sang mournful songs of old Ireland. Daniel was breathing noisily, curled up in his cot like a dog. There was no hiding place.

Now he'd known the beauty of Anna there could be no compromise. Their bodies had gripped and swirled each other in a madness of immeasurable pleasure. He'd held her arms high above her head and kissed her smooth armpits. He'd opened his mouth over her breasts, and dipped like a humming bird to find her nectar, but most of all he'd loved her abstraction. Her dignity. The unflinching concentration in her eyes and the way she thought before she spoke. She seemed so full of unsaid things. His quiet beauty. His Venus.

He and Urshie clumsily faced each other with no foreplay, no words of love and no passion. Their usual

131

mechanical routine movements didn't work for either of them, and they broke apart. 'Sorry. I'm still really tired,' he said.

She turned over and sighed deeply. 'Yeah. Tired of me.'

He was.

CHAPTER SEVEN

Saturday

I AWAKE AT 9.00 A.M. This is truly a miracle and a rare Fortune version of a long lie-in. Normally we're up at 6.00 a.m. fighting for the shower, ignoring each other and dancing with hair dryers (her, not me). We bolt toast and cereal, slurp strong coffee, look for things that we left out for the morning (and have moved during the night), pack briefcases, make phone calls and worry about the location of Me-Toom-Tum (me, not her). Just as we're about to leave a slovenly young man, in black Calvin Kleins, appears on the stairs to bombard us with a long list of 'where's my', and a pale-faced young girl, in an over-sized T-shirt, asks, with breathy simplicity, if she can have a sub.

'Sleep well?' Anna asks dreamily, her warm hand squeezing my thigh.

'Slept like a top,' I lie, knowing that our silent, miserable patch won't be admitted or discussed. But hey! Today we've got nothing to do and nowhere to go. Perhaps I can persuade the cook to be nice to me and serve breakfast in bed. I can't be the only Jew who enjoys a full plate of bacon and eggs, with fried bread, mushrooms, and grilled tomatoes, washed down with a mug of scalding tea. Then maybe a catch-up forty winks, and then . . . Now what could we do? I think I favour a mooch around Tate Modern, a pasta in Covent Garden and whatever's on at that art house movie place in Greek Street.

Anna stretches, pushes off the duvet, and the warm fug of our night escapes. She lets out a long sigh and turns to find my body. Her gentle, seeking fingers walk up and over the hill of my teddy bear tummy, while I lie there with a dopey, glazed over expression. My mouth takes hers, wide and wet, as if I'm taking the first bite of an apple. 'Don't rush, Joe, you've got all day,' but we stop moving. Our flow is arrested. 'I'll have to answer it,' I say. 'It might be urgent. Dan's on a plane, and who knows what the twins are up to?'

It's for Anna. She replaces the receiver, and gives me a down-faced verbatim report. It's bad news. The sort of bad news that makes me want to scream, and pound the pillows, and turn my guts inside out. Our precious day alone has been completely buggered. It appears that last night my detested father-in-law had a fall down the stairs. The local GP, Dr Gibson, was called, but when the poor man arrived he was greeted with a barrage of opposition and attitude from the despicable Gordon. This morning Gordon is dizzy and slurring and poor old Queenie Croften doesn't know what to do. Family crisis and Anna bursts into tears. 'Sweetheart,' I force myself to say, trying to hide my fury. 'Don't upset yourself. I'm sure he'll be OK,' but her reply is quite unexpected.

'I couldn't actually care less,' she snaps. 'I wanted to spend the day with *you*. Even if we did nothing. I just wanted you to myself. One day, Joe! Just one day when we're not obliged to put anyone else before ourselves and this has to happen.' I think I know exactly what she means, but this is behaviour I've never seen from her before. She stomps out of bed and begins an angry search for clean underwear. 'I'm going to have to go down,' she fumes. 'I can't just stand back and expect Queenie and Cyril to cope, can I? I'm sorry, Joe, but I have to go.' My obligation to go with her is obvious. We're both compelled to rush down to Monks Bottom to assess the situation, although I suspect the episode is an attention-seeking ruse. Anna decides to pack a small suitcase 'just in case'. My toothbrush isn't included.

When we arrive at The Old Vicarage my feet alight onto the gravelled drive. Stones beneath my feet, and also in my heart. Anna shuts the door of the Discovery with a deep sigh, but before we can clasp hands in harmony Queenie Croften rushes out of the front door, wiping her hands on an ever-present tea cloth. Her face is creased with anxiety, and her flustered voice follows us up the stairs, telling us the story all over again. As we approach the master bedroom she overtakes us, eager to present her patient, and ushers us in. ''Ere they are, Sir Gordon,' she says, as if she's trying to cheer up a sulky four-year-old. 'Your Anna and Joe come to see you. You tell 'em what a nasty accident you've 'ad. You're still very wibbly-wobbly-woo, aren't you? Oh dear, and that bump on yer 'ead's really comin' up.' She then turns to me. 'You'll want to give 'im the once over, won't you?' (No, I won't, actually.) Queenie disappears to attend to some homemade soup, satisfied that she has left her adored employer in the hands of his loved ones.

The wounded Fuhrer sits propped up in bed with his blue-mottled paws spread out on the broderie anglaise counterpane like a deathbed actor. 'Really Papa, what have you been up to?' Anna says, in her usual fond way of talking to him.

'Just a little tumble, sweetie,' he whispers with slow and reedy timbre, but strangely she rushes from the room. I run after her. She sits on the edge of the bath, pale and breathing deeply.

'Annie. What's the matter? Are you ill?'

She shakes her head. 'Go and look him over, Joe? I'll be OK in a minute.'

I pat her shoulder reassuringly and return to Gordon's bedroom to go through the motions of offering him a medical examination, but now we're alone he presents his true vitriolic persona. His voice is suddenly quite normal and strong. I'm advised he'd rather die than have my hands on him, and I'm emphatically ordered to get the hell out of it. Suits me. As I leave the room I notice a bottle of vodka hiding behind the curtain within arm's reach.

Anna assures me she now feels OK, and retreats to the kitchen for a calming cup of tea and a chat with the ever-kindly Queenie. I crash out of the house and walk to the top of the garden; a marathon slog of over a quarter of a mile, each step a hard and angry thump. I've just *got* to get rid of him, but I must stop filling my head with theoretical situations and do it. But how?

When I get there I realise I'm desperate for a pee, but as I'm shooting into the blackberry bushes I hear a familiar voice cackle behind me. It's Cyril Croften, Gordon's gardener (who I hasten to add is not the old rodent who took my letter all those years ago). He's sitting on a log, leaning back on a collapsing garden shed, and wheezing mirth through his emphysemic lungs. Old Cyril. Ancient, gnarled and worn-out. We've always been good friends. He hates Gordon as much as I do.

'I've bin pissin' in them bushes for years,' he splutters. 'Queen always says the vicarage blackberries are much bigger than anyone else's, and she makes smashin' jam. Must be good fertiliser. Just wish 'is majesty knew what 'e was spreadin' on 'is toast.'

I join him on the log, and we sit together to smoke. He, an old man's Rizla roll-up. Me, a thin spliff. 'That there the old wacky baccy?' Cyril asks. 'Still on the old pot plants, eh?'

'I don't change, Cyril,' I say, drawing in sweetly, 'but I might just go nuts if this sort of pantomime becomes a regular feature.'

''E were rat-arsed,' says Cyril. 'On the old Tio Pepe all day, lurchin' around all dog eyed and slurrin'. Next thing we knows, Queen 'ears a crash and she finds 'im at the bottom of the stairs. I 'ad to get our Tom to come over and 'aul 'im up to bed. Queen wouldn't believe 'e was sloshed, and phoned for Dr Gibson, but when the poor sod got 'ere 'e was told to sling 'is 'ook. Nice young bloke, very thorough, all the village says so, but 'is nibs was so bloody rude. Threatened to shoot 'im. Not that 'e'd 'ave been able to find the gun-safe in his state, let alone the gun.'

I sigh, shamed by the despicable behaviour of my wife's father. 'Well, bladdered or not, he needs some sort of diagnosis,' I reply. 'He could be having something called ischaemic attacks. It's usually the forerunner to a stroke.'

'Then we'll just 'ave to 'ope and pray for a stroke of good luck then,' Cyril titters.

'I think I'll contact Dr Gibson all the same, Cyril,' I say. 'Not that I give a flying toss, but I feel obliged to take some sort of professional interest.'

Cyril leans back, picking bits of stray tobacco from his purple lips. 'Tell yer the truth, Joe,' he says, 'I've 'ad more than enough, but it's Queen, see. You know what she's like. She farts and fusses over him like 'e was the fuckin' Duke of Edinburgh. Some days I feel like lockin' 'er up. Can you 'ave a word with 'er? Last time I mentioned it we were at it 'ammer and tongs. She didn't want to call it a day. Said she felt sorry for the poor old boy. 'Poor old boy, my arse,' I said. 'There's nothin' poor about 'im, and what about me? Aren't I a poor old boy as well?' She said she'd think about it, but I know she 'asn't.'

'I'll see what I can do, Cyril,' I say, but I'm lying through my teeth. It's the last thing I want. At least with them up the road we just about manage to maintain the status quo. What on earth would the situation be like if they trolled off? An ageing man in failing health. Maybe even a serious stroke victim. What's the worse case scenario? Anna and me up and down like yo-yos, or even worse, him coming to live with us. We've got five bedrooms. His daughter's a trained nurse and a geriatric social worker. His son-in-law's a GP. How could we refuse? Oh, my brain's racing ahead. I've got to act. Fast!

I telephone the Monks Bottom Health Centre, and have a very matey chat with the duty doctor, luckily Dr Gibson. I've no need to tell him I'm also a GP as Queenie has already done the honours. I apologise for my father-in-law's appalling behaviour by way of passing him off as an old colonial – one of the old school and too damned rich to argue with, ha-ha. I reluctantly proffer my professional views on the possibility of ischaemic attacks. 'I think his left eyelid might be down a tad,' I say. 'I'd willingly do the BP but he won't give me his arm.'

'Do you want me to visit today?' Dr Gibson asks.

'It might be wise,' I say, 'but he's still in a foul mood. Bullet proof vests issued at the gates.' We both laugh.

Dr Gibson arrives with the hour. We have a brief chat about medical training (me Oxford 1968, he Oxford 1988) and brief career résumés. I then accompany him tentatively in to Gordon, but, far from being obnoxious and rude, the patient is the epitome of charm. He insists on privacy so I slope off to the terrace for a beer, leaving Dr Gibson to it. Half an hour later he joins me and Anna and accepts a coffee. 'I think you're right about ischaemic attacks,' he says. 'His BP's well up. 230/115. Dull reflexes, wobbly on his pins and speech a bit slurred. He normally sees my colleague Jack Lyndhurst privately so I'll have to take your word on the eye droop. I've prescribed an anti-hypertensive – I've left a couple of days supply upstairs – and I'll also get our district nurse to do some routine bloods on Monday. Does that sound OK as a kick-off point?'

I nod, perhaps a little too vigorously. 'Absolutely,' I say.

'Will you still be here, tomorrow?' he asks.

'Probably,' Anna says.

'But not me,' I say emphatically, and a little too quickly. 'I'm committed to our own out-of-hours service myself tomorrow.'

Andrew Gibson and I have a very interesting conversation about the contrasts between our respective practices, concluding that doing a job swap for a couple of weeks would enlighten our understanding of the great social divide. We shake hands amiably, having cemented a sound professional footing. 'Do ring me if things change for the worse,' he says. 'I live close by and I'm on duty until six. After that the county night service takes over, but I'll make sure they know the facts.'

At 1.00 p.m. Queenie moves into the sickroom with a tempting lunch tray, and Gordon is coaxed to eat a sturdy bowl of her lentil and potato soup. 'Got to keep yer strength up,' she wheedles, and a second helping is managed after a great deal of persuading. A large portion of bread and butter pudding is waved away with a wry refusal, but somehow, faced with her concern about 'fading away', he manages that as well. Then he feels a therapeutic tincture or three of vintage port would help. Not surprisingly he becomes very sleepy, and requests closed curtains. No such luck for me. Before he settles down Anna and I are given orders to 'have a go' at all the jobs the Croftens can't cope with any more, like washing all the downstairs light fittings and scrubbing the terrace, presented as, 'well, while you're here you might as well just . . .' Just! Just! The most maligned word in the English language.

Anna and I fall into a sterile silence, neither of us able to admit our misery or discuss the situation in any way. She follows me around with buckets of hot water, liquid Flash, cloths and stiff brooms, knowing there'd be no point in attempting to create a whistle-while-you-work atmosphere. We occasionally give each other a short tight smile, but she knows I'm very angry, and any admission of the fact will cause a row; the sort of row that so often follows a day spent at The Old Vicarage. What is it about this bloody place that construes to divide us?

Christmas Day 2005: Every Christmas Day, in order to avoid a Monks Bottom muster, Joe would pull his Jewish card and volunteer to be on-call, declaring it was only fair his Christian partners should celebrate. But last year, due to a new out-of-hours contract involving locum cover, his bluff was called. He was thus forced to accompany his family to The Old Vicarage, and the situation developed into a far worse torment than usual.

On Christmas Eve they'd had a phone call from his loathsome in-law. An emergency situation ensued. Poor Queenie had been taken ill with a bad case of the old 'flu. 'Oh Lord, what a pretty kettle of fish! Could Anna possibly step into the breach? Just a question of waving a magic wand over the bird, etc.' He was sorry, but he could do nothing himself. A few dizzy spells actually. Not that Anna must worry. Of course, if she couldn't manage it he'd understand, but he'd be so delighted . . . blah, blah, blah.

On Christmas morning the Fortune family left for Monks Bottom well before dawn. Two irritable and hung-over grandchildren, one racked-off son-in-law and one very quiet daughter. The nearer they got the more withdrawn Anna became, but she greeted her father with fondness and assured him that Christmas was far from cancelled. She and Sophie disappeared straight to the kitchen to wave the magic wand (i.e. slave for hours) but five minutes later, following a large crash, Sophie reappeared. 'I think Mummy would rather be on her own,' she said, her face twisted in a pop-eyed smirk, and blowing on her fingers with theatrical affectation. Thus, Joe and the twins were given their duty-roster by the camp commandant. Joe was ordered to lay and light two log fires, polish glasses, set the table and just pop the Hoover round. Sophie and Josh were sent out into the vast garden to cut holly and look for mistletoe. Mistletoe! Who the hell was going to do any kissing? A large Christmas tree stood askew in a corner of the main entrance hall, and Gordon was in no doubt that the kiddies would have a lark dressing it. Where were the decorations? In the loft of course, and as Joe climbed up he was instructed on the shortcomings of the pull-down ladder. Gordon then hovered about, intent on doing nothing, and consequently announced he was going for a therapeutic bath.

The twins had brought no suitable clothes for gallivanting around the garden in the freezing cold, but they sallied forth. Josh, in precious new Gap Cargos and a white T-shirt.

Sophie, in a black lycra catsuit, silver DMs, long dangling earrings and make up that would make Cleopatra looked scrubbed and natural. Needless to say they were back in five minutes, empty-handed and moaning, and stood about hugging themselves. 'This place is like frigging Siberia,' Sophie grouched. 'It's colder in here than it is out there.'

She was right. The huge high-ceilinged rooms echoed with an arctic lifelessness. Conversely, in the kitchen, where the Aga burned through four seasons, it was hotter than high season Calcutta and Anna was already scarlet-faced. Sophie was heard calling to Gordon through the bathroom door, 'Grandpapa, we're ever so cold. Can we have the central heating on, please?'

'Sorry Sophie, old thing,' Gordon called back. 'The system's got a bit old and decrepit; a bit like me, ha-ha. The radiators will take off all the bath water. Once the fires are lit, it'll warm up nicely, so tell your father to get cracking. If you're that cold why don't you go into my dressing room and find one of my nice cardigans?'

Sophie thumped down the stairs, stymied. 'If he thinks I'd be seen dead in one of his moth-eaten woolley pullies he can eat cowcrap.' The twins stomped off to the kitchen to huddle around the Aga (and get in their mother's way), declaring that they had no intentions of decorating the Christmas tree as they were both suddenly allergic to pine-needles.

But Joe was entrapped on housemaid duty. He moved into the icy ambience of the drawing room to light his first fire, but, as ever, he could never enter this room without evoking the misery of that fateful September weekend in 1979. How many times had he been in this room since then? Thirty or forty, perhaps. Relatively few, given the number of years, but today, with the fury of the occasion, his most hated Monks Bottom memory visualised with the impact of a Victorian melodrama. The sad, sorry scene that precluded the twisted and bizarre parting he and Anna had suffered.

Despite the intervening years, everything still looked exactly the same; the same highly polished furniture, the same paintings on the walls and the same family photographs on the grand piano, but on that night it had been hot and humid with the hangover of an Indian summer day. He relived again Anna's burst of hate and despair. He heard her sobbing. He saw her crawling out of the door on her hands and knees, with her long, heavy fleece of hair hanging over her face.

He lifted his head and looked out of the window to see another sad scene of a few days later. A broken-hearted, scruffy young man with a pony-tail was holding a crying child. A droop-shouldered old gardener was wiping dewdrops on the cuff of his old tweed jacket, with a cream envelope tucked down the side of his old Wellington boot.

The scenes vapourised and Joe re-entered the present to lay the fire; ordered to follow the strict instructions issued from the chief to the hapless foot soldier. A dozen paper spills to be made from carefully folded newspaper, two commercial firelighters, two layers of kindling wood and a light layer of coke. He struck a Swan Vesta. The papers became a crackling yellow blaze, the firelighters and the twigs caught flame, and small swirls of grey smoke twisted up the chimney.

'For what we are about to receive may The Lord make us truly thankful,' Gordon boomed. Joe, in polite reply to his host, quietly recited a *brochah*, but deliberately repeated it three times, taking great care to cough up his Hebrew with all the charm of producing a sputum specimen. Sophie's face showed a pre-giggle slant of her mouth (the *brochah* not being part of her father's usual table behaviour) but his steely glare hauled her face back to normality. The oracle sat at the head of the table, in the stance of an entertaining wit, demanding everyone's full attention. The topics included the irritating personal habits of people they'd never heard of, drainage problems in the meadow, a tooth filling he'd needed replacing, village politics and the shortcomings of the Croftens. But after the flaming Christmas pudding had been wheeled in it was Joe who had to stand up and make a speech. 'Please can we all raise our glasses, and thank our dear wife/mother/daughter for a simply superb Christmas dinner,' but Gordon was unable to join in the toast. He shuffled noisily with his glasses and the *Radio Times*, trying to find out the exact time of the queen's speech.

Once the meal was over Anna disappeared to cope with the battlefield of chaos in the kitchen. Joe followed to embrace her fondly in a statement of unity, but their intimacy was ruined as the twins crashed in and out, thumping down dirty crocks and cutlery; desperate to be seen as 'helping' before seeking refuge with James Bond. As Joe dried the last plate (no such luxury as a dishwasher chez Morton Moore) Gordon appeared at the door holding a cigar the size of a chair leg and a huge balloon of brandy. 'My study, Joe. A quick word, if you don't mind.' Like a dog at heel Joe obediently followed. Having firmly told Joe to, 'Take a seat,' Gordon stood four square in front of him and lectured down. 'Anna's looking very tired and drawn,' he said. 'It's as plain as the nose on my face she's in a bad way. One would have thought a medically qualified doctor might just happen to notice the state of his wife's health. There'll have to be some sort of investigations, of course, and I intend to send her to an excellent chap I know in Harley Street.'

For Joe it was a stab in the heart. He wanted to grab Gordon by his old Harrovian tie and punch out his lights. He wanted to tell him that the only reason she was looking tired and drawn was because she'd been working hard all week, fighting to get small rewards for the poor and downtrodden old folk of south London, and she'd been up since well before sparrow fart on Christmas day to pander to *him*. He should have . . . but he didn't. Did he want crap doctor and X-rated loudmouth added to the long tally of his personal failings? With great forbearance Joe extracted his traditional Jewish good manners.

'I'm so sorry, Gordon,' he said, looking theatrically at his watch. 'I'm afraid it's time to go. Bad weather. Failing light. Best we make an early move. I'm sure you understand.' Joe quickly rounded up his family and announced they were leaving. No one argued. They judged his mood and were delighted to leave anyway. After shaking Gordon's hand Joe thanked him very much for a pleasant day, and assured him loudly that his kind offer of a Harley Street appointment for Anna wouldn't be necessary. Anna looked at him with a very strange and bewildered expression. 'Your father thinks you're looking at bit jaded, darling,' he said, 'but I've assured him I'll take good care of you myself.'

They call it road rage, but Joe's rage was something steeped in human failing. Ten miles up the road he was forced to stop at a lay-by to bid a violent farewell to his Christmas dinner. For the rest of the journey he immersed himself in a silent analysis of the day, and although Anna extended her hand to his knee in a gesture of loving comfort, he pushed it off roughly. 'Joe, there's nothing wrong with me,' she said, 'but I'm beginning to think there's something wrong with you.'

Once home, Josh and Sophie (expressing their amazement that they'd actually got back alive) went straight out to seek their own kind. Left alone Joe and Anna could have had the sort of Christmas evening that so many couples want, but never get. He could have poured her a drink, turned up the heating, apologised for his temper and told her how glad he was to be home alone with her. He could have, but he was unable to. His creatures of the night loomed large. The bats congregated in an oily, heaving mob and the black dog showed its teeth. He flung on his old padded jacket and banged out of the house, not knowing where he was going. Two hours later, not knowing where he'd been, he quietly returned to Sunny Lea.

The house was in complete darkness. There was no moon, or stars and the sky was black with heavy rain clouds. He didn't turn on the lights. Lights wouldn't have been right. It wasn't a grand entrance; just a shameful slithering back. What was the matter with him? He'd spent most of his adult life treating the minds and bodies of perfect strangers, so why was he directing so much hatred towards his adored wife when he knew he truly loved her and nothing was her fault? He swayed in the pitch black, trying to call up some carotene, or whatever it was that was supposed to help one see in the dark, but there was none to be found. He was as blind as one of his bats.

A blind man had once told him that he subconsciously knew when solid objects were there, seeming to loom up and announce themselves in a mysterious type of early warning system, but as Joe cautiously advanced nothing helped him. His breathing was anxious and laboured and he felt confused, as if he'd been spun around in an impromptu party game of Blind Man's Buff. He slowly shuffled his feet an inch at a time, fearful of falling into a deep pit, or stumbling over a sleeping creature. With a snail's pace his fingertips searched anxiously across the walls until he found the familiar contours of the sitting room door handle.

She was sitting on the floor by the light of a single candle, her hair falling forward over her face, her knees pulled up to her chest and the gin bottle beside her. She didn't move or look up. He removed his jacket, sat down beside her and a psychic osmosis told him that all was forgiven. She covered his hand with hers. 'Black dog?' she asked.

'Sodding hound,' he replied. She blew out the candle, and took him in her arms. The arms, and the forgiveness, he didn't deserve.

CHAPTER EIGHT

Saturday, continued . . .

STILL STANDS THE CHURCH CLOCK AT TEN TO FIVE and Anna and I are still fawning to a sick phoney. Queenie and Cyril have gone home to their council house up the road for a well-earned break and we're in the back scullery wringing out cloths and drying our hands. My favourite sage-green cords are now rendered unwearable, being mottled with white bleach splashes. Anna's hair is a damp, frizzy mess and her hands are 'coming up', a skin condition which afflicts her when she doesn't wear rubber gloves. A grating vibration is then heard from the kitchen, alerting us that the incumbent of the master bedroom is swinging the servant-summoner at his bedside. Shit! His post-lunch siesta had lasted over three hours and I was hoping he might actually have kicked the bucket and saved me a job.

Anna scurries off to kow-tow and returns with a list. She's actually looking quite green around the gills again, but she waves away my attention and concern. 'Stop fussing. I'm fine.' She doesn't look it. The ghastly Gordon has requested a pot of some poncey leaf tea that she'll make to an absurd elaborate ritual. He also fancies a large boiled farm egg (three and a half minutes exactly, and rested for a further forty five seconds with an egg cosy), two rounds of buttered toast soldiers, and a few scones served with clotted cream and Queenie's homemade blackberry jam (hopefully a dollop that's been well soaked in Cyril's piss).

150

'You're not coming back with me, are you?' I say.

She shakes her head. 'How *can* I just walk out? The buck stops with me and there's only one *of* me, isn't there? Please, Joe. Try to be patient.' She can see by my stiff face that it's a black dog situation. She reaches for my hand, but I pull away sharply. What I really want to say is that I understand completely, and offer to stay as well to help her through a bad time, but I can't. I'm clamped, once again, between the jaws of the dreaded canine.

'Best be off,' I say. 'No point in getting snarled up in the evening traffic. I'll apologise to Mum and Dad you won't be there tomorrow.'

'I'm sorry, Joe.'

'So am I.'

She wants to kiss me goodbye, but I can find no movement in my arms or my lips. As I get in the Discovery we have some sort of standard conversation about talking tomorrow, and assessing situations, but I'm out of here.

Anna watches him go, but he doesn't turn around with his usual cheery wave and a blown kiss. She wants to run after him shouting, 'Don't leave me. I can't bear to be here without you. Please don't go. I won't sleep because the evil spirits of The Old Vicarage will come to me in the night, and I'll need you to protect me,' but he's gone and it's too late. At the top of the drive the brake lights come on, but he's not had a change of heart. He's stopped to speak to Queenie. He has a few words with her, and draws off.

Queenie waves as she bustles down the drive. 'Sorry poor old Joe's on-call tonight,' she says, 'but you can watch a bit a telly, and 'ave a nice early night. I've got some lovely chicken breast for dinner with some salad and new spuds. All home-grown from the garden. Got to tempt yer Pa, 'aven't we? Be ready about eight. Why don't yer go for a little walk, dear? This time of year there's always a beautiful rose in full bloom up by the blackberries.' She moves forward and pats Anna's hand. 'Now you've not to worry about all this. 'E's gonna be all right. Our Cyril'll see to 'im later, and run the Remington over 'im. Then I'll pop 'im into some clean jim-jams.'

Anna has no wish to hear domestic details concerning the cleanliness and appearance of her father, but she smiles, or at least forces her lips apart and shows her teeth. She can't tell Queenie that she'd like to drive a stake through his heart (if he had one). 'Thank you, Queenie,' she says. 'You're both so kind.'

It's a warm, mellow evening. 'Go and see the rose,' she'd said. Surely it can't be the same Albertine rose that's still blooming? Anna walks slowly up the long lawn, around the ornamental fish pool, over the ha-ha bridge and across the meadow to the far, far away part of the garden she and Hugo used to call the jungle.

The old garden shed still survives, but its window-panes are cracked, smoked black and cobwebbed. The wood is desiccated to a light grey and slowly rots. The roof has started to slip, but the Albertine has endured as a woody overgrown giant, its blooms hanging in heavy trusses of salmon-pink clusters. She turns the shed's loose, rattling door handle. The door sticks, but it shudders to opening. Inside it's hot and full of rubbish. Old pots of varnish, empty cans of creosote, piles of scrap wood. Broken things. Dirty things. Things that look as if they've never had any useful purpose. She remembers the burning sun on her naked back. She remembers the smells of lawnmower oil, blood, hoof and bone, the rotting sweetness of grass cuttings and the sharp, rubbery smell of condoms. She stands for several minutes, eyes closed and eclipsed. Many bad things before, many worse things after, but this was a golden time in a mire of hatred. She turns, closes the door behind her, walks back down to the fish pool, and removes all her clothes. She feels mad. Perhaps she *is* mad. The mad are always the last to know themselves. The water draws her in. The sun has shone on it all day, and it's warm, thick and slippery. The fish noisily splosh, diving for cover. She lowers herself down amongst the water lilies until only her head remains above the water line.

I slam the front door. Fuck-rat and arseholes! I angrily tear off my bleach-stained cords and kick them into a corner. My new yellow polo shirt has suffered the same fate, so that goes flying as well. A whole outfit ruined, a waste of a precious day, and now an absent wife. That evil bastard has won again. I should have thrown a tantrum and insisted she come back with me. I should have got onto an agency and arranged an emergency nurse. I should have done something instead of poncing off in a cob. But could I? No, Joe. Stop kidding yourself. You know there's absolutely naff-all you could have done to change things, except to act with grace and not a complete and utter wanker. Or? Yes. Or eliminate the archetypal villain.

My only sustenance today has been a poxy bowl of soup and dollop of bread and butter pudding so I dial a Chinese, smoke a glorious fat spliff, and down a bottle of Spanish plonk. What a rip-roaring way to spend Saturday night. Even the sodding cat's done the disappearing act and my balls ache. There's no message on the ansaphone from Dan, so I can only hope and pray that he reached South Africa safely and the funeral 'went off all right'.

After I've gobbled down the take-away I reach for another bottle and tip it to my mouth. I raise a respectful toast to the body of my first wife, and the sorry absence of my second, but then another wave of hideous guilt for my shameful behaviour looms out of my inebriated state. I lift the phone. 'Annie, it's me . . .' I'm so pissed I don't know what I said, but I think it was the traditional sort of grovelling apology. Do I deserve her? I'm sixty miles from where I should be, I'm drunk, and I'm full of self-loathing. I crawl up the stairs and flop out on the bed to stare at the old velvet monkey, sitting slumped on the windowsill. I reach over and pick it up, stupidly wishing we could have a deep, sympathetic exchange. Tears burn my eyes. I hug the monkey to my chest, lie down in the cold, loneliness of our kingsize and await the night visitors.

September 1979: Joe's love affair with Anna was now over two months old and his domestic situation with Urshie hadn't changed one iota, except that she'd found them a large, sunny flat in Headington. Despite the enforced move, Joe had bottled every opportunity to announce his departure, never finding the right time, or the right words, or the right sort of courage. Their relationship, thus, still endured between a stagnant pond of indifference and full-scale war. She'd spent the intervening time in intense study, and had passed yet another exam. He'd spent the time indulging in emotional and sexual overdose, explaining his long absences from home as studying for an exam of his own, and trawling out the good old library alibi from his boyhood.

But he was in love. Completely and insanely. Not only had he found unplumbed depths of passion in Anna's body, her gentle presence had become a salve to his mental exhaustion. At the end of the working day, after painful hours ignoring each other, they crashed into her flat, and into each other, like two drunken drivers. His nights on-call were spent together in his hospital room, where they would lie, wedged hard together in the single bed. Before every parting he held her in a compulsive bear hug, promising her that he'd leave Urshie soon, but she was never sulky, or petulant, or demanding. Their last snatched meeting had been a rushed lunch hour and she'd caught his hand as he rose from her bed. 'Will you come to Monks Bottom and stay with me this weekend?' she pleaded. 'My parents will be away in Scotland, golfing. Please, can you come?'

'Of course I can,' he replied, without a pause. But could he? With *his* domestic circumstances! How? He needed something a bit more convincing than the library lie to be able to disappear for a whole weekend. A sudden Fortune family death? Go missing and blame amnesia? Pick a row and stomp off?

The row picked itself without any prompting. There'd been an horrific coach crash on the A40, involving thirty children, and Urshie had been required to put in a twenty-four-hour presence for nearly a week. Daniel had been to the childminder during the day, but at night he'd been all Joe's responsibility. Urshie eventually came home, but the minute she walked through the door she barked a charge sheet of all Joe's shortcomings. His reply was that if she was so bloody particular he would leave all domestic duties to her exacting standards.

'Can't you see I'm exhausted?' she yelled.

'And I'm exhausted as well?' he bawled back, 'but don't worry. I'll be out of your hair this weekend. I'm going to stay with Felix. We're going to a *bar mitzvah.*'

'Whose *bar mitzvah*?'

'David. Eli's grandson.'

'Who's Eli?'

'Mitte's cousin.'

'Never heard of him.'

'Yes you have. He's married to Wanda, the one with the ginger wig.'

'But I'm on duty again at the weekend. Things are still chaotic. What about Daniel?'

'Can't he go to Doreen?'

'Why the hell should he? So you can go to a *bar mitzvah*! Good God, Joe, you can hardly light a candle for *Shabbat* these days. Sounds like a good excuse for pissing off to me. Perhaps Daniel would like to go to a *bar mitzvah* as well?'

'OK, I won't go.'

'Oh, that's right, blame me. Tell your precious family it's all my fault. OK. Sod off then. I couldn't give a flying fuck what you do.'

'Shut up, Urshie. Some mother you are, teaching your child four-letter words.'

'And some father you are dumping your kid to go off gadding. Don't tell me you won't be sniffing around the clubs in Soho with that over-sexed cousin of yours.'

They started to fight. She aimed a knee for his crotch which missed. He grabbed her leg, she overbalanced and fell on the floor. Her arm locked round his ankles, and although he made every effort to stay upright, he fell forward knocking a tray of cold tea onto the floor. Cups and saucers crashed, and Daniel started to scream, and scream, and scream. Joe swept him off the floor, ran out of the flat, and marched blindly up the London Road, but he could have been humping a sack of coal in his arms; his normal tenderness being replaced with the tight limbs and jerky movements of abject fury.

He went into Bury Knowle Park, and sat down wearily on a swing, but as he pressed his face to Daniel's damp head something began to make him feel nostalgic. But what? In the distance a small gang of teenagers jeered, jostled, and chased each other with bawdy talk and bursts of laughter. It was the park at Peckham Rye that was coming back to him. The happy times of his youth he'd spent sitting on the swings with the local gang. The laughing, and foul-mouthing, and the jokes. The carefree times when his life was ahead of him, and the joy of not knowing where it was going to take him. Where *was* his life going to take him now? As dusk began to fall he walked slowly home carrying a near-sleeping Daniel on his back, but he stopped at a phone box, rang Felix, and arranged cover for his illicit weekend.

As Joe drove through the high, black iron gates the Indian summer day was turning into night, and in the dusk of evening The Old Vicarage stood with overpowering grandeur. The vast Edwardian villa twisted and turned in an unbridled celebration of Gothic architecture; an asymmetrical, rambling fanfare of mellow russet bricks, stained glass, moulded mullions, sculptured finials and pointed gables. How could this sort of opulence be justified to one commonplace parish priest in such a small village? Through undrawn curtains he could see that within the house lamps were lit, creating a comforting, magnetic welcome. A heavy heat still hung in the air. Birds sang sleepily, crickets chirruped and a bat flew over his head. With his eyes closed it could have been Africa, but even with his eyes wide open it could have been Africa. It was a foreign land he didn't know.

Running steps crunched on the gravelled drive, and her voice called out his name. An exhalation of her warm breath hit him, her hair swung round his head and she clasped him tightly with a passionate, excited greeting only to be expected at the start of a sex saturated weekend. He'd longed to hold her in his arms all day, but as she hurled herself into him his body suddenly became rigid. He was clearly expected to whirl around in a dervish-like celebration of the occasion too, but he was strangely deflated.

The greeting scene was clearly strained, but she smiled kindly, took his hand, and led him up a wide, curved mahogany staircase to the Tapestry Room; a large, ceremonial guestroom that overlooked the garden. Tonight he would sleep in a four-poster bed, its tapestry drapes depicting mediaeval peasants cavorting amid lambs and sheaves of corn; the hey-nonny Anglo-Saxon world that neither Joe, nor his ancestors, had had any part of. Would it be the first time a Jew had slept in this exclusive Christian preserve? The darkening view from the window showed a long, wide lawn, herbaceous borders and towering hardwood trees. Floodlights illuminated an ornamental fish pool and in a distant meadow a silhouetted group of horses stood as still as statues. The splendour of The Old Vicarage filled him with sad diffidence. What could he give Anna? Certainly not a fraction of what she was used to.

They ate in the kitchen at a long oak refectory table. Cold pheasant, salad, a selection of cheeses, fresh fruit and a chilled Chardonnay. Conversation, usually so fluid and easy between them, stumbled sparse and stilted; the long silences amplified only by the echoing tick of the grandfather clock in the reception hall, and kamikaze moths striking the window panes. When plates were clean they laid down their knives and forks and smiled at each other, trying to assure normality. 'Cheese, darling?' she asked, offering him the board. He shook his head. 'Perhaps some fruit then? The pears are ripe.' He declined. 'More wine? Perhaps a coffee?'

'I'd rather have a glass of beer.'

It was gone ten o'clock before they moved into the drawing room, the biggest room Joe had ever seen in a private home. Perfectly proportioned, the ceiling was embellished with ornate plaster cornicing, and long, perpendicular windows overlooked the garden. It was furnished with large chintz sofas and armchairs, an antique knee-hole desk, mahogany bookcases and a grand piano. Oil paintings, in heavy gilt frames, covered the walls. Dark landscapes of gloomy fells, moody lakes, bad weather and indigenous animals in various stages of violent death, but the heavy brass standard lamps created a soft, comfortable light.

On the piano a large collection of silver-framed family photographs was displayed. An official school pose of Anna, aged about eight, with long fair plaits. The wedding of her parents showing her mother, whom she resembled almost exactly, wearing a stunning Dior-inspired wedding gown, and laughing with the joy of a happy bride. Her father in contrast looked an austere man, considerably older, with a thatch of prematurely grey hair. Sepia tints of this man's colonial Indian childhood displaying game hunters wearing pith helmets and puttees, proudly posing with dead tigers and beaming wallers. Joe thought of how the whole of the Kitchener Street house would have fitted into this one room. That little house of utility furniture, candlewick bedspreads, cracked brown lino and thin, unlined curtains. Biscuit tins for saving up, fingers crossed over football pools coupons, the insurance man and the Rabbi calling at the door. Patte and his father, washing and shaving in the scullery with their braces hanging down. Mitte on her hands and knees scrubbing the front door step, and his mother's knitting needles clicking furiously as she made him yet another embarrassing garment. He thought about the child he'd been and the man he was today. He was now a responsible professional; a saver of lives, a custodian of skill and knowledge, and a humanitarian. Against all odds he'd made it into a revered profession, but at the end of the day who was he? Still the scholarship boy and the son of working class Jews. Kitchener Street or The Old Vicarage? He'd sailed away from one, but there was certainly no safe harbour in the other.

Anna drew the heavy red velvet curtains, poured herself a gin and tonic and handed him a bottle of cold beer. But Joe was unable to settle. As he swigged from the neck he moved around the room, prowling like an animal, looking up at the ceiling, down to the floor, staring with horror at the paintings of death, running his fingers over beautiful artefacts that had no purpose other than their value. He stopped by the piano and scrutinised the photographs. 'You've got a twin brother,' he said. 'Where's his photograph? Where's Hugo?' She left the room and returned with a recent snapshot of her brother; a wild, heavily made up punk with bleached spiky hair, leopard skin singlet and tight leather trousers. Now known as MoMo, lead guitar and vocals in an American band.

'Papa's finished with him,' she said. 'That's why there are no photographs.'

'Why is he finished with him?' Joe asked.

'Isn't it obvious?' she replied. 'He's let the side down. Sex, drugs and rock'n'roll isn't the image my father expected. Oh, he paid lip-service to his music, when it suited him. Hugo's enormously talented, and he lived for his music, but he was expected to turn his back on it all and turn into a fiscal genius. Officially he's working on Wall Street. Poor Hugo. He went off nearly a year ago. He said he's never coming back, but he's always kept in touch with me. You'd like him, Joe. He's so brave and funny.'

A barren silence then enforced itself; she, seeming to retreat from the subject; he, knowing that to say more would be folly. She sat down on the thick vanilla carpet, sipped a large draught of her gin, and leaned back on the sofa. Not knowing exactly what to do or say, he came and sat down beside her, but made no attempt to touch her or humour her. They both tried an opening gambit, but the words failed. 'Have I done something wrong?' she asked timidly.

'Sorry. I'm a bit tired,' he replied.

'No,' she said. 'It's nothing to do with being tired. It's this house. It's got a curse. It spoils everything. It's full of spooks and spirits. It was built to be the house of God's disciple, but it's evil. I hate it. I hate being here.'

'Then why did you ask me to come?'

'I thought having you here would make things feel better, but it's made everything worse. I just don't belong here. *We* don't belong here. It's a horrible place.'

'Anna, what on earth are you talking about? It's ... It's ... Awesome. Only one person in a million has had what you've

had. I've never known this sort of beauty, this comfort, this …
this other sort of bloody life. It's the riches of Croesus to me.'
He tried to make her laugh. 'Matter of fact, anyone with an
inside bog impresses me,' but she didn't laugh.

'You know nothing about my sort of life,' she rounded on
him. 'Things aren't always as they seem, Joe. Your quartet
have looked after you, and loved you, and no matter what
you do they'll stand by you and be proud of you. This *is* a
lovely house, but that's all it is. It's not a home and we're not
a normal family. Papa's people were in India, but now they're
all dead anyway. Years ago Mummy had a sister but she
stopped coming, and there must have been some family in
France, but she never speaks of them, and I know nothing of
them. The only one I ever had was Hugo. Things were just
about bearable when he was here, but now he's gone.' She
burst into tears. 'Why are we talking like strangers, Joe? Have
you stopped loving me? If you have stopped loving me just
say so and go home.'

'Of course I haven't stopped loving you. I'll never stop
loving you.'

'I loved Hugo when there was no one else,' she
mumbled. 'He always said there was someone in the world
who was out there waiting to love me, and look after me, and
it turned out to be you. Now I've told you. That must be
enough. The rest belongs to me, and we'll never talk of it
again.' She let out a slow moan that changed to a melancholy
wailing. With tears falling she turned onto all fours, crawled
out of the room and up the stairs to the Tapestry Room. He
followed her slow progress, patiently and without comment.

Without looking at him, or acknowledging him in any way, she threw off her clothes, slid into the bed and pulled herself into the foetal position.

The next morning Joe woke to hear the church clock striking nine. When he opened his eyes he saw that Anna was already awake and smiling brightly, showing no signs of the previous night's despair. 'Are you feeling better?' he asked carefully.

'Yes. I'm sorry about last night. Must have been the gin talking.'

They shimmied together, but her bizarre behaviour was still bothering Joe, seeming to thrash and scrape like a wounded bird in a cage. 'Anna. About last night. I know you don't want to talk but we've got to. We must discuss all our worries and anxieties. Identify all the hurdles we've got to get over.'

'OK,' she said, pushing some pillows up behind her head. 'But you first. Tell me some more about the quartet.' He made her laugh with his impersonation of Patte, shouting out as he sold his fruit and veg from the stall. Mitte, throwing her arms up and remonstrating because he wouldn't eat. His father cleaning the windows every Sunday with diluted vinegar and screwed up newspaper, and his mother . . . well, he couldn't think of much his mother did, except to knit jumpers for Daniel and to walk up to Lipton's with her string bags.

'They sound lovely,' she said. 'I do hope they'll like me.'

Well? What would the quartet think of her? He could find nothing encouraging to say. In their eyes she'd be 'the other woman' who'd toppled the daughter-in-law they were so fond of, forcing their precious grandchild to become the quarry between two warring parents. A posh girl from a privileged background, evoking their immediate fear that Joe would move into an upper-class world and leave them behind. She was also an Aryan. The dreaded and much maligned *shikse*. Joe had assured her that Judaism would never come between them, but had he ever considered the reality?

'They'll adore you,' he lied. 'Now it's your turn to talk to me, but don't talk in riddles and start at the beginning. It can take all day and all night if needs be,' but she suddenly sat bolt upright, and flapped with her hand.

'Listen. It's the door bell. I'm not answering. Whoever it is will go away.' After several more shrill rings there was a pause, but then a man's voice was heard calling from the garden below the window.

'Annie, love,' the man called up. 'Where are you, Sweetie? Darling, I've come to take you to the races.' The man's voice was cultured, and clearly the dulcet tones of the upper-crust county set. The hideously over-refined accent Joe recognised as that used by the new-wave satirical comedians to depict a silly-arse fop. Anna slipped out of bed and crouched down on the carpet, in a needless gesture of hiding.

'It's Oliver Frockton,' she said. 'I don't want him to see me.' The man called out again a couple of times, but ultimately gave up, and his car was heard leaving.

In life, we've all had at least one moment we can't explain. The irrational and shameful behaviour we're unable

165

to suppress. The inexplicable trigger we pull that releases an explosion of hatred we immediately regret. That September morning was Joe's time. His one moment of cruelty, when his multiple insecurities erupted with jealous aggression. Who *was* this up-market jerk who dared to come looking for Anna? Love! Sweetie! Darling! 'Who's that bastard?' he yelled. He leapt out of bed, lunged towards Anna on the floor and grabbed her wrist tightly. 'For God's sake, don't tell me you're two-timing me.' She tried to pull away from him, but he continued to hold on to her, his fingers squeezing intense pressure on her wrist. She screamed. He released her, but in jerking back she knocked her head on the edge of a wardrobe. She scrambled away from him and drew herself tightly into a corner, shaking, muttering and balling her body like a hedgehog. 'Anna, who is he?' Joe asked, now trying to make the sound of his voice normal, but finding that his tongue was stiff and a jagged tick twitched diagonally across his mouth. 'Tell me you haven't got someone else? Please! I couldn't bear it.'

She slowly got up and went to sit on the edge of the bed, her face flushed and tear-smeared. 'That was Oliver Frockton,' she said. 'Lord Frockton's son. You must have heard of the Frockton brewing family. They live at The Park. That big place with the high stone walls you pass on the way into the village. My father wants me to marry Oliver. You see, even money's not enough for him. He wants me to move up the social ladder as well, but it's the last thing I want. It's the last thing Oliver wants, actually. We're very fond of each other, but we're just friends. That's all. Just friends.' She paused and swallowed. 'Joe, you've got no idea what I have to put up with. You just haven't got a clue.'

She left the room and came back holding Joe's birthday present, the monkey nightdress case. It was ruined. Shrunken, wrinkled and colourless. 'Do you remember I told you I had to come home for my birthday party? It was the last place on earth I wanted to be, but it was an excuse for my father to show off and impress himself with the guest list. I was just the commodity. 'Look at my daughter. Doesn't she look lovely, and darn me, if the Frockton boy isn't just crazy about her.' I had to dress up in a long velvet evening dress, and diamond earrings, and pretend I was enjoying myself. We had a marquee in the garden, fairy lights in the trees, waitresses, and champagne, and a ridiculous, old-fashioned dance band. I hated every minute of it, so I pretended I had a headache and went up to my bedroom. I sat on my bed in the dark, hugging my precious monkey and thinking about you, but my father barged in, yanked it out of my arms and yelled at me to get downstairs. Then after the speeches and the toasts he announced there was going to be a team game. 'Right chaps,' he cried. 'Let's rugger this little bugger.' He gave the monkey a huge kick in the air and all the male guests thrashed about, and barged each other, and fought over him like jackals tearing at a carcass. They ran down the lawn, and he was passed between them with whoops and roars and touchdowns. They were rampant and wild, like it was some sort of vile bloodsport, and when they got bored and breathless they kicked him up into the air again and he landed in the fish pool. Then they all cheered, and sang some stupid rugby song like a tribal war cry. Can't you see how desperate it all makes me? I love you, Joe. You're the only man I'll ever want in my life, but for my father you're the wrong sort.'

Of course he was the wrong sort. Joe knew that already. He found his clothes and began to dress. 'Please don't go,' she said, pressing her face into the carcass of the dead monkey.

'Why should I stay?' he said. 'What hope is there for us?' but as he looked at her he knew he could never leave her.

The word sorry was a shoddy compromise. Life with Urshie had always been so violent and vicious. Had it reduced him to a cruel bully? 'Please forgive me, Annie,' he pleaded, 'but I'm so jealous.'

'Oliver's never been my lover,' she said. 'We truly *are* good friends, but that's all. That Darling and Sweetie stuff is just the way people like him talk. We've never even held hands. But, Joe, you must understand that I'm insanely jealous too, and with reason. Put yourself in my place. When I'm alone at night, longing for you, all I can see is you and Urshie lying in bed together. The thought of it makes me sick, but I have to share you with her, don't I?' Joe, caught off guard, failed to answer. After the ferocious row he'd had with Urshie the night before last he'd sloped home from the park and put Daniel to bed. He and Urshie had silently got into bed and lain flat on their backs, staring into the darkness, but gradually the inches between them had lessened as she shifted towards him. She'd crawled onto him, crouched over him like a jockey and hardened him.

Strangely, he'd been fiercely satisfied, but not with lust for Urshie. It was the need for release, caused by the vast range of angry emotions he'd had to confront. Afterwards they'd got up, washed, and returned to bed without one word being exchanged.

'I haven't slept with her for weeks,' he lied, 'and I'll never sleep with her again.'

'Does that mean you're going to leave her?'

'Yes,' he replied, but his face was unable to show any sort of joy.

'Don't say it if you don't mean it,' she said, 'but if you don't mean it we're finished. We didn't go through that fight for nothing.'

'I do mean it, but leaving my wife and child does involve rather more than just packing a bag.'

'I know,' she said, stroking his forearm. But Joe doubted she would ever know the agony he was suffering. The joy of her as his future wife, counterbalanced with the prospect of losing Daniel. He took her head in his hands and kissed her crown. 'Go back to bed. I think we could both do with a cup of tea.'

Making tea was everyone's answer to a crisis, but it was only ever an excuse for a diversion; a breaking of a silence or the diffusion of a tempest. Joe didn't need tea. He needed to enter his own mental courtroom of analysis, and confrontation. In a melodrama an actor would drop to his knees in mock appeal to the audience, his hands clasped in a plea for absolution. Joe's only audience was himself, and he was challenged only by himself, how can one man be both the accused and the jury? But the conflict had forced his hand. Confrontation and confession to Urshie was the most terrifying thing he'd ever have to face in his life, and Daniel's sweet, innocent face loomed up at him. Although Anna would join his life, Daniel would all but leave it. As the innocent party, Urshie would be awarded custody and he'd lose his son in a morass of scandal, alimony, and legal visiting arrangements. His adored child was now with the child-minder, happily playing, while his future was poised for collapse. Suddenly anxious to hear that he was all right, Joe rang Doreen Harris.

Doreen was a happy, matronly woman, who delighted in the innocence of a child's world. She'd looked after Daniel, with complete devotion, since he was six weeks old. Joe could imagine him now, standing on a chair in her kitchen with a teacloth knotted around his waist, helping her to make cornflake whispers. Bossily insisting he be allowed to stir in the melted butter and golden syrup on his own, and getting more on himself, and round his mouth, than into the fluted paper cases. 'Doreen. It's Joe. Is Daniel OK?' he asked

'Right as ninepence,' she replied. 'It's such a lovely day we're going up to that big sandpit at Shotover Park. Then me and my little helper are going to pick some blackberries and make a crumble for Bob's tea. Urshie's coming for him around six. Don't worry, Joe. He's fine.' Joe replaced the receiver and put the kettle on.

The day was becoming even hotter and the air was suffused with sultry overtones of tropical humidity. When Joe went back upstairs with the tray of tea he placed it on a chest of drawers, but made no attempt to pour it. He threw himself into bed and kissed Anna energetically, each of them finding a conscious desire to make this act of love special for its unification and forgiveness. But the heat of the day created a sweating, prickling discomfort and vacuums of hot air puffed in their faces. Their ribcages became wet and slapped together. Trickles of perspiration fell from their armpits and foreheads. The demands of foreplay obviously required too much effort and their passion slowly fizzled down. The sounds of early autumn wafted in through the window; the buzz of sleepy bees, a distant lawnmower, and the occasional hoot and cry of village football. Anna turned away from him, and settled down to go back to sleep. Joe too drifted off.

He awoke, with an urgent demand from his bladder, to find a completely different atmosphere. The hot power of the sun had gone and the sky was hazy. No sounds came through the window. The bees had found flowers, the distant lawn had been cut and the village football match completed. His watch showed it was past midday. Anna still slept, her hair covering her face like a shroud. He rose, and quietly moved to the bathroom. On coming out he dawdled on the landing. Consciously, or subconsciously, he knew that this was a house of secrets. He began to open other bedroom doors. What was he looking for? Or was something looking for him? What exactly was the ambiguity, and what were the strange words she'd used last night?

'I loved Hugo when there was no one else, but now I love only you. He said he always knew that there was someone in the world who was out there waiting to love me, and look after me. It turned out to be you. Now I've told you. That must be enough. The rest belongs to me, and we'll never talk of it again.'

Joe's only resource in trying to fathom the behaviour of other people had been his bare, basic training in psychology. Judging by his own erratic behaviour he knew very little, but perhaps he knew enough. The door he'd just opened must have been Hugo's old bedroom, clearly untouched from the day he left. On the floor lay a heap of the *New Musical Express*. A violin stand lay on its side alongside untidy piles of sheet music and a smashed guitar. He then looked around him and immediately understood. From every square inch of the walls the beautiful 1960's face of Catherine Deneuve looked at him. A sharp, dramatic, monochrome exhibition of posters and stills from Roman Polanski's cult film *Repulsion*. He remembered seeing the film at the age of about fifteen on one of his solitary escapes to the cinema as a trapped schoolboy. The story was a bizarre and terrifying depiction of Carole, a young French girl, repulsed by men and sexuality. After several days of festering loneliness in an empty flat she'd gone insane and butchered two men to death, with a violence made even more frightening by Polanski's avant-garde direction. Hugo's personal depictions of the film were just as disturbing. One whole wall was dedicated to Deneuve's beautiful face. Her eyes – her sad, sad eyes – stared down hypnotically. What were the eyes trying to say?

Another wall was covered with sequenced copies of a bizarre scene, strewn like a frieze, showing a hundred hands reaching out of a wall, trying to catch the terrified Carole as she ran down a hall in a flimsy nightdress.

Joe lay down on the bed and pressed his face deeply into the pillow. The faint, but unmistakable fragrance of Anna filled his nose. As he turned his head her doppelganger was staring at him from every corner. The same eyes, the same expression of gentleness and innocence, the same burning sex appeal, but he felt no jealousy, or anger or disgust. He understood it for what it was. Others perhaps would not, but he accepted it as a redemption, a saving and a protection. A strange but comforting love, and the only one they could find together in this sterile, hateful house. He left the room as he'd found it, and no doubt how Hugo expected to find it, if he ever returned.

In the distance he heard a telephone ringing. There was a shrill desperation in Anna's voice as she called his name, and the thump of her footsteps rushed to find him. 'Joe. Your cousin Felix is on the line.' Her breath came in gasping pants. 'Daniel's seriously ill. He's been rushed to A and E.' In the distance a low rumble of thunder was heard as the weather broke up.

CHAPTER NINE

Saturday, continued . . .

ANNA STANDS IN THE OLD VICARAGE KITCHEN. Her long, cotton dress is clinging to her wet, naked body. There's pondweed in her hair and she's holding her underwear in her hand. Cyril makes jokes about a mermaid. Queenie makes jokes about Sharon Davies. They both laugh, and Anna laughs too, but it's a hollow performance. 'Swimming in the fish pool!' Queenie mocks kindly. Anna can tell by her strange expression that she's seriously bewildered. The sort of face that says she's witnessing a peculiar mental derangement. Maybe she is. 'What a dafty you are. Come on, dear. Let's go upstairs and get you sorted. I'll run you a bath, and while you're 'aving a nice soak I'll make up the bed in your old bedroom.'

An hour later, Anna goes downstairs to find Queenie pulling on her cardigan and gathering up her shopping bag. 'Hello, dear,' she says. 'You feeling a bit better? Anna nods. 'Yer Pa's eaten a good supper and 'e's settled down with 'is book. 'E's worn out, poor old soldier. I'm sure 'e'll be out for the count all night, but being right next door you'll be 'andy, just in case. Don't rush to get up in the mornin'. I'll be over about nine as usual, and it's rare for 'im to be awake before I take 'is breakfast in. I'll say nighty night. Yours is there on a tray.'

Anna sits down at the kitchen table to contemplate her meal, but just as she lifts her knife and fork her mobile rings. It's Joe. He's drunk, but he's trying to build bridges. He's saying how sorry he is, and she can tell he's crying. She doubts he hears a word she says, but she soothes and reassures. He tells her he loves her, but he has no need. Even when he's at his worst, she knows he loves her. Even when he's at his worst, she still adores him. 'Put the phone down, Joe,' she says. 'Go to bed. Don't make such a big deal of it. I love you too. Of course I forgive you. Please, darling, go to bed. We'll talk tomorrow.' After a lot of mumbling and muddle his words peter out, and the phone goes dead.

She stares at her plate, but she finds she just can't eat a thing. She needs a drink, though, and pours herself a dangerously large gin and tonic. She goes upstairs and after a perfunctory word with her father she feigns exhaustion and bids him good night. She then hauls the bedding from her old bedroom into the Tapestry Room on the other side of the landing. She wants to be as far away from Papa as possible. She'll keep the door firmly shut, so she won't hear his voice if he calls, but she knows she won't sleep. She'd like to run away. Should she call for a taxi? Go to the station and get the last train? Of course she'll do nothing. She's a coward. She slurps her gin deeply and speaks to the spooks and spirits and evil things in the house, begging them to leave her alone. She gets into bed and lays flat on her back, with a thumping heart.

1973: Anna was thirteen. She'd passed the entrance examination to St Cecilia's, a prestigious girls' public school near High Wycombe, and Papa was very pleased. But Hugo was in big trouble. Despite a year of private coaching, he'd failed to get into Papa's *Alma Mater*, Harrow. 'You'll have to go to Spencer's Court instead,' shouted Papa, 'but you do realise that they only take idiots like you, Hugo, and the fees are extortionate for the honour of mopping up the failures.'

That week there was a smart dinner party at The Old Vicarage for ten guests. 'We've chosen Spencer's Court for Hugo, haven't we, darling?' boasted Papa, 'but we think it's well worth it. We're so impressed with the high academic standards and the emphasis on music. Another bonus is that it's practically on the doorstep, so it means we'll still have him at home. Now come along, Hugo. Entertain us.' Hugo played Beethoven's *'Moonlight'* sonata on the piano, and Gluck's *'Scottish'* symphony, on the violin. The guests clapped loudly with genuine admiration and told Papa he had a supremely talented son.

Later on in Anna's bedroom Hugo was very angry. 'One minute I'm crap and the next minute I'm trotted on to perform like a circus dog.' He got very red in the face and threw her alarm clock across the room. His breathing was noisy and he was trying not to cry, but Anna put her arms round him and cuddled him like a mummy. But she kissed him nothing like a mummy.

1974: Anna was fourteen. She lay on the floor of the garden shed watching the Albertine rose moving through the glass paned roof. Its long, straggly branches swished on a warm summer wind. Light – dark – light – dark. He looked like a man. He had strange friends and he went to secret places. He drank beer from cans, and smoked something he called ganja, and took pills, but it was she who was his real addiction. He got up, sat on an old garden lounger, picked up his guitar and sang to her. *'You fill up my senses, like a night in a forest'*. They both hated John Denver's melancholy tribute to Annie, but Hugo sang it all the same

1975: Anna was fifteen. Mummy had to go away 'for a little holiday'. The doctor said she was over-tired. She'd thrown Jeyes fluid and creosote all over Papa's Jaguar. Hugo said, 'Why couldn't she have thrown it over Papa, and done us all a favour?' The whole village was buzzing with the news that a gang of yobs from Cow Lane had defaced the beautiful car, and poor Mrs Morton Moore was so distressed she had to go off to France to visit relatives and have a rest.

Mrs Huckstep asked for an appointment to see Papa. She said she was very upset and insulted that he'd publicly blamed the boys from Cow Lane. She said that there were only six teenage boys in Cow Lane, and four of them were her sons. The other two were honest and respectable and well behaved as well. She knew it was a lie, because she had a damned good idea who'd really thrown the stuff. She was very sorry but she and Arthur had to give in their notice.

Mummy came back after a couple of months, but she had to take a lot of medication, and was very pale, and got into lots of muddles.

1976: Anna was sixteen. When she came home from school Mummy was often drinking gin with Alex Fuller. Mummy was very happy now and Hugo said he knew why. He said that Mr Fuller's nickname in the gents' bog at the Golf Club was 'Dobbin' because he was hung like a horse.

Papa and Mummy were holding a lunchtime cocktail party, and she and Hugo were required to hand round drinks. Mr Fuller was there. He and Mummy were playing flirty games with each other when they thought no one was looking. Swift eye contact. Raised eyebrows, sidelong glances and sweeping lashes. The occasional mouth twitch. A two second touch on the back of a hand. Then both of them leaving the room separately, thinking they wouldn't be noticed.

That night Mummy walked into a lamppost. She moved into the spare room but she kept on walking into lampposts.

1977: Anna was seventeen. Oliver Frockton stood in the drawing room with his parents. Anna stood bashfully, like Mary Poppins, smiling at her date for the evening. 'Well, these two young things have certainly taken a shine to each other,' said Papa. 'Rugby Club do tonight, I gather? Well, off you go and enjoy yourselves.'

Hugo and Anna drove Oliver to a small terraced house in Uxbridge where his real date for the evening was waiting.

The twins then went off to a punk club in Soho where Hugo was playing his guitar in a band.

July 1978: Anna was eighteen. Miss Murray, the headmistress of St Cecilia's had paid a surprise visit to The Old Vicarage. 'Oh, Miss Murray,' Papa gushed. 'Please come in. May I offer you a sherry? Let me just give my wife a call. Is it about the benevolent concert for Oxfam? I'm sure I can rustle up some sponsors.'

'Mr Morton Moore,' she beamed. 'I've got very good news. The Radcliffe in Oxford have contacted me to say they will be delighted to offer Anna a place as a student nurse.'

Mr Morton Moore wasn't pleased or proud. He was furious. 'I fear you've been misinformed, Miss Murray. What on earth's all this nonsense about nursing? Anastasia's going to finishing school in Switzerland. It's all arranged. She's practically engaged to Lord Frockton's son, you know. Hasn't she told you?'

Miss Murray was not to be intimidated. 'Mr Morton Moore. You're quite aware from our sixth form brochure, and our parents' evenings, that we encourage every girl to achieve fulfilment in whatever their chosen career might be. Their own choice. Not those chosen for them by their parents or well meaning teachers. Our mission statement is to achieve academic excellence and a fully rounded citizen. Anna's a very able and compassionate girl, and I know she'll make a gifted nurse. I've already written to the Matron and expressed my delight. No doubt, Mr Morton Moore, you'll be happy to do the same.' She rose to go. 'You know, it really is the done thing these days for young ladies such as Anna to pursue a career. You're so fortunate to have such a lovely, well balanced daughter, and it's been a pleasure to educate her. Goodbye, Mr Morton Moore, and I'll certainly take you up on your kind offer to find sponsors for our Oxfam appeal. I'm so sorry to have missed Anna's mother, but I look forward to seeing you both at prize-giving on Friday. Did Anna tell you she's won a first prize for her voluntary work project at the nursing home for the elderly near the school?'

When Miss Murray had gone Papa lurched for Anna and grabbed her by her forearms. He shouted that girls like her hadn't been brought up to be public servants or get their hands dirty. 'Nursing's a filthy business,' he yelled. 'How can I approve of a daughter of mine mixing with all that dirt and disease, and as for nurses, they're all tarts. Don't forget I've been through a war. I know what nurses get up to. And another thing. What about Oliver? He won't wait around for ever.'

Anna had known that Miss Murray was coming and she'd promised her that she'd be strong and stand up for herself, but she hung her head, mumbling and shaking. 'But Papa,' she managed to blurt out. 'There's no talk of marriage with Oliver. I'm not in love with him, and he's not in love with me.'

'Love! Love! What's love got to do with it? Oliver Frockton's the catch of the county, as well you know, you stupid girl. Good God, the chance of becoming a Frockton, and you stand there telling me you'd rather be a nurse!' He grabbed her again and began to shake her, but then Hugo walked slowly and quietly into the room. He didn't say a word. He was holding a small, sharp kitchen knife and walked towards Papa. Papa took a step backwards, but Hugo advanced. He gathered up Papa's shirt front and held the knife to his throat. 'Lay one finger on her, and I slit your throat,' he hissed.

Mummy then walked blindly into the room, oblivious to the dramatic scene. 'Who vaz zat voman?' she slurred. 'Whoever she vaz she has just vacked into ze new Daimler doing a three point turn.' As she moved towards the drinks trolley she stumbled and fell. With gratitude for the diversion Anna ran out of the room.

August 1978: Hugo was sitting in his bedroom, picking out a tune on his guitar, and singing softly to himself. Papa burst in with a scarlet face. He'd just received Hugo's A level results. Although he'd got an 'A' grade in music he'd failed maths and English. 'Disgraceful results,' Papa bawled. 'A small fortune invested in you, and all you can do is dress up like a pantomime wizard and strum a bloody guitar all day long.' There was an explosive exchange of traded insults. Hugo told Papa he was going to be a musician and he'd decided to go to America with a band. Papa snatched Hugo's guitar out of his hands and smashed it against the wall. 'If you think you're going to pursue such an inane and pointless way of life after all the advantages you've had, Hugo, you've got another think coming. You'll sit your A levels again, and do as you're told.'

Hugo grabbed the guitar back and swung it round Papa's head. 'You're a fucking, sadistic pervert,' he shouted, 'and this time I really am going to kill you.' Anna was screaming. Mummy was standing at the bottom of the stairs with an empty, glazed face, a drink in one hand and a cigarette in the other. She neither reacted, nor even looked vaguely interested, as Papa fled down the stairs with blood pouring from a head wound.

Anna and Hugo grabbed some clothes, jumped into Mummy's Mini and ran away. They got on a ferry to Dublin and bought a tent. They hitched down to County Kerry and found a little village called Kilcuddy. It was a long hot summer and the south-west tip of Ireland was touched by the Gulf Stream. They bought bread, butter, cheese, apples, crisps, chocolate digestives and Guinness. They had few words. They just needed each other, and loved each other, as they'd always needed and loved each other. They were in their own world of shared thoughts and sadnesses. Theirs was a special kind of love that had started in the womb, and was nurtured by a lifetime of protective symbiosis. Other brothers and sisters would have wasted time quarrelling, and setting parent against parent in the usual power struggle of siblings. Not they. They loved each other, because their parents didn't love them, or each other. In muted moonlight their bodies drew together in a fast moving reef knot to seek the comfort of the angels.

CHAPTER TEN

Sunday

I CAN'T OPEN MY EYES. I've got a thumping headache and such a thirst I could drink the Thames. Shouldn't have had that second bottle last night. Just as well it was only the old monkey that bore witness to my pathetic misery. I stretch out a very aching leg but it meets only a stone-cold loneliness. No doubt she's already running up and down the stairs and pandering to his every whim. Bastard. A gallon of black coffee is urgently sought so I stagger to the kitchen, but I can't find the frigging kettle because the worktops are littered with the gooey silver cartons of an oriental feast, and the detritus of a boozy night. God, what a start to the day.

I ring Anna. She sounds tired, and says she didn't sleep well, but I'm delighted to hear that Gordon *has* spent a good night. He's already tucked into two fried eggs, three rashers, a grilled tomato, and several rounds of heavily buttered toast. He's now sitting up, propped by ten pillows, with the Sunday broadsheets and a pot of his poisonous tea. How can she cope with this alone? She needs me. 'Darling,' I say, 'I've been a complete turd. I'll come back down right away.'

'But it's your mother's birthday,' she reminds me. 'You can't disappoint her. You're the chief guest, and you've got the lovely news about Dan's baby to announce. They'll be over the moon, Joe.' Over the moon? Will my father really be over the moon to hear that the House of Fortune has come to an end?

'Then I'll come down straight afterwards and stay over.'

'But you can't. I don't want the kids coming back to an empty house tonight. You know what devils they are for forgetting their keys.'

'I'll text them. Tell them I've put some spare keys in the shed. They can cope.'

'I'd be happier if you were there. Just in case either of them has an emergency. Look, Joe, I know you don't want to hear this but I've got a feeling this is going to be a long haul.'

'What do you mean a long haul?'

'I mean it'll be quite a few days.'

Whatever she means it's the same thing I voiced to old Cyril. That we're moving into a very serious phase of Morton Moore tyranny. 'You're not to worry,' I say, trying to make my voice sound gung-ho and supportive. 'After today's out of the way I'll come down and commute from Monks Bottom until things get back to normal. As long as it takes. Promise. I'll ring you when I get back from Orpington tonight for an update.'

I spin out a very long and loving goodbye, peppered with jokey up-beat phrases of reassurance, but, as I replace the receiver, my spirits sink with misery at the commitment she's being forced into and the piss-balling inconvenience I've just signed up for. My temple begins to throb with a resurgence of my hangover and behind me there's a vigorous shaking as the black dog rouses itself. The most pivotal moment of my life has arrived.

There used to be programme on the television when I was a boy. God knows what it was called, some sort of talent show, but it kept the quartet in ribald rivalry. Who'll be the winner, then? The margarine sculptor, the one-armed pianist, or the yodelling dog? The catchphrase was 'Make Your Mind Up Time.' I'm finally compelled to *really* make up my mind with no comedy involved. Put up or shut up. My long years of planning Gordon's demise have (let's face it) been just a pipe dream; a way of channelling my boiling anger for his hatreds and prejudices and manipulations. The odious old fucker has now *really* got to go, but I need to find the courage of an astronaut and the conscience of a terrorist. I sit looking at my hands, knowing that the ten experienced fingers *can* do it. Joe Fortune, BM, BCh, MRCGP is equipped to kill, but the huge, towering shadow of sin looms up in the corner. For several minutes I'm paralysed in my chair, knowing that when I finally get up the pendulum will have swung. But swing it does, with the realisation that my dream scenario is laid out for me with the perfection of a film set. He's laid up in bed and he won't be going anywhere for a few days. A captive victim. I'll drug him up. Swift needle up the bum and 'Goodbye, Gordon.' My mind is now fully made up and there'll be no retraction. My heart thumps with anticipation, and I grin like a huge, contented Cheshire Cat, but the thought of my impending day does rather take the smile off my face.

Lunch with my parents is a duty I must endure about once every six weeks, but today it's birthday tea as well, with the close ranks of the Fortune/ Moisemann family. My offer of hosting and funding the event in a tasteful London restaurant had been flatly turned down in favour of a 'home do', but it's a 'do' I could well do without. I would prefer to ring up and feign illness; anything not to suffer the mental torture it'll cause me as I bob about pretending to be a dedicated super-son. Oh, Joe! Pull yourself together. Stop crawling up your own arse and have a little humanity. It's her eightieth birthday for God's sake, and who knows how many more she'll have. More than Gordon I'll safely predict.

I shower, dress and crank myself into some sort of presentable state. There's a birthday present all arranged – a week for her and my dad in a five star hotel in Eastbourne – but I can't find the booking details, and I've no time to look for them. Thus, I traipse off to Sainsbury's for champagne and flowers.

My parents' house, Jacochel, is situated half way up a gentle, tree lined rise in Orpington; the name dedicated to Jacob, my Patte, and Rachel, my Mitte, who both departed to the special place long ago. An immaculate thirties detached, with a nice little garden and a gabled garage. Bought with the money they received from the compulsory purchase of Kitchener Street and a hand out from Moisemann's.

My mother opens the front door resplendent in a frilly, lime green apron, purple trousers, a shocking-pink cardigan and a rope of bright blue beads around her neck. She looks like a box of Smarties. She's carefully made up with Judy blobs on each cheek, a scarlet bow mouth, and her white hair dyed to a strange shade of orange. 'Shalom, Shalom,' she cries, standing on tip toes and reaching up to embrace me. How was I ever small enough to have come from this tiny little bird? 'Daddy, Daddy,' she calls happily. 'Our boy's here.' My dad (whom I've never called Daddy in my life) appears, bustling, excited and smiling.

'Shalom, Shalom.' A firm hug, and a kiss on both cheeks. He's wearing a brown acrylic cardigan that holds no hope of meeting in the middle, high-waisted crimplene trousers and the essential Orpington accessory; a cravat depicting fox heads and hunting horns. 'Sorry Anna couldn't come,' he says. 'She rang us earlier on. It's grave news about her poor old dad, isn't it?' I agree, but the only grave required is one freshly dug (and soon to be ordered). I can never understand why everyone always refers to Gordon as poor. I suppose 'poor excuse for a human being' could justify the word.

I sniff the air with feigned interest. 'Something smells good, Mum.' I make an educated guess at a glutinous lamb joint, roast King Edwards, carrots, peas, and Bisto gravy, rounded off with a sloshy, thick-skinned rice pudding, referred to as dessert. The whole menu will be announced as 'Our Joe's favourite,' which it isn't and never was. The matriarch rushes off in a big flap to the kitchen. 'No help needed,' she declares, even though I haven't offered.

'Fancy a beer?' asks my dad. Oh well. Hair of the dog. We sit on a fancy ornamental bench in the garden which clearly wasn't designed for the generous proportions of my father and myself. Precariously balancing our broad beams on twelve inches of wobbly planking, we pull rings on a can of gnat's piss apiece. I offer him a cigar which he accepts. We lean back to smoke and ruminate together, but just as we're comfortably settled my mum rushes up the path with a big paper bag and a colander. 'Fancy shelling peas?' she asks, beaming. 'Fresh from Guernsey. Our Jack dropped off such a big bag we'll be eating them for a year.' We shell peas, hunched up like two garden gnomes. Lunch is always booked in for 1.00 p.m. but (in traditional maddening-mother-mode) here we are at 1.30 and still preparing the vegetables. I thus drift into gentle conversation with my Dad about this and that, and nothing in particular, bracing myself for the announcement I have to make.

'Dad,' I say. 'I've got something to tell you . . . er . . . two things, actually. Dan turned up on Friday night with some really sad news. Urshie died suddenly. A stroke. He's gone over for the funeral, so I'm afraid he won't be here later on.'

'Is that so?' he says, shaking his head and sighing. 'What a shock. Far too young to die. Must be getting on for twenty years since I've seen her. Our Dan's *bar mitzvah* if my memory serves me. Never heard much about her after that. I know you and her together were like two bloody ferrets in a sack, but up until your split-up we liked her well enough. What a tragedy for Dan.'

'But there's something else, Dad. Breaking news, as they say. Graznya's having a baby. Some time in January, I think.'

He slaps his knee and laughs out loud. 'Well, blow me down. My son a Patte! Time marches on, all right. Your mum'll be real excited. You know how she loves babies.' He sits shelling peas in silence, seemingly unable to enlarge or find any further comment.

'Dad,' I say. 'It's really knocked me for six. Do you remember that night in the back room at Kitchener Street?

The night before I went up to Oxford when you talked to me about being a true Jew. I remember it like it was yesterday. You talked about the long line of our forefathers, and keeping myself for the perfect Jewish girl. OK, it was a pep talk, but it was the turning point in my life. After that I really tried to be the perfect Jew you wanted me to be. I was good. I conformed. I married Urshie. I know we definitely *were* like two ferrets in a sack, but out of it all we had Dan. Our line was unbroken –just as you wanted – but now it's going to be broken after all. What do you really think, Dad? Are you as cut up about it as I am?'

'Of course I remember that night,' he says, smiling somewhat sweetly to himself. 'Whatever I said was for your own good and I meant it at the time. All parents, especially our lot, want what's best for their kids. We were about to lose you. Hilda and Harry were worrying themselves pig sick about what Jack and Felix were getting up to, and we were no different.'

'But it was more than that, Dad,' I say. 'It was about the House of Fortune. All our ancestors stretching back to Abraham. How tall they stood, how proud. After the holocaust and all that. The pride. The continuity.'

My dad stops shelling peas and sits looking puzzled, searching for the words he needs. 'Dan's a very special boy,' he says at last. 'He's come through all your troubles with a smile on his face, and every time I look at his *bar mitzvah* photo I'm so proud of him. He'll always be a Jew, just like you are, but his heart's followed his head, same as yours did. When you took up with Anna I must admit it took us all

189

some squaring up to, but we couldn't have been happier to see you married to such a lovely girl. I suppose at the time we were hoping she'd convert, but let's face it, do we really think of conversion as becoming a real Jew? We've always loved Anna as if she was one of our own, anyway, and we can tell the love's still pouring out of you both. Granted the twins don't give a tuppenny toss for Judaism, but that's the way things are. They're smashing kids, but don't forget, Joe, we're still part of them. When they look over one shoulder we're there for them to be proud of, and when they look over the other one there's all the gentry, and the colonials that made this country what it was. Gone down the pan now I grant you, but there's a lot of history there. Same as this coming child will have. Us on the one side, and her people on the other. Don't they call the world a global village now? Mixed marriages are the norm between every race and creed on earth. You must see it every day, dealing with the rank and file, like you do. I'm getting old, son. I've led a decent life, and been very happy, but no one leaves the world exactly as they find it, do they?'

My heart turns over. So nothing matters any more. The world's decided to change and Harvey Fortune has changed with it. This isn't the answer I thought I was going to get. I wanted an understanding hand on my shoulder. Comfort and solidarity. The pain of a fellow sufferer. Now I want to shout, 'Hypocrite! Bloody impostor. You changed my life, Dad. My whole free life was waiting for me, and I sacrificed it because of what you said. I listened, I cared and I was a good boy. My whole life was directed down a path that was chosen for me and my feet are still bleeding from its sharp stones.'

'Excuse me Dad,' I say. 'My guts are playing up a bit this morning. Chinese take-away last night.'

He smiles kindly at me. 'They don't call it fast food for nothing, do they?'

At 2.30 p.m. my mother calls, 'Dinner's ready,' and we troop into the dining room. On the sideboard, without realising it, my parents have created the whole of my life in a showy display of family photographs. A shrine to Mitte and Patte surrounded by candles and artificial flowers. Their own shivering, teenage wedding. Me, at four days old, naked and newly circumcised, with my pretty young mother. My first day at The Apprentices Hall, proudly wearing a stiff, over-sized school uniform. My official graduation pose; a sombre, sad-faced, lonely man. Me and Urshie, holding our beautiful newborn son, with rare, genuine smiles. Me and Anna, happy and laughing on our wedding day. Traditional school poses of the twins.

Hanging on the wall behind, the four generations of the family *bar mitzvahs* are flaunted. Patte's in 1911; sepia brown, foxed and faded to nearly nothing. A tiny boy standing in the back yard of Kitchener Street. Five years later a boy soldier fighting for England in France. My father's in 1939; studio posed against a backdrop of 'Israel,' with potted palms and a bamboo table. Five years later a boy soldier fighting for England in a real life African desert. My own in 1963; an ostentatious, giant-sized monochrome. Professional photographer hired for the occasion at great expense. A clear-eyed good-looking lad, wearing *kippah*, bow-tie and embroidered waistcoat. The deified victim, word perfect with his Hebrew recitation of the Torah. Clapped, spoiled and hugged; his pockets heavy from the silver that was showered on him. The reception costing the quartet more than the price at the time of the new Mini Minor car. Five years later fucking for England over the junk shop in Rye Lane and dreaming of a new, free life at Oxford University. Daniel Elijah Dov in 1988; my handsome young son in full colour, standing between his estranged parents who are attempting to hide all signs of their loathing for each other. Five years later . . . What? A bloody miracle, that's what. At eighteen-years-old a well balanced, and contented young man, in his A level year at Radley. Happily bonded with his stepmother, and rough housing with his young brother and sister on the floor at Sunny Lea.

On a special display shelf (between two small Union flags) a place of honour is also given to the handsome bastard I was in 1979, shaking hands with the queen at the opening of the new oncology research unit. I was smiling. Of course I was smiling. I was at the height of a passionate, adulterous love affair with a beautiful English rose, ten years my junior. An hour earlier I'd lain in post-coital collapse in her bed, my cock as red and raw as a hunk of fillet steak. She'd caught my hand as I rose to leave her. 'Will you come to Monks Bottom and stay with me this weekend?' she pleaded. 'My parents will be away in Scotland, golfing. Please, can you come?' Although I see this same photograph on Anna's bedside table every day of my life, I pick it up, as I always do when I come here. Was it on that warm summer morning, Anna, that our child was conceived? Our love-child I was never able to love. My mother, noticing that I've gone a bit tight-chested and sniffy, touches me gently on the arm. 'Proudest day of our lives as well, son.' Ah well, if it makes her happy.

We light a candle and my dad says the *brochah*, the familiar Hebrew shooting from his mouth with the speed of light. As we eat I fill my mother in with the news of Urshie and a genuine tear is shed for her premature death. Then the news of my coming grandchild and she's all smiles again. She waves her knife and fork in the air and bounces up and down on her chair. 'Oh, that's wonderful news. Can you believe it, Harv? Our son, a Patte. Oh, I'm so excited. My hands are itching to get on with some knitting.' We then talk easily about trivia and catch up on the news of Sophie and Josh. With their A levels now completed their futures hang on the results. With good luck it'll be Oxford for Josh, to read jurisprudence, and Cambridge for Sophie, to read medicine. Gap years are being discussed that involve some sort of (very expensive) foreign travel. They're rude, noisy and selfish (and they think I'm a prat), but I shine with pride and love for them. 'They're both fine,' I say, bumbling my way around excuses as to why they too have failed to turn up for the family occasion. Gordon's illness is then brought up and they seem a little surprised when I can't (be bothered to) give them an exact medical profile. They've only met him once but he's remembered as a charming man and a real toff. They sympathise and grimace about the sadness of being alone when you're getting on.

My dad then relates the latest gossip from the old Market Traders' Association. Aziz on the curtain material was mugged for six quid, Bert on the china was done for receiving, and Kit Kennedy, the old bag who ran the junk shop in Rye Lane, dropped dead last week at Catford dogs. 'You must remember her, Joe,' he says. 'She was a right weirdo.' Oh, Dad, did I ever remember her? I swallow hard a few times, and my hands clutch the paper napkin on my knee.

'Yes,' I say brightly, 'I used to tidy up for her when I was at school.'

After dinner I'm shooed away and my parents do the washing up. She washes, he dries, moving around each other with the swerve and glide of Torvill and Dean. Despite Moisemanns doling out a large, yearly profit bonus to my parents, they've steadfastly refused to buy a dishwasher. 'We like doing it together,' they say. As usual, they're completely nuts.

An hour later the Moisemann family arrive. Auntie Hilda and Uncle Harry, Jack and Naomi, Felix and Nola (who you may remember still has the hots for me), and gay Melvin. The women all disappear to the kitchen to prepare tea and discuss the castration of whoever's turn it is. Harry and my dad go to the dining room to talk about the good old days, and the four blood-brothers commandeer the sitting room. Crystal glasses are produced, a fine malt is poured, and a short respectful toast is drunk to the first Mrs Fortune. A second shot is raised for my coming grandchild and our boys' gossip commences.

Centre stage is Mel, Moisemann's financial director, and known officially in the family as 'a confirmed bachelor'. Anthony, his partner of thirty years, is a retired high court judge (you can tell how old he is by the term 'retired') and always referred to by the older generation as 'Melvin's friend'. To me and his brothers, Rump-Hole of The Bailey is the more usual term. The flamboyant and queenly Anthony is now a senile, sick old man, and Mel is, in wifely terms, his carer.

'How's Anthony?' I ask.

'Oh, dead from the neck up and the navel down,' he sighs sadly.

'How are *you*, Mel?' I ask.

He smiles, and puts his finger to his lips. 'I've got a lovely boy, dear heart. Very young and a touch petulant, but he's got a donger like a donkey. I have to spoil him, but he makes an old man very happy.'

'I hope you're taking good care of yourself,' I plead, donning my doctor's hat.

'Of course I bloody well am, you cheeky cat,' he snaps, 'but talking of safe sex did you know that there's a new tasty one from the States? Southern Comfort. Gives the term stiff whisky a new ring.' We all laugh like drains and put in our orders for the novelty value.

We then catch up with all the other personal news. Jack, like me, is monogamous and happy, and passes round the latest snaps of the grandchildren. Felix has the usual tale of wobbling infidelity, and gives us the low-down on his current nooky in Broadstairs. He's got the wind up. This particular fat and jolly bit-on-the-side has decided her biological clock is ticking. Ergo, stop all the clocks. Time for a sharp exit, but he's got his eye on the new rabbi's sister. 'She's got an arse like a hot air balloon,' he gasps, closing his eyes with dreamy desire.

Soon we're summoned to the dining room. It's birthday teatime, and the star of the show sits centre stage, surrounded by her close and loving family. Champagne flutes are raised, there are kisses all round, and fortunately no-one seems to notice that Nola's tongue nearly disappears down my throat. The table is laid with all my supposed favourites again. Fish paste or Marmite sandwiches. Peak Freans Iced Gems, Twiglets, Jaffa Cakes, Jammie Dodgers, Mr Kipling's exceedingly good somethings, and a trifle (top secret family recipe, but not worth passing on). The Harrods birthday cake, donated by Jack and as big as a tractor wheel, is trollied in, ablaze with eighty flaming candles. I manage to find room for a large slice but then I decide I really can't stand another minute of it.

'I'm ever so sorry,' I say, 'but I'm going to have to go. I'm on-call tonight.' My parents understand completely. They're proud I'm on-call. Only important people like their son, the doctor, are on-call. They love the thought of me lurching around the hell-hole of south London in the dead of night, with my medical bag chained to my wrist, and risking my arm getting torn off for the small amount of heroin I carry. We all embrace. The usual doorstep Hebrew, and five-pound notes for my spoiled children. The whole cast assembles on the doorstep and I kiss the two ageing dolls goodbye. I get into the Discovery. I smile, I wave, I pull off, and that's it for another six weeks, thank fuck.

When I get home there's a short message on the ansaphone from Dan. 'Funeral done and dusted. Still things to do and sort out so returning home in a few days. Be in touch soon.' I'm relieved, but I'll feel even better when he's safely back home again. I phone my beloved, and pass on my parents' genuine concern for her father. God, how I miss her. Gordon has apparently spent a good day and a jolly evening of Canasta round the bedside with Queenie is planned. 'I'll be down tomorrow night, darling,' I say (and kill the nauseating old tosser).

'Any plans for tonight?' she asks.

'Nope. Just a quiet night in for me and Me-Toom-Tum.' We bid fond farewells and I settle down in an armchair with the cat on my lap. The day with my family has, not surprisingly, exhausted me, and although I must get my head round the logistics of Gordon's demise again, I find my eyes closing . . .

September 1979: Within minutes of hearing that Daniel had been taken seriously ill Joe had thrown himself in the Morris Minor. He couldn't remember arriving at the hospital, or where he'd parked, or if the blue Laura Ashley dress accompanying him contained a body. Did he say goodbye to her? He didn't. He fell into the casualty unit remembering how, as a junior doctor, he'd seen so many seriously sick children rushed in to endure the pain of blood tests, lumbar punctures, and drips and drugs. The distraught parents would wring their hands and cry, but on those occasions he was a professional physician and allowed to be detached. But not today. Today he was a shell-shocked parent, just like them.

Daniel had been transferred to the paediatric isolation unit and Urshie was sitting hunched up in a side room. He rushed to her and took her in her arms. 'What happened?' he pleaded, his voice a pinched howl of grief. 'Urshie, I rang Doreen this morning. He was fine. I bothered . . . I promise you I didn't forget him . . .' She nodded, twisting a wet handkerchief in her hands. 'They were up on Shotover Park,' she said. 'He'd been really happy, playing in the sandpit and being his usual self. He ate a banana sandwich, and drank his milkshake, but then they went to find some blackberries and he started dragging his feet and grizzling. Doreen just thought he was tired, but he started to burn up and he was sick. Then he covered his eyes and screamed, and thank God, she recognised the signs. She was wonderful, Joe. She ran to the car park and begged someone to bring him in here. And that was it. They got me out of theatre and I rang Felix, so thanks for getting here so soon. South London to Oxford in under an hour, Joe? It's a miracle.' The significance of her statement swung heavily between them. There was a brief silence but she suddenly clung to him.

A couple of hours later Joe and Urshie were looking through the glass side of the isolation room watching their unconscious, naked little son. His eyes were tight shut and the dimpled flowers of his hands had balled into fists. He was attached to a drip, a monitor screen displayed his functions, and a fan blew cooling air over his burning body. He'd had his lumbar puncture, and every blood test possible, but there was nothing that either of his medically qualified parents could do for him. The paediatric team had taken him over and Daniel's life now belonged to them. Joe and Urshie were just impotent bystanders. Nonentities. In-the-way people. Voices muttered things they couldn't hear and weren't meant to hear. Decisions were made and executed. Eye contact was avoided and the echoing voices of the old hospital carried on as normal, showing no reverence to a dying child. They sat close up, gripping hands intensely, and feeling completely useless. For nearly five years they'd hissed and growled at each other in hate and frustration, but today they were parents united in grief. Exhaustion overtook Urshie. She curled up in an old armchair and wrapped her arm round her eyes. Joe sat beside her, unable to sleep, forced to admit that their intense unity was but a brief and transient illusion. Unlike the night of Daniel's birth, there was to be no fools' love because it was nothing to do with how they felt about each other. It was love for Daniel.

The local rabbi came to comfort them and pray. The nurses were kind and endless pots of tea appeared. Colleagues crept in quietly to support Joe and Urshie – the Fortunes – a couple in crisis. There were long hugs, and reassurances, and sympathetic noises from everyone. 'His skin's still pink,' they all said. 'It's a good sign; there's no bruising.' They both knew that. They were doctors, so why were they being treated like a couple of ignorant imbeciles? Was this how all parents in grief felt as the hospital process swallowed them up? Joe put his head in his hands. He wanted Daniel to be saved. He wanted to be kind to Urshie. He wanted to cry. He wanted a puff. He wanted to go to sleep and wake up and find that he'd imagined it all. Perhaps he slept – he couldn't be sure – but suddenly it was morning and another day of agony lay spread before them.

They passed it largely in silence, having no ground to go over and no news to dissect, but in the early evening they were suddenly aware of Peter Butler, the paediatric registrar, standing over them. Results of all the tests had come through. Daniel didn't have meningococcal meningitis. He had viral meningitis. His temperature had dropped, his white cells were going up, and with cautious optimism he was likely to make a full recovery. Joe and Urshie collapsed into each other arms. They had no tears left, but they let out two long, primitive groans of gratitude and turned to look at Daniel, now sleeping peacefully under a light counterpane. They put the palms of their hands against the glass barrier wall, staring at their cherished child with God-given thanks.

It was now gone 10.00 p.m. Urshie was moribund with exhaustion, her eyes red and sunk into green pools, caused by the constant friction of her knuckles. Although they still stood close together the agenda they'd been holding at bay began to form an unseen barrier. 'Urshie, you're completely done in,' Joe said. 'Why don't you go home and get some sleep. Take the car. I'll stay in my on-call room tonight so I'll be on hand. We'll talk tomorrow.'

'Oh, we certainly will,' she said. They parodied an embrace, but their bodies were now rigid and no kissing was attempted. They both knew there would be lots of things to say, and fight over, but today was Daniel's day. A porter then came in and handed a small bunch of freesias to Urshie. She read the card, stared hard at Joe with a trembling lip, and threw them into the wastepaper bin. The flowers were the only bright splashes of vibrant colour he'd seen all day, and he scrambled to take them out of the bin, wanting to savour their brightness and perfume. 'No, Urshie,' he cried. 'Take them. Please. Enjoy them,' but by the time he turned to hand them to her the swing door was juddering. They were from Carina.

Joe stood alone outside the isolation room, watching Daniel's ribcage rise and fall as he slept. His son might have won his fight for life but what would his future life be like? He wanted to pick him up, sit him on his lap, and talk to him. To say how sorry he was that he hadn't been there when he started to feel ill. To tell him that there would be big changes in his life, because Daddy loved a lady called Anna, and he was going to have to leave Mummy to be with her, but it was he, Daniel, whom he loved most in the world.

Joe left the ward with a lumbering stiffness, his throat sore and his eyes tight with tiredness. He stumbled to his on-call room, but when he opened the door he saw Anna framed in the darkness, holding the velvet monkey. It was neither the time, nor the place, for passion. They said very little, apart from reassuring nods, and smiles, and short kisses of gratitude for Daniel's recovery. Later, when they lay pressed close together in the single bed, Joe couldn't stop talking about his son. 'I want you to get to know him when he's better,' he told her. 'We can take him out to tea at the Cadena. He's very well behaved and he always says 'please' and 'thank you'. He's got the vocabulary of a six-year-old. He watches *Playschool* on the television and he loves the Jemima doll best of all. The one who always refuses to sit up. He can sing all the verses of '*One potato, two potato*' from the LP.'

She heard all about his toys. A Fisher Price jack-in-the-box, a red telephone, a huge basket of Lego, a plastic tea set, Ladybird books and a hideous, stinking golliwog Joe's mother had knitted. Why did it stink? Because he dipped Golly's hand in the yoghourt as a substitute for a spoon. Oh well, perhaps his table manners were a little less than perfect. She heard all about his clothes. He wore OshKosh dungarees, either with T-shirts or jumpers made by Joe's mother; most of them made from odd balls of wool picked up cheaply from the local street market, so they were bright and hippy. He had a blue quilted anorak with a hood, red wellies, *Magic Roundabout* pyjamas, and *Captain Pugwash* slippers. Joe became exhausted. His words drifted off and stopped all together. Anna too began to drift off and dream, but did she hear a noise? Was she asleep, or was she awake?

A spectre of quiet, determined purpose had entered the room. Very soon it would act, but first it needed to gather its formidable strength for armed combat. It took a few deep breaths and sniffed the air; its nostrils dilating like a predatory animal. Poised to attack, the spectre became an angry, bitter woman and moved in for the kill. Anna was dragged out of bed by her hair and sprawled naked on the hard, cold linoleum. Prey taken by surprise. A night attack on a weak, defenceless victim. Hard vicious kicks to the body, and attacked around the head with a steel spike. Muttered words of 'filthy bitch' and 'whore'. Joe awoke, bleary and half-comatose, but he hurled himself out of bed and turned on the light. In the glaring brightness Urshie was standing there, as if paralysed, holding a stiletto-heeled shoe. She looked at Joe, she looked at Anna, and back to Joe again, her mouth open and an expression that portrayed disbelief.

Joe dropped down to the floor beside Anna, traumatised, his hands fluttering, not knowing what to do or say. Urshie walked slowly to the door and left the room, but Joe sprang to his feet and followed her out. An intense, threatening caucus of angry words raged between them like machine-gun fire. Then a scuffle and a thump, followed by a single scream. Joe returned, his face drained to an alabaster whiteness.

He helped Anna to get up onto the bed and gently probed her wounds. Lower back and buttocks bruised and burning. Multiple head lacerations; one on her hairline, one deep gouge on her eyelid. He felt her pulse, took her blood pressure, and shone a torch into her pupils. 'You haven't got any cerebral signs,' he said, 'but I'll monitor you every ten minutes. If you start feeling faint or sick I'm going to have to take you to straight down to casualty.'

Above their heads rain slashed on the skylight window, the first rain they'd had for two weeks, and the dull light of dawn revealed a sullen sky. He re-examined her. 'I want you to have an X-ray on your kidneys, and some of those wounds might need stitching. I must go down and see Daniel, and I'll have to show my face on the ward, but then I'll find out who's on duty in casualty and see if I can get you through quietly.'

'It's the end, isn't it?' Anna said, declaring a fact.

'No! It's not the end. Can't you see, she's handed it to us on a plate? She's mad. She's shot herself in the foot. Surely you can see that?' He kissed her gently and left the room. 'I promise you I'll be as quick as I can.'

Daniel had been moved from isolation to a single room. He was sitting propped up in a metal-sparred cot, flushed and heavy-eyed, while Urshie stood over him, holding a plastic beaker of Ribena to his lips. As Joe came through the door the child's face showed no animation or interest. Urshie too, ignored him. Her top lip was swollen and she'd acquired a bruise to her cheekbone. His first thought was to embrace Daniel, but as he leaned forward Urshie pushed him off. 'You'll spill the Ribena,' she snapped, but the bright red drink had already slopped all over the white sheets. 'Now look what you've done.'

Joe picked up his son's hand and kissed his warm fingers. 'I'm sure a drop of Ribena won't leave any lasting scars, dear wife. That honour goes to you, and the war wounds of your hatred are on full view upstairs.'

Urshie shook her head with a look of amusement and sarcasm. 'Do you know, I really thought it was going to be that Alton cow. But then I find a child in your bed. You're pathetic, Joe. She's hardly out of short, white socks. Fairy Tinkerbell to a real life Peter Pan.'

'Her name's Anna,' Joe replied, staring at Urshie with a look of utter contempt. 'Unlike you, she's a beautiful, mature woman of great sensitivity and elegance. I'm in love with her and I intend to marry her. Thanks to your behaviour of last night our divorce will be an uncontested *fait accompli* and complete custody of Daniel will go to me. When I leave here I'll put in a token appearance on the ward. Then I'll make sure she goes to casualty. They will, of course, see a gentle, young student nurse who's been severely brutalised, and they'll expect her to tell them the facts. Being a truthful girl, she'll tell the truth. Then the whole circus will get involved. You know. All the hospital top brass, and just in case you need reminding that means the services of the police surgeon, and a full medical report. Photographs too. Full close-ups of your handiwork on full view in court. You'll be judged mentally unstable and you'll probably be struck off.'

'Oh, just listen to you. Don't threaten *me*, Mr Squeaky Clean.'

'I put my hands up to the sin of adultery, but it's actually a consensual and pleasurable activity. Vicious assaults by respected registrars are not. Medical ethics apart, you're a disgrace to your sex, and I'm sure even the fish and bicycles brigade would throw you on the slagheap. Now, why don't you just shut up and start planning your lonely future?'

Daniel's eyes had followed them wearily as they traded curses, his tired face showing a sad bewilderment, but then the door opened and a smiling nurse came in with a balloon. 'Got to cheer the little chap up on his birthday, haven't we?' she said, tying it to the end of his bed. They'd both forgotten it was his fourth birthday. Joe lifted him out of the cot, and told him that today he was four-years-old, and when he was better he would have the best birthday he'd ever had. They would go on a lovely holiday to somewhere warm with a nice lady called Anna, and when they got back he and Daddy and Anna were all going to live together. Urshie stared at him with slitted, angry eyes. 'You're not having Daniel!' she snapped. 'OK, your floozie got a smacking, but you're the biggest sinner in this story.'

Joe lay Daniel back down in the bed, kissed his forehead, and looked at his watch. 'Nice try, Urshie, but it won't wash. Just off for a quick ward round, and then I'll get Anna down to casualty before it starts filling up. Shall we formally shake hands on our divorce?' Her answer was the remains of the Ribena, hurled full in his face.

Above her, through the small metal skylight, Anna could see dark, plodding clouds and the occasional wind socked bird. She was cold and she started to shake. Her back throbbed, and as she slowly moved her head on the pillow dried crusts of blood moved like sharp shards, pulling her hair. The door opened and closed again as someone quietly entered. 'I haven't come in anger,' the person said, 'I've come to say I'm sorry. Hear me out, will you, Anna? Can I call you Anna? I didn't know your name before, but I've seen you around. How could anyone miss a stunner like you? They call you the Ice-Maiden, don't they? I think hot stuff might be nearer the truth, but you high-class tarts are all the same. Noses in the air, but gagging for it. Especially with someone else's husband. Still, Anna, I really am sorry. I never meant it to be that bad. All I wanted was a showdown, but I just lost control. You see, I thought you were someone else and I got such a jolt when I saw it was you. I'm afraid you're in for a bit of a shock, dear. You're not the only one he's screwing. Professor Alton's wife as well, actually. Another posh bitch. I'd never suspected a thing, but a while back someone was kind enough to write and tell me all about it. It beats me what he sees in that skeleton, but they say variety is the spice of life, don't they?

'I was so angry. I felt such a fool. Just another cuckold. Of course I confronted him, but he denied it. Well, he would, wouldn't he? But after that I watched his every move and I could tell he was deceiving me. All that nonsense about studying in the library for an exam. I knew he was up to something and then yesterday happened. Our son at death's door and his daddy missing. So where was his daddy? Well, officially it was a *bar mitzvah* in Peckham, so managing to get to Oxford in well under an hour rather blew his alibi, didn't it? Just as well that double-crossing cousin of his was in on the act. Then last night, when the crisis was all over, he was more than keen to get shot of me. The prof's in Finland, and I put two and two together, but ironically I still made four.

'I must tell you something else as well, Anna. He might act the big horny lover, but when we got together the poor lamb must have been the only twenty-four-year-old virgin at Oxford. I suppose I felt sorry for him, but then the stupid, bungling, dumb cluck got me pregnant, and that, as they say, was the first day of the rest of my life. It's not been heaven, but we've had a marriage of sorts. Not the one that either of us would have chosen from a mail order catalogue, but we're far from being completely washed up. We still have a proper relationship in every sense of the word, although I'm sure he's told you a different story. Our sex life's never been that great, but having you and the Alton slut waving their randy fannies in the air doesn't leave much more than a fag-end of his passion for me. Now when was the last time we got romping together? Quite recently actually. Only a couple of days ago. The night before he disappeared to *bar mitzvah* you. I bet that's a surprise? We'd had a flaming row, but making up a row always heightens the pleasure, doesn't it? Or haven't you had your first big fight yet?

'Oh, I know he doesn't love me, Anna. I'm not a fool. He'd love to dump me and lead a much more dazzling life with a beautiful, sexy wife like you flattering him all day long. Poor love. He lives completely in his dreams. But listen, Anna. This is the most important bit. Where you come from all the goodies in the world are handed to you on a plate. You think you've only got to snap your fingers and everything falls into your lap. Well, Joe Fortune isn't for sale at Harvey Nichols and you're not having him. He'll never leave me, even for a gorgeous creature like you, because of Daniel. He worships him. His love for Daniel is so intense, he'd kill for him and he'll never walk out on him. I'm sure he's told you what a lousy mother I am. Well, I am, but I'm still the innocent party. I've kept my side of the marriage vows and he hasn't. I will *not* lose my son. I'll fight Joe through every court in the land before that happens.

'Now, Anna, here's the pleading bit. My only concession to humble pie. I know you don't care about turning *my* world upside down, but think of Daniel. Does he deserve the mess you're going to inflict on his life? He doesn't need *you*. He needs his daddy, and his daddy needs him. Will you please go away and leave us alone? I mean really go away. Leave the hospital. Find another job in Timbuktu. Go and wreck someone else's marriage or screw up someone else's kid. Go back to your own kind and leave us alone. Fuck off, I suppose.'

Anna remained still, unable to gather any strength to fight her corner. Yes. It really was the end. Joe's little boy had moved out of the mist. An innocent child of only four-years-old. She looked back in time and opened the photograph albums at The Old Vicarage. She saw herself and Hugo at four years old. Tightly holding hands. Small and innocent. Still in full expectation of a happy future. Childhood only happened once. Hers had been ruined. Daniel's couldn't be ruined because of her. His life had to come before her own.

'I'll go,' Anna said, 'but only for Daniel's sake. I'm certainly not doing you any favours. I don't like you and I don't care about what you want. No matter how much you try and fool yourself, Joe loves me. I'll go, but I'll never really be gone, so you'll never be happy. One day, when you're not expecting me, I'll come back for him. That's not a threat, it's a promise. You'll always be looking over your shoulder.'

She struggled out of bed, but wavered, feeling dizzy, and clutched the end of the bed. 'Perhaps I ought to go down to casualty,' she said, 'just to get checked over.'

'Be best if you don't go,' Urshie said sweetly.

'Some caring doctor you are,' said Anna. 'I'm quite aware you want me out of the hospital so I don't point the finger at you, but don't worry. I won't wreck your precious career, but I need a proper medical examination. You can drive me to The Hartington near Henley. It's a private hospital my family uses.' Anna slowly and painfully started to get dressed, and as she struggled Urshie moved forward to try and help her. 'Leave me,' she recoiled. 'I couldn't bear the touch of you.'

Tucked behind a mirror in the small cold room was a recent photograph of Joe shaking hands with the queen, smiling and bending forward in full reverence to the tiny monarch. Anna put it in her handbag. She found a scrap of paper and a pencil, and wrote herself out of Joe's life. She gritted her teeth, slowly descended the fire escape, and let Ursula Fortune drive her out of it.

On his return Joe found a short note.

Dear Joe,
I know this is a dreadful way to say goodbye to you, but I must go. I'm going away to make another life for myself, far away from here. Please don't come looking for me because it has to be the end. I can't bear to wreck a child's life. You belong with Daniel and he mustn't suffer because of us. And Urshie too, Joe. She may have an unbelievable way of showing it, but she must love you to do what she did. She fought for you. Now she's won you, so I must go. Please try to make them both happy and try to be happy yourself. You'll always be my truest and my only

love. We've been so in love, haven't we? Let's hope we always will be.

Forever, your loving Anna.

All men are creatures that crawled darkly from the sea. He began to drown. Water blurred his eyes. His lungs collapsed and a long plaintive groan escaped. 'Oh, Anna,' he cried. 'You're wrong. Wrong. Of course Urshie doesn't love me. I've lived with the vixen for over four years and apart from the night of Daniel's birth we've never known a minute of sweet, genuine affection. When has she ever laid an understanding hand on my shoulder, or sought my arms for comfort? When have we ever, in mutual passion, made love? She's never listened to me or talked to me. We've never laughed together, apart from forced gaiety produced for Daniel's sake. When has she ever flirted with me or teased me? Her ice has always been feet thick. I could have been the good husband but I've always been rejected, my presence only seen in terms of achievement. No, Anna, you're wrong. Urshie hates me. Urshie hates everything except herself and her career prospects.'

He had to find Anna. First to get her injuries assessed and to ensure she received the correct medical treatment. Then to assure her that she was wrong about everything. That he was leaving Urshie, as of now, and that although the future ground was littered with mine shells they would survive to be united.

It was early evening by the time Joe, at last, escaped the demands of the oncology department. A couple of quick attempts at phoning Anna's flat had proven fruitless, but he was sure she must be there. He walked in a tired daze along the Woodstock Road, holding the lynched velvet monkey, and quietly let himself into her darkened flat. 'Anna,' he called. 'It's only me,' but she didn't call back. Overcome with both physical and mental exhaustion he lay down on her bed and closed his eyes. Her note of goodbye was nonsense of course – just a gesture, written in the depression of the moment. She would never leave him – or would she? Where was she? Who was looking after her? But then his bleep suddenly screamed. He was wanted urgently on the paediatric ward. He slung the monkey over his shoulder, and rushed out of the flat.

Three minutes later he was back on the ward, his heart pounding. A relapse? A missed diagnosis? But he could see Daniel was sitting up in bed, wide awake, while Peter Butler, the paediatric registrar, was talking to Urshie. 'Ah, there you are, Joe,' he said. 'This little lad of yours seems to have made an amazing recovery, but he'll certainly be needing his Mummy and Daddy for a few days. Urshie's been doing a bit of string pulling and I'm more than happy to let him go home. I'm so glad we've had such a wonderful result.' He shook hands with them both, and they thanked him.

'I phoned the prof in Finland,' Urshie snapped. 'We've both got a week off. Think we can manage to convalesce our son without killing each other?'

'Of course,' Joe said. 'He's much more important than either of us.' Daniel then saw the sad, wrinkled monkey hanging limply over Joe's shoulder, and he reached out his arms for it.

'What a disgusting thing,' said Urshie, with her lip curled.

'It's spotless,' he replied, 'but of course it came from Anna's bed. Not the shit tip we sleep in. And talking of filth, Urshie, I'll go back to the flat and make sure it's clean enough to take a sick child back to. Then I'll spend the night with Anna and be here first thing in the morning to collect him.'

'Did she go to casualty?' she asked, feigning indifference.

'Wait and see,' he replied.

He returned to the flat in Headington, but despite it being newly built and with modern facilities, it was the same mess and despair. Their marital bed stank like a dog's blanket and the sink was, as usual, full of washing-up. The sad scene of a failed marriage. He cleared up, washed up, changed the beds, gathered up a large bag of Daniel's clothes and went to the laundrette. The little garments circled mesmerically in the machines. Falling dungarees and T-shirts whirled with little vests and pants. The arm of a pyjama top. Flying socks. On removing the warm, clean clothes he pressed them to his mouth with a surge of thanks for the life of his child.

With his domestic duties completed he drove to Anna's flat to see if she'd come home. She hadn't. Had she gone to casualty after all and been admitted? He rang the unit anonymously, posing as a close relative of Miss Morton Moore, but they hadn't treated anyone of that name. He rang

The Old Vicarage. No answer. Was she there, choosing not to pick up the phone? It was now 11.00 p.m. First he would check on Daniel and then drive to Monks Bottom.

Quietly he entered the dimly lit paediatric ward where he found Daniel was still awake and whimpering. Joe leaned down and stroked his cheek. 'Daniel, I've got to go somewhere in a minute but I'll be back first thing in the morning to collect you. Then we'll go home.'

The child began to cry; the whingy, whining cry of overtiredness and he clutched tightly at Joe. 'Don't go, Daddy. Don't go.'

The staff nurse came over and looked caringly at him. 'He's been very distressed since Urshie left. He's had some phenergan to calm him down, but it's not been much use. Can you stay for a bit?'

'Of course I'll stay' he said.

Daniel stopped crying and reached under the bed covers for Anna's monkey. He took one of its long, dangling arms and patted Joe's face with its paw. 'I love my monkey,' he said. 'He's my friend. He smells of flowers.'

'It's called perfume, Daniel,' Joe replied. 'It's what lovely ladies wear.'

Eventually the exhausted child fell asleep, but Joe sat up with him all night, wide awake and staring into space.

CHAPTER ELEVEN

Sunday, continued . . .

M E-TOOM-TUM'S SHARP LITTLE CLAWS wake me up from my siesta. I've been asleep for over an hour, and despite catering overload at Jacochel I find I'm ravenously hungry. I dial for an Indian, and while I'm waiting for it to arrive I have a bath and change into my *thobe*. At 8.00 p.m. I eat the curry, and have another little doze. By 9.00 p.m. I'm wide-awake and bored witless. What the hell am I going to do? Nothing on the telly I can be bothered with. Read? I've got a pile of racy thrillers that friends have passed to me, and a stack of primary care research papers I've been meaning to get round to, but I just can't be arsed with any of it. I can't really settle to doing anything that requires concentration seeing as I have a murder to plan. However, despite the memory of last night's alcoholic orgy, I find my usual thirst has returned. I down two large slugs of whisky, and smoke an enormous spliff, but as I begin to unwind I find that I'm sinking into a miserable mid-life-crisis type of philosophy. How weird that this weekend the five women who've formed the mainstay of my sexual and emotional life should all be jostling for my attention.

Kit Kennedy, who dropped dead last week at Catford dogs. What can I say of Kit? The unique and lovely woman who taught me how to make love as an art form. Who gave me her passion and her time and her intelligence. Thank you,

Kit, for the privilege of knowing you, and all the things you did for me. Rest in peace, you sweet and honourable lady.

Ursula Fortune, whom I detested with venom, but who gave me my wonderful son. Now dead and gone. No more to be said.

Carina Alton, who satisfied my wants and needs in the famine of my lousy life. Her slender, classy body forever desperate and clawing for me, and me, blindly obliging, thinking only of myself. I'm ashamed to say I can't really remember what she looked like.

Anna, my beautiful and refined wife. The lady who holds my deepest love, respect and passionate yearning. She who suffers the slings and arrows of my vile temper and deep, black moodiness, but remains devoted, and kind and desiring of me when – let's face it – I behave like an absolute arse-hole. How desperately I want her love and presence, without which I'm the floundering victim of a shipwreck.

My mind falls to Nola. Not much honour there, and a bit of a thorn in my side; forever reminding me that I only have to give the nod and it's all on again. Damn the woman, but there again, good old Nola also gave me her passion, and her time and her discretion when I had doodle shit in my life.

My reverie is broken by the shrill ring of the doorbell. Ah! Perhaps it's the kids arrived home early? Oh, I do hope so. Even their babble and bickering is better than the silence of an empty house, but when I open the door, it's Nola. What do they say about talking of the devil?

'Oh, God,' she says, as I open the door. 'Love the nightie, darling. Is it your transvestite night?'

'What do you want?' I say. 'I'm not in.'

'No you're not, are you?' she smirks. 'You're on-call, but don't flatter yourself. I don't want *you*. I've come to see Josh. I just wondered if he'd fancy a summer holiday job goffering for me at Lincoln's Inn. Do his Oxford interview no end of street-cred.'

'Clearly you weren't listening this afternoon when I mentioned that he and Sophie had gone away for the weekend.'

'Can't say I recall that,' she lies, marching into the sitting room and flopping down on the sofa. 'My, my, Joe. Love the smell in here. Shades of Belsize Park. Curry, scotch and the weed. Doesn't take you long to collapse into type without the fragrant Annie fawning all over you. Aren't you just a teensy-weensy bit pissed?'

'Pissed off being here on my own,' I say. 'And just for the record, madam, although I miss my wife, your snatch on a plate is not required.'

'You should be so lucky,' she says, lowering her lids, but then she starts crossing and uncrossing her bare brown legs. Oh, good God. She's been watching too many films.

'Come on, Nola,' I say, picking up her handbag and waving it at her. 'We both know why you're here. I can't play games with you. Let's live to fight another day.'

I try to shoo her out, but suddenly she's all over me like a turbocharged Hoover tube. I've had enough garlic tonight to see off a dozen devils but it has no power over this one. 'Joe,' she pleads. 'Darling monkey man. We were so good, you and me. There's never been anyone like you. Just a little taster for old times' sake.' She gets a little taste, but seeing as it's enhanced with high notes of curry, alcohol and grass I can't imagine it's a very nice experience. She appears to be enjoying it, though. She says she's only ever awarded twenty out of ten once in her life, and that was to me. She wants me, and if I don't do something drastic she's going to have me.

Suddenly, there's an explosion of stars in my head, my mouth hangs open and my loins leap to the height of Nelson's column. She shoves her hand up my *thobe*, and begins to rummage around, but it's quite obvious I've managed to get there all on my own. There's a flurry of her garments being hurled around the room. 'The monkey,' she demands, and I know exactly where I'm going. It's been well over twenty-five years, but I still remember every spectacular leap and bound. We slither down together on the floor and I'm carried off on auto-pilot, disappearing into a fabulous place full of bright lights and happiness and freedom that carries me on with an impetus I can't control. It's wrong, it's wrong, I know it's wrong, but all the bitterness, and anger that I've relived over the past three days roars like a rocket in my head. My soul is exposed.

The spectacular pleasure peaks with a head-on blast of fireworks. I collapse, my heart thudding and my mouth drooling. I'm a bastard. I've done it. Two minutes ago I was an ever-faithful husband. Now I'm an adulterer again. Was it worth it? Reverse, reverse – but of course, it's too late. Nola's petite size eight is pinned beneath me, and she's fighting for breath. When I shift to release her she turns round, gently enfolds me, and reads the despair on my face. 'Don't look so sad,' she says. 'I know you love her, and I love Felix. I *do* love Felix. I'm sure you think that's something I've trawled up for the occasion, but even before, when you and me were at it like jack-rabbits, I really loved him. He just can't find anything to love about *me*. Don't let's have a moment of guilt about this, Joe. We go back far too far. Let's just think of it as two consenting adults enjoying a nice meal or a smoke together.' We kiss weakly and eventually stagger to our feet. 'Well, monkey man,' she says, pulling on her silky thong, 'we may have to call it a smoke, or a meal, or even a walk in the moonlight, but we both know it was a shag to die for.'

I stand at the front door watching the tail lights of her Lotus Elise disappearing out of the forecourt, but before I can hold a post-mortem of remorse, the phone rings. 'Oh, Daddy,' says a distressed and tearful female voice. 'I'm in the most frightful state. Boffin and I had a big bust up, and he buggered off, and I've just been mugged by two girls in a pub bog, and they've nicked my bag and my mobile and I haven't got any dosh or car keys, and I've got to get home and . . . oh, Daddy (she starts to sob), I want to come home and I'm so frightened and . . .'

Dear God, what can I do? I'll have to go and get her. She might look and act like a worldly woman, but she's really only a little girl, isn't she? She's in the Green Dragon, a pub in some godforsaken village outside Epsom. I just hope I manage to drive in a straight line, and can remember how to turn on the headlights. I'm just about to leave when the phone rings again. 'Dad! Thank Christ you're there. The Polo's completely fucked. I called the AA but they can't fix it.

The big end's gone. I'm on the M25, in the Happy Eater just past Junction 29 eastbound, but you'll have to go to Junction 28 and go over . . .'

'Josh,' I say, trying not to sound furious. 'I'm just about to leave for some poxy hell-hole near Epsom to pick up your sister. She's had her bag and her car keys nicked. Can't you get a taxi to a station and get a train?'

'No spondooly, Dad,' he says. 'Cleaned out. Heavy time.'

'Then I'll send a cab for you,' I say, wearily. 'Now exactly where are you?'

I ring and arrange a cab. 'Hundred and sixty quid round trip,' says the extremely pleased cabby.

Through the window of the Green Dragon I see my beautiful daughter, sprawled in a comfortable armchair, slurping a pint and talking to an audience of young men. Her mother's melon breasts are hoisted over the top of a skimpy camisole, my own curly, black biblical hair falls to her waist, and her long, blue-jeaned legs are splayed to display her crotch. Only a child? What of me at eighteen? Do you remember me? A young man, naked in a bedroom over a junk shop, my legs splayed too, posing for a lover twice my age, vain and preening and putting all my goods on show. What about her mother at eighteen? Thrusting on top of me with the perfection of a steam-powered Victorian pump. We were no children, and neither is she.

When she sees me she gets up and throws her arms round me. 'Oh, Daddy,' she cries. 'I'm really glad to see you, but do you know the most amazing thing's happened! This is *such* a hoot. You didn't really need to come after all. These guys only live in Bromley.' Really? Well, stone the crows. I'm splitting my sides. The young men ignore me, preferring to ogle my daughter, so seeing as no one is likely to buy me a drink I slope off to the bar and hitch up on a stool. An hour later a happy smiling Sophie bounces up to me. 'Are you ready to go, then, Dad? I'm knackered.'

Ah-ha. I know what you're waiting to be told. That I was stopped on the way back home and breathalysed! Sorry to spoil your day, but no. I managed to weave home without attracting the fuzz and I'm just about to crash exhausted into bed. My son and daughter are downstairs, screaming with laughter and swapping bad luck stories. Do they really know what bad luck is? I climb into bed, bash the pillows and try to find a comfortable position. What with one thing and another I've had a very busy day, but it's not over yet. I still have a perfect murder to plan. A script, stage directions and props are required that leave no room for error. The bats are quiet, the black dog is unconscious and twitching, and the jeering crowd keeps its distance.

Half an hour later I've accomplished a brilliant and perfectly crafted production. I turn out the light, but I don't get very far down the long green road to sleep before Nola Moisemann looms up to haunt me. Oh God, Nola. Welcome aboard. Here we go. Thanks for crawling back into The Crowded Bed.

September 1979: Joe was unable to pursue Anna due to his parental responsibilities. He and Urshie took their compassionate leave, and Daniel was discharged, but it was a Daniel they didn't know. He cried constantly and wouldn't eat so they fed him all his favourites. Jelly squares, chocolate Instant Whip, tinned spaghetti and Penguin biscuits. He threw it all back up. They bathed him, sang to him, read to him, and played his *Playschool* LP, but still he cried. They took his temperature and his pulse, looked in his ears, eyes and throat, scanned his skin, and felt his tummy, but could find no physical reasons. They pulled together all their professional expertise, and consulted their textbooks, but inevitably they began to argue again, honing their frustration in a tennis game of poison words. As a last resort they took him back to the paediatric ward for a reassessment.

'The poor kid's depressed,' Peter Butler said. 'It's a common post-viral pattern in children. He just needs cheering up. Why not take him to the country or the seaside for a few days? Get some fresh air into his little lungs?' There was very little fresh air around Urshie's parent's sub post office in Birmingham, and even less around Kitchener Street. It would have to be the caravan at Westgate-on-Sea. The last thing Joe wanted was to be banged up in a confined space with Urshie, but there was no other choice.

They packed the Morris Minor Traveller and drove to Kent; their hostile silence broken only by Daniel's incessant crying. There were constant stops on the way, when they argued about what he wanted, or what he needed. Urshie eventually lost patience and smacked Daniel. Joe smacked Urshie. Urshie smacked Joe. It was touch and go whether they abandoned the trip or killed each other.

The old family caravan was now spartan and worn out. There was one small double bed, assembled from a sofa with sagging cushions, a rack of narrow bunks, a hissing gas fire, a primitive cooker with two rings, and a cold water tap. A small compartment held an ancient, rusty version of an army field closet. Perhaps not the best place for a child to convalesce after all. As Joe entered the claustrophobic living space, a sour, rank smell hit him, but the absorptions of a damp autumn day weren't the only odour. The caravan was a zoo cage, permeated with stomach-churning memories of himself, cooped up and captive; the good boy, eaten up with frustration and dreaming of suicide.

He connected the services, buttered some bread and opened a tin of tomato soup. Urshie humped in the bedding, and made up the bed. She then decided she was deaf and dumb, lit the small gas fire, wrapped the duvet round herself, and immersed herself in a textbook on lung function during heart surgery. It was clear she wasn't going to manufacture any maternal interest for the occasion, so Joe found an old bucket and spade. 'Shall we go and play on the beach, Daniel?'

A sharp north wind screamed in competition with the gulls, and cut like a sword around their ears, but Joe affected the usual over-the-top parental effort of trying to provide holiday fun. His voice became high and excited, and he leapt around with dramatic over-acting, but all he evoked was the pathos of a failed clown. However hard he tried to entertain and energise his son, his words and gestures failed. The small, pale boy remained static and inanimate. He stared with a vacant, bored expression that said 'thank you for trying, but you're wasting both my time and your own'. With one last attempt at jollity Joe whirled him up on his shoulders, and galloped down the sands, pretending to be a charging elephant. Daniel usually loved that game, but that day he began to grizzle. With no point in carrying on Joe took him back to the caravan and laid him to sleep on a bunk.

As the exhausted child slept he tried to talk to Urshie about the permutations of their forthcoming separation. The practical and financial considerations of 'who would do this, and who would do that'. 'Sorry to disappoint,' she sneered. 'If you think for one minute I'm co-operating you can think again. Anyway, I suspect your precious new domestic arrangements are a bit buggered. Tinkerbell's done a bunk, hasn't she?' Joe was too tired to either quarrel with her, or lie. 'I hope not,' he said. 'I love her, Urshie and I know she loves me, but even if she has left me, you and I are finished. Nothing you can ever say or do will make any difference. Daniel and I are still going to leave you.' At that point Daniel sat up and vomited his tinned soup.

Later, Joe counted out a large pile of coins and walked to a phone box on the promenade. He phoned Anna's flat. No reply. With shaking fingers he dialled The Old Vicarage. "Allo,' said a flat-toned, female voice with a hint of a foreign accent. Could that be her mother? Joe was polite, pitching his voice with no hint of London vowels.

'I'm so sorry to bother you, but would it be possible to speak to Anna?'

'Go avay,' the voice rasped. The receiver was replaced. He rang again and repeated himself. The receiver was replaced again. But hang on. What was her mother doing there? Today was Wednesday. Weren't her parents supposed to be in Scotland until Saturday? Was Anna there or not?

Joe spent a cold, sleepless night in the sagging bed, carefully detached from Urshie, listening to the wash of the ever-moving sea. As it began to get light he edged towards her. 'Urshie. Would it be possible for you to get up and see to Daniel? I don't feel so well.'

'No!' she snapped, rounding on him. 'You've chosen to be a one-parent family, Joe. You've made it quite clear that you can do without me, so you can just get used to doing without me.' He rose, and caught sight of his face in the cracked mirror that hung over the kitchen sink. Red-rimmed eyes, deep lines around his mouth, his long hair greasy and matted. He'd aged ten years in three days.

Daniel was hiding under his blankets, quietly crying. He'd wet the bed, and he knew his mother would be short-tempered with him for being a careless boy, but Joe removed the soaked bedding, washed the plastic mattress over and fitted a clean sheet. 'It doesn't matter, Daniel,' he said. 'You couldn't help it. You're not a naughty boy. Daddy used to wet the bed when he was a little boy, too.'

Joe boiled a kettle to wash him, and dried him with a towel he'd warmed in front of the fire. The child wobbled on one leg, and stepped shakily into his pants and dungarees. He held his arms high over his head while Joe slipped on his vest and jumper. His tiny feet stretched out for two pairs of socks and his *Captain Pugwash* slippers. 'Come here,' Joe said, taking him in his arms. 'I love you, Daniel.'

'I love my monkey,' Daniel said, waving its floppy legs and arms about, and doing a little dance.

The weather was much improved by periods of sunshine and a mild southerly breeze. Joe bought a set of miniature skittles and a kite, and he and Daniel played all morning on the sands with whoops of enthusiasm and laughter. The child was now full of energy, and his cheeks glowed with vitality again, but his laughter was somehow depressing. Full convalescence meant his return to normal, but his future life was going to be far from that.

By lunchtime, the vigour of both father and son had started to flag, and they wandered into a noisy, low-grade pub that didn't seem to mind a drowsy child-in-arms. The child crumbled his way through an outsize cheese roll and drank Coca-Cola. The father downed three pints of strong ale and smoked steadily. They slumped together in a dark corner of the bar and slept, inebriated in their separate ways, while a strangulated voice from the jukebox banged on about Cathy coming home.

Two hours later Joe roused himself and staggered out. His head was fugged and hungover, his eyes smarting from their long wash in nicotine, and his neck sore from the weight of a sleeping child. He walked to the phone box, rang The Old Vicarage, and carefully attempted to repeat his chosen words without stumbling. This time the foreign female voice was distinctly slurred. Was her mother drunk? 'Anastasia is not vell. Plizz don't ring again. Plizz leave her alone. It's for ze best. Plizz don't make any more trouble for her,' and the phone went dead. A dismissal with no room for manoeuvre. But from somewhere he found the courage not to be deflated. He would get in the car right now and drive straight to Monks Bottom. He would demand to see Anna and tell her parents the whole sordid story. To pull himself up to his full height and inform them he was taking her away with him, and he didn't give a stuff what they thought. But then he immediately lost confidence. She'd told him not to come looking for her. He was terrified of having to stand on the doorstep while she stood, stone-faced, and asked him politely to go away. To watch her turn and walk back into her own world while her powerful father shut the door in his face. His only resort would be to write her a long and loving letter and beg her to come back to him.

By next morning he'd had enough of the caravan and Westgate-on-Sea. He packed his and Daniel's bags, but before he left he sat on the edge of the bed and talked to Urshie as kindly as he could. 'Urshie, I'm sorry, but this is it. I'm leaving you now so you'll have to get the train home. From today our marriage is over. I'm taking Daniel, and I'm going to Kitchener Street for tonight. When I get back to Oxford we'll stay at Anna's flat. I've discovered she's at home with her parents and I'll see her soon. After that we'll have to take things one step at a time, but I'm still seeking a divorce and full custody of Daniel.' Urshie suddenly seemed stunned and frozen. She rubbed her face in a strangely sensitive way, reached for her bag, fumbled shakily and produced a typewritten letter that looked as if it had been read a thousand times.

> Mrs Fortune,
> Did you know about the affair between your husband and Carina Alton? Can't have him getting the sack can we? I should do something about it if I were you.
> A Wellwisher

So it *had* been a letter. Presumably from the same source as the one Carina had received. Who would do such a thing? Who had so much malice in their hearts to make so much trouble? 'I'm so sorry you had to get hate mail,' he said, 'but for the record Carina got one as well. Of course I lied to you, Urshie. I did have an affair with her, but she meant nothing. She was only my escape. I really wanted our marriage to work, but from day one you didn't even try. Before we met I'd had years on my own and I was desperately lonely. All I wanted was some affection and encouragement. I wanted the comfort of togetherness but you made me feel like a filthy animal. It's too late now. It's Anna I want, and I really want her, but I apologise for cheating.'

Her head fell forward and she leaned her chin on her chest. 'The night he was born,' she said, raising her eyes to look at Daniel, 'it nearly happened, didn't it?' She made no attempt to say more or to kiss Daniel goodbye. As Joe quietly closed the door behind him, he thought he heard her crying, but it could have been the wind off the sea.

CHAPTER TWELVE

Sunday, continued . . .

MIDNIGHT, AND THE OLD VICARAGE SLEEPS its evil, haunted sleep. The only sounds Anna can hear are the regular tick-tocking of the grandfather clock in the reception hall, and the odd scream of an owl. Anna didn't sleep at all last night, and she knows it won't come tonight either, so she gets up, slips on her mules and wraps herself, sari-like, in a vast Indian bath towel. She walks down to the kitchen to make a cup of tea. She takes her cup into the drawing room, and curls up on the sofa, but she can feel the eyes of ghosts and spirits peering down at her from behind the picture frames and round the curtains. The same spectres that have always made her crazy. The vicious tongues of night convey the fear that isn't there by day. She gets up and walks out into the garden. In the light of a hazed-over moon she picks a bunch of flowers, walks to the top of the drive and turns into the churchyard. Here, amid grassy knolls, their quiet neighbours lie. Marble gravestones straight and new; stone gravestones crumbling and collapsed. The churchyard has ghosts, but they don't have cruel stories to tell. They're just observers of her misery and protectors to Hugo. She places the flowers on the grave, kneels down on the damp grass and presses her palms onto the flat, coldness of the headstone.

Hugo Gordon Alexander Morton Moore
July 1960 – April 1980
A dearly loved son and brother

The night is warm. Powerfully warm. She throws off her shroud and folds it to use as a cushion. For now she will sit there, eyes wide shut, and pray for Papa's death.

September 1979: The strong and triumphant Ursula Fortune had driven Anna to The Hartington Hospital. Their close proximity had been a torture for both women and the journey had passed in complete silence. When Anna got out of the car no last minute empathy, or underlying unity of womanhood, emerged. There was nothing to say. Not even goodbye. Anna admitted herself. She told a story of a violent row at a party with a drunken man she didn't know. Her kidneys were X-rayed, but there was no rupture, or permanent damage. Six lacerations to her scalp were stitched, but the gouges to her eyelid and temple were not, being more like open wounds, but she was warned there might be some scarring. She was counselled and advised to involve the police, but she refused. She was washed, sedated and allowed to sleep. She lay, weak and completely destroyed, but she was determined that this wasn't the end – just a temporary sacrifice. She'd worked so hard to win his love and the same steely grit gave her the strength for survival. She'd been clever, manipulative, and determined. Like a heroine in a wartime spy drama, she'd stalked her victim and played the game of capture.

230

Over several weeks she'd secretly followed him, disguised with headscarf, dark glasses and shapeless old clothes. She just had to look at him and enjoy the sight of him doing ordinary things. She watched him at the laundrette, washing and folding clothes. She slowly trailed a trolley after him in Sainsbury's, watching him dither over frozen food and compare prices of baked beans. She followed him in her car to the childminder, and watched him come out with his little boy, but the little boy was just a child in a mist and Joe was just enacting the role of a father. She never cared that he was married. She knew his wife was just a nothingness in his life. Everyone talked about them: how they rowed and how sorry they felt for him, being married to a shrew like Urshie.

On a day when she knew both Joe and Urshie were at work, she descended the damp, mossy steps to their sad basement flat. Through a chink in the dirty lace curtains she saw a bedroom with tired, dated wallpaper and cheap furniture. At the foot of the bed was a child's cot, strewn with a rumpled pair of *Magic Roundabout* pyjamas and some toys. At one side of the bed was a photograph of a baby in a shawl, a plastic child's beaker, an alarm clock, an empty beer can and a torch. That would be Joe's side. At his wife's side was also an alarm clock and a pile of textbooks. Anna envisaged no passion, but she knew that routine, loveless connections still occurred in this despairing, slovenly bed.

But Joe's domestic life wasn't the only side of him she discovered, and what a shock she got. She'd followed him one night to a large, Gothic house in Norham Gardens. A slender, angular woman, probably several years his senior, opened the front door. She was wearing a short cotton dressing gown and her fair hair hung in a long plait over her shoulder. He quickly walked inside. About an hour later he slipped out and walked back to the hospital for his car. She went to the central library and looked up the address on the electoral role. Carina Alton! The prof's ritzy wife! Hot sex and no strings. The prof was in Canada, but what a risk Joe was taking. What a danger to his career, and what strong competition!

Anna's love was obsessive and she was becoming impatient. She wanted Joe so much she became tinged with madness, so whenever she was in close proximity to him she played a clever little game called body language. Cold indifference, but cunning, careful flirtation. It was a very skilled art, but Anna was a natural performer. She knew she had an exquisite body and a beautiful face. She knew that with clever manipulation he'd find her irresistible. She denied him eye-contact, she swayed her body, she inhaled deeply so as to project her breasts, she swept her lashes down in slow shows of modesty, and posed her profile where it caught the best light. When lowering herself into a chair she elegantly revealed covert inches of sleek, inner thigh, and in bending over she angled her bottom to incite his sexual appetite. She slyly watched his reaction to her slow dance of desire, and knew her victim was falling prey. His full seduction would come in the fullness of time, when he was besotted, but there was one last trump card to play. He and Urshie needed a serious quarrel, something much more dividing than their on-going cat-scraps, and Carina Alton had to go as well. She typed two anonymous letters. No real details in either of them of course, but enough to destroy the status quo. And that was all. It worked. He became her lover and they fell in love. Truly, madly, deeply, and for ever in love.

Now, lying in an iron lung of misery, her tears fell. First silently, with her rib cage pumping. Then a wailing emerged, like the hollow, sucking howl of a chimney in a gale. Exhale. Inhale. Her tears fell in rivers. Salty and stinging, running down her cheeks, dropping from her chin and overflowing down her neck. Their grand passion was over, but their love would survive until the time came for its restoration. They would never forget each other, nor cease to want each other. They were too close, too bonded, too inextricably woven. Perhaps in the intervening years he'd take lovers, perhaps so would she, but it would never be truly over. For now she had to go away, but she'd come back, perhaps in ten years time, when Daniel was old enough to understand.

Her crying lasted until she was dehydrated, and her mucous membranes so swollen she could hardly breathe or swallow. A doctor was called to her bedside. There was talk of a psychiatrist and she was prescribed extra sedatives. Through the blur of her troubled mind she lay with her hand on her belly, willing that the final phase of her master plan be accomplished. She dreamed a dream of little black swimming creatures, with prehensile, slithering tails. Compelled by nature's magnetic forces, they thrashed like eels, searching to find the wide Sargasso Sea of her womb. She willed the eels onwards, higher, higher, into the upper reaches of their journey, fighting and striving to reach her fertile golden yoke. She knew when it happened. A blue shock of lightening threw itself around her; her right ovary stung, and then glowed. The glow expanded until the whole of her body was warm and the God that existed for believers took her hand and told her she'd done a good thing, and forgave her.

When she awoke her fever had broken, and she knew she wouldn't cry again. She had plans to make. She'd promised his wife she'd leave him, and she would honour that promise, but surely Joe would come looking for her? She would leave the country immediately and go to Hugo in America. She would go back to The Old Vicarage, quickly pack a case, and gather up as much money as she could. Papa always kept a huge stack of used banknotes under his bed, and she'd steal it all. She would write a short letter of goodbye saying she had no plans to return.

She discharged herself from The Hartington, paid the large bill, and called a taxi. How often, Anna thought later, do we think of small moments of time – seconds sometimes – that change fate? Such as 'if only I hadn't gone back into the house for my gloves I would have got to the chemist before it closed. If only I hadn't been stopped by that traffic light I wouldn't have been in the place where I knocked the cyclist off her bike.' If only bad weather in Scotland hadn't sent her parents home . . . If only she'd got back to The Old Vicarage an hour earlier . . .

As her taxi drove through the big black iron gates she knew she was too late. The metallic bronze Daimler was there, sneering like a golden Cerberus. Her father was running out of the house in full battle cry. A huge warlike presence. The hated enemy. Before there had always been Hugo to protect her, but this time she was truly trapped.

The taxi door was opened, Anna was pulled out, and money was stuffed into the driver's hand. A flock of birds soared to the sky, the silver birches bowed in the wind and rain flew in her face. Like a butterfly in a net she was captured. He dragged her into the house by her hair, yanking her tender, bruised body forward. It hurt. Oh, how it hurt, as her wounds were pulled and stretched by his angry, uncaring hands. Her mother stood aside with the inevitable glass in her hand, her expression blank, her eyes lifeless, and knowing there would be no point in caring.

With Anna's hair distressed to a frizzy, matted bush, and falling all over her face, her father couldn't see the gouges on her eyelid and temple, or the stitches in her head. He was too distracted to see her as a living person anyway. She was, as ever, just a 'thing' to be overpowered. He bore down on her with a venomous attack, his voice echoing inside her head like gunfire. Hard words, and accusing words. Questions! But no answers sought. Questions! But no answers listened to. 'What on earth's been going on here, Anna? I know you've had a man in the house. You're a slut. A cheap, filthy strumpet. The Tapestry Room's like a tart's boudoir. Bed all rumpled up, my lady, and your underwear all over the floor. Wet towels in the bathroom. Dirty dishes and beer bottles all over the show. I know what you've been up to so don't try to deny it. I wasn't born yesterday. I expect you thought Mrs Miller would be in to clear up the mess for you. Just your bad luck that we gave her the week off, isn't it? His name, Anna! His name!' She remained mute. He yelled, he postured, his fist lashed out and struck her on the side of her eye. She screamed. She fell to the floor in front of the fireplace to crouch on her hands and knees. A rill of bright phosphorescent lights dropped down past her eyes. Black flicking specs, like musical notes, danced in her head, and she heard loud tinny rings, like the bells of a Buddhist monastery. Her father kicked the coal-scuttle across the room and strode out. Her mother moved forward like a zombie to extend a shaking hand to her daughter. Clearly she was trying to be kind, but it was far too late for her to be a mother again. Together they climbed the stairs, but it wasn't obvious who was helping whom. Anna slid exhausted into her bed and her mother, not knowing what to do or say, swayed out of the room without comment.

Later in the afternoon she came back and sat on the end of Anna's bed. 'Ze bastard 'az given you a black eye,' she said. 'But I sink you 'ave uzzer injuries, yes? 'E vaz too busy shouting off 'iz mouth to notice, but I saw zem. Let me see, plizz.' She lifted Anna's hair to view her stitches, and then smoothed her fingers over the damage to her face. 'Many injuries, Anna. Oh, plizz do not love a man the same as your Papa.' Her mother then started to cry, but she was loose and mumbling, with the gin seeping through her tears. 'I vaz a beautiful young girl, just like you are, but 'e ruined me, screwed me under 'iz foot like a dog end on ze pavement. You must leave ziz brutal man. Don't protect 'im. Don't be so stupid as me. You must get avay before it 'appens to you too.'

Anna could have told the whole story, but there would have been no point. It was too late. Her mother was too drunk, and too vague, and too detached from her to offer any unity or safe secret. She, herself, was too dazed to make a sensible story of it anyway. 'It's all over,' she said. 'I've already left him.'

'I 'oped zat vaz ze case. Your Papa's been through your bag. 'E knows you've been in ze Hartington. 'E 'az found ze receipt.'

'I can't ever talk about it.'

'No, Anna, neizer can I, so ve vill not talk of it ever again. He sez you must go avay. To ze finishing school in Svitzerland. I 'ave to take you there on Friday.'

'It's no use saying I don't want to go, is it?'

'No. But it's ze only chance you 'ave. Get avay before you end up like me.'

Anna looked at her mother, trying to feel some affinity. How could the bloated, lined face have once been beautiful? The young photographic model who'd enchanted the middle-aged banker; the stunning bride displayed on the piano, and the smiling young mother in the photograph album. All poor broken-down Eugenie had now was her bottle and her cruel husband. But Anna knew she could never love her or sympathise. Her mother was guilty of a crime that could never be forgiven. She'd chosen the wise monkey philosophy; neither seeing, hearing or speaking of the evil inflicted on her children.

The next day Anna's father said he was glad she'd got rid of it and had shown some sense in the matter. 'But Papa, I haven't had an abortion,' she said.

'Don't bother lying, Anna. The Hartington is a Godsend to stupid bitches like you. This disgusting episode will never be mentioned again. What an absolute mess you look, and you can get right away before Oliver sees you in this state.' Again, Anna was too exhausted and sick to exonerate herself. What did it matter anyway? What did anything matter?

Her car keys, cheque-book and passport were confiscated. The Radcliffe was informed she was leaving immediately due to severe exhaustion, and removal men were hired to clear her flat. She was to be packed off, out of sight and mind, to Switzerland where she was to complete a course of cordon bleu cooking, flower arranging and other essential etiquettes. A fitting preparation for marriage to a Lord's son.

A couple of weeks after she'd been abandoned in Switzerland a thick brown envelope arrived for her. The address was written in Papa's familiar handwriting, but inside there was another envelope, sealed and imprinted with the Frockton crest.

Dearest Anna
I'm so sorry to hear from your father that you're unwell, and I
hope that the fresh air of Switzerland is helping you. I guess

there's been some awful drama in your life, and I want you to know that I'm so sorry. Things are going very badly in my life too. They've had enough of me, Anna. You must remember my grandmother who died last year? They're sending me away to her place in Southern Ireland. It's a wrecked old farm, but I've been told to lick it into shape, and get some malt barley going. They just want me out of the way. If they could send me on a one way ticket to the moon they would, but I'll be pleased to go. I've got to do something with my life, and Ireland's far away enough not to have them bearing down on me all the time. Aren't families a bastard? Why can't they let us be? Why do they have to rule everything, and decide everything? Being born with a silver spoon isn't what it's cracked up to be, is it? Mine is shoved so deeply into my mouth it's going to choke and kill me one day.

I love you very much, and I care very much about what happens to you. I wish I could say I was deeply in love with you, but you know the truth of that one. Dearest Anna, can we help each other out? Please will you come to Ireland with me as my wife? It's virtually what we've both been ordered to do, anyway. I promise you it won't be that bad. We'll make the house a home, and I'll (we'll) be very busy. We both know it won't last for ever, but will you come?

Your loving (and I mean it)
Oliver F

Miss Anastasia Morton Moore, and the Honourable Oliver Frockton, were married at St Margaret's, Westminster within weeks. The reception was held at the Dorchester and the bride's father was overflowing with largesse and smiles. Her mother was (sadly) in hospital. Everyone said it was a match made in heaven. All the usual speeches, photographs, confetti, champagne, smoked salmon, and caviar, but the bride and groom's endearing hugs and kisses were Oscar-winning performances. It was to be a strange marriage. Oliver knew that if the child looked like its father the next generation of Frockton would be an Israeli, but he was delighted. 'Sod them all,' he said. 'We've been treated like a couple of pedigree dogs, anyway. Let's just say the wrong stud scored, but how fantastic it'll be. Carrickmore's the perfect place to bring up a child.'

The happy couple left for a two-week honeymoon in Bermuda, and on the second day, with stately presence, a beautiful, turbanned young Indian boy arrived. Dapinder Khan was greeted by both Anna and Oliver with equal welcome, and thereafter the vast bridal suite bed was christened hourly by the bridegroom and his true bride. The strange trio then flew to Ireland to begin a three cornered version of married life.

The Carrickmore Estate was situated in an isolated part of County Waterford; a place of vivid Irish greens, fast changing skies and liberation. At last a place for them all to enjoy independent movement. To talk and walk when they chose, and to think for themselves. Within the cold and draughty Georgian manor house an atmosphere of warm and loving harmony was created. Oliver and Dapinder led a mature and sober life together. They donned green wellies, wax jackets, hats, scarves, gloves and long, old man's underwear. They worked from dawn to dusk, ploughing and draining, and hedging and ditching, to prepare for sowing in the spring. They laughed, cracked jokes, and made endless love. Anna lit the fires, and washed and cooked for them. Sometimes she cried for her child's father, but Oliver and Dapinder looked after her like surrogate husbands. They took her to the doctor. The doctor said she was a healthy young heifer, the baby was a fair-sized bruiser, and it'd be born in the middle of June. They laughed and called her Buttercup. They talked endlessly about the coming child and decorated a nursery. They loved her, and Anna loved them both, but it was the love for her child's father that became her life. But it was never a sad depressive illness; just how she coped with things. Each minute of each hour, talking to him.

'Dear, Joe. How are you today? I still love and miss you so much. I can't bear to think of you leading a life that doesn't include me, but I know this is only a temporary sacrifice. Daniel needs you, but one day our child will reunite us. How is Daniel today? Have you played with Lego? Have you watched *Playschool*? Have you read to him? I wonder if he still dips Golly's hand in the yoghourt. Oliver and Dapinder have just called home for lunch. We had hot potato soup and some cheese scones I made this morning. I wish I could cook for you, my love, but all I can do is create our child. No one else knows it's your child, Joe. I promise you that no one else knows. When the baby is born we will say that I gave birth to Oliver's child prematurely, and of course, we'll be believed. I'm sorry about that, but it has to be that way. For now. All will be so proudly revealed in the fullness of time. Now for some really exciting news. Hugo is coming to Carrickmore. I think it all went wrong in America, although he's not saying much. Anyway, it'll be wonderful to see him again. Perhaps he'll stay for a while. I do hope so. There's enough room for a battalion here, and Oliver and Dapinder could do with some help. I get very tired, but now the boys have gone back to work I'm going to curl up in a chair, beside the old iron range, and listen to *Woman's Hour* on the radio. Maybe if I doze off I'll dream of you.'

At the end of February Hugo arrived at Carrickmore. He was emaciated, disorientated and deeply depressed. He said he was trying so hard to get off the stuff, so Oliver and Dapinder took him to Dublin, and found a doctor who arranged a rehab programme for him. Anna nursed him through his fevers, and nightmares, and tears and gradually he started to recover. The week before Easter he said he felt so fit he wanted to go to Dublin, to buy some new clothes and get his hair cut. He asked Anna for some money and she was pleased to give him as much as he wanted. One thing the Frockton couple weren't short of was money. He came back, loaded up with treats and presents for everyone, and bubbled over with happiness. He said he was now cured. Completely clean. He would never slip back again and they should all celebrate.

During his convalescence Hugo had been loving, supportive and emotional about Anna's pregnancy. He would sit close up to her, on a sagging old sofa, and press his ear to her bare belly, laughing with delight at the pushes and squirms of the baby. Once he tried to slip his hand a little further down, innocently saying that he just wanted to feel the place where the baby would come out.

'No, love,' Anna said. 'It's not right now.'

'No it's not, is it?' he replied. 'But you're not ashamed of us, are you?'

'No, Hugo. Never ashamed. Never. It was precious part of us, but I belong to Joe now.'

Joe's absence in her life was the only dissension they had. 'Where is he, then, this saintly Joe? If he really loved you he'd have come looking for you. He'd have chopped down every tree in the world until he found you.' But Anna was patient and defending of Joe, knowing that Hugo's mental state hung precariously on the edge of a ravine, and that if he fell in his recovery would be a long, uncertain haul out again. Thus she soothed and appeased him. 'It's only a temporary situation. Joe and I will be reunited one day. You've not to get upset. Just get better.'

For Anna, night time at Carrickmore was a beguiling place of isolated comfort. It was now spring. The rain and cold blasts of winter had been replaced with the mellow voices of new leaves opening, the occasional creaking door of a farm building and the odd yowl from one of the farm cats. Despite her broken heart and loneliness its ambience made her secure. She felt the presence of Oliver's grandmother, Charmian, whom she remembered from her visits to Monks Bottom; an autocratic, but kindly old lady, who spoke with a gentle lilting Irish voice. Someone who genuinely loved Oliver, and had never imposed her prejudice and hatred upon him. It was a happy house. When she got into bed, and turned out the light, her room became a dark, protected haven; a shrouded black tent with no distractions, where she could escape to dream of Joe and to enjoy her baby's night time dancing. She would lie flat on her back waiting for it to start. Little fists and elbows would push out, and her belly would shudder with its turns. Her fingers would massage the fierce protrusions, as if they were playing games, or trying to hold hands. She pressed, and the baby pushed back, kicking her hard, seeming to convey its bond immediately. Such a strong baby. A strong character in a strong body, showing that it had so much of its father's personality already. Her sorrow was that Joe's hand would never feel the magic as well, but he came to her in dreams . . .

That night she felt his warm breath on her neck, and the firm press of his body, but as she began to wake up a tongue was rasping her face. It wasn't Joe's tongue, and the voice mumbling her name wasn't Joe's voice. She cried out, but he silenced her by covering her mouth with his clumsy kisses. She struggled to break free, but her long hair was trapped beneath her shoulders, making her head and neck immobile. All the time he was saying mad muddled words that made no sense. Her legs kicked out, and she tried to slip from beneath him, but had to restrain for fear of hurting the baby. She pushed hard with her arms to try and force him off, but the writhing of their two bodies caused a skewering movement, and she started to fall out of the bed. Her head hit the floor and she was suspended vertically as he grabbed her ankles. She arched her back and contorted her body with one last effort to escape, but he lunged at her, grabbed her pelvis, and forced himself inside her. His crazy words continued as he thrust into her with the rhythmic power of a battering ram. She screamed and they fell conjoined to the floor.

The light snapped on. Oliver and Dapinder dragged him off. Their sweet natures knew no aggression, but, in rare incitement, they punched him with the strength and venom of underworld gangsters. 'I'm so sorry,' Hugo slurred through swollen lips, 'but I wanted her and she wouldn't let me. I love her.'

'I think it's your little habits you're in love with,' said Oliver. 'What are you on, you pathetic coward?' He rushed off to Hugo's room and wrecked it, searching for his poison. He came back with a blister pack. 'Barbiturates,' he said. 'I knew he was on something. Haven't you noticed how wild-eyed and crazy he's been these last few days? He must have got them in Dublin. What a bastard.' Both he and Dapinder threw Hugo out of the room. 'Get out of my house,' Oliver shouted. 'Get out of here for ever. Just go.'

An hour later the pains started and then the bleeding. In the early hours of the morning the baby just slipped out, with no chance at all. Twenty-four weeks gestation, but dead. She was tiny and pretty. She looked just like Joe. Anna called her Joanna Rose Fortune. She wrapped her in a soft, angora shawl she'd knitted for her, and held her all night to keep her warm. She showed her Joe's photograph and talked to her. 'There's your Daddy,' she said. 'He's shaking hands with the queen. Can you see him? He's wearing a white coat, and he's smiling. He doesn't know about you, but he would have done, later on, when things were different. We loved each other. We still love each other. You were a very wanted child and he'd have adored you. I'm so sorry that I ran away from him, but I had to, you see. He had to be with your brother Daniel, but me and Oliver and Dapinder would have looked after you. Your Uncle Hugo didn't mean it to happen. I know he didn't. He's a gentle, lovely person, but the drugs possessed him. It wasn't his fault. All his sorrows, like mine, go back to the house of hate. I'm so sorry, and I love you so much.'

In the morning she cut off the fine wisps of Joanna's fluffy hair and sellotaped them to the back of Joe's photograph. 'We won't call the doctor or an undertaker,' she said to Oliver. 'They'll take her away from us, and we'll lose her. She mustn't be touched by strangers. She must live here.' Oliver dug a deep hole beneath a wide spreading beech tree on the outer reaches of the estate, and she was laid to rest, wrapped in the angora shawl.

Hugo was found in a barn, lying still and cold. Put to sleep by his own hand. The three of them accompanied his body to Monks Bottom and he was buried in the churchyard, to bow-headed reverence from the whole village. Her father made sure that the official cause of death was given out as a car crash. They said Dapinder was a close friend of Hugo's, but Papa didn't speak to him. The Frocktons knew who Dapinder was. They didn't speak to him either. Anna held herself like a statue at the graveside. Her heart too frozen for displays of grief.

The strange trio then returned to Carrickmore. The deaths of Joanna and Hugo forged an even deeper loving bond between them, and Anna's sanity and survival were completely due to the care and tactility of her two surrogate husbands. At night when they heard her crying they came into her bedroom, and, with one on either side, got into bed with her, and wrapped themselves around her, and talked to her with soothing words that superseded any need for professional counselling.

Thereafter life settled down to a regular pattern, and the peace of Carrickmore allowed Anna to visit Joanna, and to grieve. As she became stronger she went into Waterford and took up some voluntary work in a geriatric hospital. After a couple of years she felt ready to leave. 'Look after each other,' she said to Oliver and Dapinder, 'and most of all look after my daughter.' She filled a small wooden box with soil from Joanna's grave and moved to Belfast to finish her nursing course.

CHAPTER THIRTEEN

Monday

I WAKE WELL BEFORE THE ALARM, but it's not really surprising, is it? The memory of last night's infidelity has slung its noose round my neck, and will tighten for the rest of my life. However, I can't wallow in the aftermath of my foolish lapse just at the moment. An even bigger sin looms large, so I must get a grip. After tonight I'll be a murderer. Such intensity of life, but there'll be no flinching.

I rise and prepare a small overnight bag, carefully packing a clean *thobe* which I'll wear when I do the deed; a disdainful and flamboyant pose in reverence to myself, the proud Israeli. Please don't form the impression that I'm sailing calmly into this event without nervous anxiety. This is my one big chance, and I'm obviously agitated and excited. It'd be prudent for me to take the day off work, and prepare myself psychologically – as a boxer or tenor would – but as an actor on the stage of public servitude I don't have the common man's privilege of 'throwing a sickie'.

At 8.30 a.m. sharp I'm poised and ready at my desk for whatever Ravenswood Health Centre throws at me. Every Monday morning my column in the appointments book says, 'Dr Fortune. Emergency Clinic,' which is self-explanatory. The usual barnstorming South London weekend always creates a small army of walking wounded who, having lost all faith in the local hospital's casualty unit, find my services much more convenient and user-friendly. I already have a queue a mile long, and the usual battle-scarred punters troop in. Sprained wrists from fist fights, hangovers which I'm led to believe are brain tumours, a stream of black eyes, ten morning-after pills and a clutch of bad trips.

At twelve noon, having seen thirty patients, and saved the NHS a small fortune, I phone my beloved. 'Hi, darling,' I say brightly. 'How's the patient this morning?' (Does my voice sound different? Please God it doesn't say, 'I had very gratifying intercourse on our sitting room floor last night.')

'He's still rather laying it on,' she says, 'but an awfully nice district nurse turned up this morning to take some bloods. Unfortunately she was one of those hand-patting types, and recommended bed rest for a few more days. Of course he lapped it up. I'm really sorry, Joe, but it looks as if I'm going to have to stay until at least the weekend. I've contacted work and they've been so understanding. Compassionate leave until we get things sorted.'

'No more than you're owed, my sweet,' I say cheerfully. 'I'll be down after work, tonight. Love you lots.'

I replace the receiver and move clumsily out of my consulting room. 'Just going to do my home visits,' I say to my reception staff, but I've lied. I have no home visits. I drive up onto the elevated greensward of Ravens Hill, park up and find a bench to overlook this rare oasis in the metropolis. Here I've walked, talked and enjoyed time with Anna and all three of my children; kites in autumn, toboggans in winter, bird feeding in spring and licking Cornettos in summer. Here I'll ask my God to forgive my infidelity, but is adultery *really* such a sin? Is it as bad as it's cracked up to be? Surely, as Nola says, it's no big deal. Dick in, dick out and QED. No more important than a smoke, or a meal or a walk in the moonlight. Without true love it's bugger all. I love Anna with an all-consuming passion, and although I know last night was an horrific betrayal, she will (thank God) never know. When Nola and I next meet at family gatherings we'll lower our eyes and ignore each other. It's over. I've been flattered that she's itched after me for so many years (what man wouldn't be), but perhaps last night had to happen as the final scratch. Real sin, though, needs true revenge and Gordon's revolting, supercilious face leers at me. 'Eye for eye,' is still my battle cry.

September 1979: Having left Urshie in Westgate-on-Sea Joe drove to Kitchener Street where he and Daniel were received by four sets of open arms, all falling on their faces with gratitude at the restored health of their grandchild. But they were alarmed at the sight of Joe. Baggy-eyed, dishevelled and morose. Hungover and half-stoned. He confessed to the quartet that he and Urshie were having 'relationship problems', but didn't elaborate more. After a lot of hand-wringing and muttering they didn't condemn. They could tell he was desolate. They listened, made sympathetic noises, and brewed predictable pots of tea, but did they know how he felt? No one on earth knew how he felt.

After settling Daniel in front of the television, to watch *Tom and Jerry* with the quartet, he disappeared up to his old bedroom. He had a letter to write, but despite a hundred false starts all he produced was a pile of screwed up paper.

After much time and frustration he at last wrote what he hoped would pass for a love letter. A desperate outpouring of his passion for Anna, begging that they be reunited and pledging his commitment to their future.

When he went downstairs his mother and Daniel were cuddled up together singing nursery rhymes, and Mitte was clucking about food. Patte sat quietly in a corner, pursed-lipped over his accounts, and his father was chuckling over *The Benny Hill Show*. Joe sat down, trying hard to join in their simple domesticity, but the claustrophobia of Kitchener Street was already beginning to irritate him. He felt guilty and ungrateful, but he pulled on his sweater and mumbled about some fresh air. 'I won't be long,' he said. 'Just a turn around the block. The old place won't be here for much longer, will it?'

He fled the house, and lurched around in a deep and troubled state. The company and support of his cousins would have helped, they were, after all, his own generation and men of the world, but they were all missing. Jack was driving a lorry up to Heathrow to collect pineapples, Felix was pursuing fat and happy totty in Chelmsford, and Melvin was ensconced with an adoring lawyer in Golders Green. But was he really fit company for any of them? All he had to offer that night was his own philosophy of a miserable life? *I am, but I wish I wasn't. I would like to be, but I know I won't. I used to be, but now I'm useless.*

The empty streets were greasy and depressing. Lumps of soggy newspaper lay rain-swollen in the gutters, empty cans rolled and rattled, and under the streetlights puddles shimmered in psychedelic swirls of purple and green. A rat leapt from a dustbin, and from a derelict house shadows bobbed in candlelight. It was becoming a slum. Soon this whole area would be razed to the ground to make way for a vast shopping complex that the planners had decided was preferable to stable communities.

As he slowly walked he could hear it. He stopped. It stopped. He looked behind him. Nothing. But he knew it was there. Young, sleek and black. Slithering on its belly. Symbiosis they call it. The symbiotic friendship of the black dog had arrived. Deep inside him there was movement. The other black things, that had been there since he was a tiny child, were moving. The deep, hidden away hang-ups and resentments. The parts of himself he didn't like and the parts of other people he didn't like. The parts he'd been forced to bury deep down in a private mineshaft, but that night the bats bounced up to the surface, with a crescendo of bubbles and mud, and embedded themselves in his brain.

He shuffled to an off-licence, bought a bottle of whisky, entered the back yard of a boarded-up shop, and sat amid the detritus and squalor of an abandoned business. Happily he embraced oblivion. A vice tightened around his chest and he slumped sideways against a crust of decaying refuse. He cried the short, silent, painful tears of a man, and spoke an inward prayer. 'Please God. I have never called on you before, but tonight I beg for your support. Please will you grant that my love be restored to me.'

Just before midnight he crept back to Kitchener Street to find that Mitte had waited up for him. The fire burned low, the table lamps threw the same familiar shadows on the walls, and discarded knitting lay in the armchairs. Did he love it or despise it? All he knew was that when the heavy metal ball swung through the window a part of himself would be demolished as well. He gathered her in his arms.

He awoke early with the sealed letter to Anna on the bedside table. He would drive down to The Old Vicarage, deliver it in person, and pray again for their reconciliation. He strapped Daniel into the Morris Minor Traveller and headed for Monks Bottom. Two hours later, as the rooks cawed and the wind moved through the silver birches, he watched his precious letter retreat away from him in a sour old Wellington boot.

By the time he returned to work Anna's official notice had been received by the hospital. 'Such a lovely girl with superb aptitude and dedication,' his colleagues said. Joe received no reply to his letter, nor received any other communication from her. The Fortune family resumed life in the Headington flat and his wife reclaimed him with a newly acquired enthusiasm. Despite his misery, he showed a face to the world that said good husband, good father and good doctor. The chapter closed quietly, but despite the page turning there was no emergence of love or passion between him and Urshie. Their life together continued in the same blind mime of pretence, but he could tell that he was now her hard won trophy. The 'Anna episode' was never thrown up in any way between them, but his head couldn't allow the same detachment. His lost love continued to haunt him. He'd fall into a shallow sleep thinking of her, and she'd be there as he groggily emerged into consciousness. She arrested the word on the page, and moved beneath him on the rare and bland obligations of marital union.

As the days turned into weeks, and weeks turned into months, he suffered a deep internal depression that swung between grief, despair, anger and entrapment. Mostly he just missed her quiet movements, the sound of her voice, her perfume, her gentleness and the touch of her fingertips. Everyday he yearned for communication and the postman was eagerly awaited, 'just in case'. Every time a phone rang he prayed it would be her, and in every situation he looked for her. He saw her for years in queues, in shops, in orchestras, in choirs, in *Pan's People*, on trains, in traffic jams, on page three and in endless ale-soaked public bars.

It was only Daniel's presence that made his life worthwhile. He taught him to read, and before long became himself a captive audience to daily endurances of *The Three Billy Goats Gruff*. Urshie took him to a Jewish mother-and-child group, where he wore a *kippah*, and an embroidered waistcoat, and learned to sing simple Hebrew songs. He attended a multi-cultural nursery school, where he played, and painted, and fought over toys with children of all races, creeds and skin-tones. Out of sheer boredom Joe began to work hard. He passed a couple of oncology and surgical exams, and Professor Alton promoted him to senior registrar. To any observers, and even sometimes to themselves, the Fortunes appeared to be like any other professional medical couple living in Headington at the turn of the eighties. Of course they weren't. Carina, who'd known nothing of Anna, eventually held out her arms again to Joe, and their affair was rekindled with the same grateful intensity. But this time they would meet at the Alton's weekend cottage, hidden down a country lane in the remote Cotswold village of Lower Slaughter; a place far away from prying eyes, and vicious, jealous people who wrote poison-pen letters.

July 1982: It was a hot midsummer night and Joe and Carina were standing together in the low-eaved bedroom, looking out onto the tangled, cottage garden. It was dark, but an external light illuminated the scene. A smell of honeysuckle filled the air and jumbled balls of night insects danced in frantic movement. 'Marcus is talking of early retirement in five years time,' she said. 'It's a bastard. Can you imagine me stuck out here, day in, day out? But listen, love. He really wants you to take over the firm when he goes, but he said you need more bite, more ambition. You've got what it takes to be a consultant, but it won't happen without much more hard work. It'll be yours for the taking, but you've got to pass more exams, write more papers, do some research and put yourself about a lot more.'

'Don't *you* start,' Joe said. 'You're beginning to sound like my wife. I *have* been working. Why does everyone keep nagging me? I love oncology, but I'm not sure where I want to be next year, let alone for the rest of my life.'

'I want you to be here for me,' she said. 'I can't bear the thought of losing you again.'

'But Carrie, this is nonsense,' he said. 'You've always made the rules. We fuck. End of story.'

'But I love you,' she said, turning round and kissing his heart.

October 1982: Joe decided not to inform Carina that something dramatic was happening in his life that would completely scotch her plans. After many weeks of letters and phone calls that Joe wasn't privy to, Urshie announced she'd been offered an exalted position as consultant anaesthetist on Isaiah Goodman's pioneering cardiac team. An amazing accolade at her age. 'I've got to take this promotion,' she said. 'We've tried hard with our marriage but it's not been brilliant, has it? I'm off to London, and it's up to you whether you come or not. If you don't, I'll understand, but Danny comes with me.'

'Urshie,' he said. 'Whatever I am, and whatever you think of me, I love that child more than anything else, including myself. Where he goes, I go. Whether you want me or not, I'm coming too, and you can't stop me.'

It was time for Joe to say goodbye to Carina. He'd obliged her with a loveless congress in her marital bed, and although she'd been full of her usual ardour he could only perform in a half-hearted way. His mind was fifty miles away, high up in a hospital laboratory in north London, where he'd been appointed director of a small pain-relief research team. The challenge excited him, but the thought of Carina's life to come, with the pompous and impotent Marcus Alton, filled him with a sorrow he could do nothing about. She was crying and pulling on his hand. 'Please don't leave me. I know you don't love me, but we're all right, aren't we? Marcus is devastated you're going. He really wants you to take over . . . You'll be made, Joe . . . A consultant by the time you're thirty-five . . .' Joe was dry-eyed, staring into space, not knowing what say or do. He looked at his watch. One last embrace and he made his excuses to leave. Danny's bedtime, etc. He left and didn't look back. He promised he'd keep in touch with her, knowing he would not.

Joe and Urshie rented a small house in Belsize Park, and Danny, now seven, was enrolled in a fancy little private school, with a very fancy uniform of brown corduroy knickerbockers and a hat with long tassels; only the best for a child deprived of true parent bonding. In response to their new domestic circumstances it was agreed there would be an untraditional domestic arrangement. Joe's new position gave him the freedom to be flexible in his working practices, and thus Urshie became a wholly detached and fulfilled career woman who left the house at 7.00 a.m. and returned at 7.00 p.m. with swollen ankles and a pained expression. Joe was more than happy to devote himself to Danny, and in the near permanent absence of Urshie he threw himself into being a good mother. He collected him from school, cooked his tea and did his washing. He tried to be jolly and to give him a nice time. He bought a television and they watched *Jackanory* and *Blue Peter* together. He took him to the public swimming baths, the cinema, a trampoline club, a children's drama group in Islington, and to White

Hart Lane for home matches. He read *The Lion, the Witch and the Wardrobe, Peter Pan,* and *The Wind in the Willows* to him at bedtime. They played with plasticine, Lego, Mr Potatohead, and Scalectrix, and became fiercely competitive chess rivals. Danny said he wanted to go to judo, so he went to judo, and it did him good to rough house with other children without being scolded by Urshie for being too boisterous when he wanted to play-fight with Joe. She detested other children coming round to play, so he made sure the house was always full of his noisy little friends. To counteract the frivolity she arranged *cheder* classes for him, but to Joe's surprise he enjoyed them. Daniel may have been fulfilled but Joe was damned lonely. But not for long. Cue Nola.

Cousin Felix, like Joe, had inevitably been forced to conform to family pressure. Both a wife and business partner were required. Fat and jolly Christian barmaids didn't fit the bill, but the brilliant little Jewish lawyer did. Enter Nola; seven stone in her socks and the only bride to commit adultery before her marriage had been consummated. She handed Joe a time and a room number at the wedding. 'No conscience needed, Joe,' she said when he arrived. 'I've just discovered that chiselling bastard I've just married spent his stag night holed up in the Hilton, humping a fat cow from Colorado with a laugh to cause an avalanche. What's good for the gander, is even better for the goose.' For the purposes of speed, and with the encumbrance of a white lace meringue to cope with, a unique position was invented: 'the monkey'. Thereafter, Joe became her monkey-man, and he was happy to oblige. A simple arrangement that suited them both.

March 1983: Six months down the line the status quo in the Fortune marriage had been maintained. There'd been no dramas, or major upsets, and a comfortable routine had been established. Joe wasn't normally one for waxing lyrical, but as he waited for Danny outside the school gates as usual he felt strangely happy. It was an abnormally warm day for March, and as large puffball clouds scudded across an azure sky, his heart soared. One of his pain control trials, involving acupuncture, had been accepted for publication by *The Lancet*, the previous night Nola had been very, very nice to him in the isolation of his lab, and he'd just bought two bunches of daffodils. His life was unconventional, shapeless, and unstructured, but so what? The love of his life had been gone for nearly four years and he was resigned to compromise, but one way or another he'd accepted his parameters.

Danny was always one of the first to hurl himself through the big double doors, his hat askew, and his satchel slung round his neck, but on that day Joe just stood and waited. And waited. The flurry of chattering children, and their equally chattering parents, gradually dispersed and he found he was standing alone on an empty pavement. He thought he'd better go in. He entered the building diffidently, peering round the corner, but expecting Danny to leap out at him yelling, 'Surprise, Daddy!'

'He's gone to the dentist, Dr Fortune,' his teacher said, packing her briefcase, and smiling at him. 'His mummy came for him after lunch.'

Joe returned to Belsize Park, and as soon as he opened the front door he heard an echo of emptiness. Danny's Tottenham duvet had been ripped from his bed and his wardrobe hung open and empty. Everything else had gone as well. His books, puzzles, and boxes of board games. Action Man and all his kit, the model farm and the little grocery shop. Star Wars figures, soft toys and the endless beakers of crayons and felt-tips. The only thing that remained was a cruel note propped up on the kitchen table.

Urshie had left Joe for the world-famous cardiac surgeon, Isaiah Goodman, a taciturn, conceited autocrat, over twenty years her senior. The forwarding address was his elegant Georgian house overlooking Hampstead Heath. She'd seen a solicitor, and in the absence of any joint property, or savings, or pension funds to share out, their only asset had been wrenched from him in a blatant act of possession.

Joe was pistol-whipped with pain and he crumpled to his knees. Blood rushed to his head and his ears roared. Once again he was drowning, but this wasn't the deep and complex pain of lost passionate love. This was a different severance. The physical and brutal snatching of his little boy. A declaration from Urshie of, 'I don't want or need you any more. I've found another father-figure who is rich, and much more successful'. Joe's emotions surged full of violent intent. The bitch wasn't having him.

He ran straight round to Heath Road and a messy doorstep scene ensued. Urshie yelled at him to go away. Danny howled and struggled, but was restrained by a beefy Dutch au pair girl and her even beefier boyfriend. Joe punched the boyfriend and Isaiah Goodman called the police.

'I'm sorry, sir,' the police constable said to Joe. 'I understand your problem, but as a point of law you're causing a breach of the peace.'

'But she's kidnapped my son!' he shouted, imploring sympathy.

'I'm afraid that's a domestic matter,' the officer replied. 'Best get yourself a solicitor, but you must leave or I'll have to arrest you.' So he was ordered by the law to leave; his only crime being that he loved his son. With a feeling of complete helplessness he sloped back to the empty flat in Belsize Park, where two bunches of daffodils lay dying in the hall.

Joe sat at the kitchen table and cried like a widow at a graveside. Daniel Elijah Dov Fortune, his beloved Danny, was now a legal tug-of-love child and his life to come would revolve around an ambitious and humourless mother, an old, sack-faced father substitute and an indifferent Dutch au pair girl. An alien trio, not one of them caring a tuppenny toss for him. His spliff became too soggy to smoke. He became too drunk to hold a glass. At 3.00 a.m. when he crawled into bed on his hands and knees, he found he had company. The old, velvet monkey lay slumped on his pillow.

Joe begged Felix to intervene, but his reply was not encouraging. 'You won't win,' he said. 'In cases like this the mother always wins, unless you can prove she's an alcoholic, a drug addict, excessively violent or certifiably mad.' Perhaps Joe could have trotted out the shameful act of violence she'd inflicted on Anna, but it would have done his cause no good. The infidelity card was already being played. 'I've had a letter from Urshie's solicitor,' Felix said. 'She claims you're always having affairs. Is it true? Because if it is, you haven't got a snowball's chance in hell.'

'Affairs,' Joe shouted. 'What's she doing with Goodman if it isn't an affair?' but he knew a double-edged sword was poised over his head. Nola's name was not required reading and he reluctantly shrugged.

'Matter closed then, Joe,' Felix said. 'We don't want all the gory details hung out on the clothes-line, do we? Oh, and by the way, she says you smoke dope.'

Joe raised his eyes. 'For fuck's sake, Felix, don't go all pompous on me. We all smoke dope.'

'Joe, we might all smoke dope, but the Families Division won't look at all kindly on a habit. I'll ask her, off the record, to remove that accusation, but I think the best I'll be able to get you is visiting rights.' So all Joe got was visiting rights. 2.00 p.m. Saturday, to 2.00 p.m. Sunday, and he tried to make it the happiest time of the week for Danny. It was certainly the happiest time of the week for him.

On that particular Saturday he turned up promptly to collect Danny. He'd bought him a new Tin-Tin book and the latest Tottenham strip, and had booked tickets for a boat-trip on the Thames. Afterwards they would go to the Hard Rock Café, with a colleague from his lab, who had visiting rights to his ten-year-old daughter. Urshie opened the door with her usual look of repugnance. 'He's not coming,' she said. 'Izzy's taking him to a children's lecture at the Royal Society. Do him much more good than stuffing his face with burgers and watching television all night.' Isaiah Goodman, a diminutive, round-shouldered troll in a grey cardigan, hovered silently in the background, nodding his head.

'He bloody well is coming!' Joe thundered.

'Go away, Joe,' Urshie sighed, unmoved to any sort of emotional exchange, but as she spoke Joe could hear Danny crying.

'Danny,' he called out. 'Where are you? Come here.' From upstairs Joe heard a door being kicked, and a handle being rattled. 'Go to the window, Danny. I'll talk to you.' Joe ran back out onto the pavement to see the blurred mush of his son's wet face staring down. 'Do you want to come out with me, or go to the lecture?' he shouted up. 'If you want to go out with Izzy I don't mind at all, just say so.'

'Daddy, Daddy, I want to come with you,' Danny's muffled, sobbing voice shouted back.

Joe leapt back to the front door. 'My son will not be imprisoned,' he yelled. 'You heard him. He wants to come with me, so let him out.'

'Clear off, Joe,' Urshie said with venom. 'You're nothing but a damned nuisance. Every time he comes back from seeing you, he's uncontrollable.'

'Let him out or I'm coming in to break the door down.'

'If you enter this house it's unlawful trespass, and I'll call the police.'

'You can call the whole bastard Met for all I care,' Joe screamed. 'He's legally mine for one fucking day a week, and I'm going to have him for one fucking day a week, so screw yourself, bitch!' He pushed past Urshie and collided with the puny troll in the hall. As the troll fell to the floor Joe rushed up the stairs, kicked the door lock until it gave way, threw Danny over his shoulder and ran out of the house.

Urshie stated to her solicitor that Dr Joe Fortune, her estranged husband, had assaulted her. Goodman stated that Dr Joe Fortune, his fiancée's estranged husband, had subjected him to severe physical abuse causing injuries so serious he was forced to cancel his operating list for a week. They both stated that Dr Fortune had wrecked their house, used foul and abusive language, and physically removed seven-year-old Daniel Fortune from the premises against his will. Thus did the court deny all Joe's visiting rights. He was issued with an order allowing him to see his son once a month for only two hours, at a venue chosen by his mother, and with her present at all times. He was told that any more of his nonsense would result in all contact being denied.

Joe was finished. Totally beaten. A physical and mental depression descended and seeped into him. How he grieved for Danny. How he missed him. How he loathed the thought of him banged up in Hampstead with a superbitch and an old troll. A grief made more poignant by the hand-wringing of the sad and bewildered quartet, whose loss was as painful as his own.

Urshie chose Regent's Park Zoo as their monthly venue, and Joe's two precious hours with Danny were spent, not peering at the poor trapped animals in detached silence, or forced stilted exchanges, but in a verbal river of joy and physical closeness. They would glue themselves together like Siamese twins, and walk around the familiar paths so well trodden by other estranged and odd little couples like themselves. Urshie would follow, ten paces behind, silent and numb with boredom. Father and son would round up the visit in the zoo café, where, in defiance, they ate beefburgers, with onions and chips, and double ice-cream sundaes with chocolate sauce and nuts. Then the bewildered child would crawl onto Joe's knee, and cling to him, and beg him to take him back home to Belsize Park. At the end of the allotted time Urshie would tap on the window and point at her watch. Joe was thus forced to pull apart from Danny and to push off his frantic grabbing and pleading. To walk away, to ignore his loud beseeching screams, and to abandon him.

Divorce followed just before Danny's ninth birthday, and despite Felix making an excellent case for Joe to be granted improved access, the courts decreed that the same astringent rules prevailed. Felix also informed him that Urshie was sending him away to The Unicorn School, a prestigious preparatory school in Oxford, and Joe was obliged to pay half the fees. Having stolen him from his father, she was happy to give him away to the care of strangers, and there wasn't a damn thing Joe could do about it. Complete mental breakdown might have beckoned, but he was just too tired and dispirited to indulge himself. He'd had more than his fair share of drama. Nola was still delighted to be his accomplice in regular binges of sexual excess, but all he ever wanted, and would continue to want, was Anna. Might there be a chance that they could rekindle their love affair, now that he was free and alone?

He drove down to Monks Bottom in the showy, single man's accessory he'd indulged in; an immaculate classic Austin Healey 3000, in a bold shade of scarlet. As he drove through the big black iron gates he could see that The Old Vicarage looked exactly as it had on that weekend five years before. Mellow September sunshine basked on the ruby-hued bricks, and the maples were turning into a hundred shades of russet through to gold. A warm breeze moved through the drying leaves of the silver birches, and he could hear the distant cawing of rooks in the oaks down by the meadow. There was no one at home. He looked through the window into the drawing room, and it hadn't changed either. He walked round to the back of the house and looked up at the window of the Tapestry Room, shielding his eyes with his hand. On that fateful weekend another man had stood in the same position. Oliver someone. How Joe wished he could erase that scene from his memory. He'd been so cruel to her. 'Oh, Anna,' he silently mouthed. 'How I was beguiled, but circumstances never smiled.'

Behind him the gravel crunched and he jerked round. A gardener stood there with a trowel and bucket in his hand, but it wasn't the rat-faced old bastard who'd taken his letter. 'I've come in the hope that Anna Morton Moore might be here,' Joe said. 'I'm an old friend.'

'Ah, yes,' the gardener said politely. (Joe's classy car and grey business suit obviously impressed this time.) 'That'll be the daughter, won't it? I've not worked here that long and I've not met her yet. All I know is that she's married into the Frocktons – you know, the big brewing family from The Park up the road. Far as I know she lives in Ireland. Husband's into farming. The guvnor's up in Scotland golfing, but he'll be back on Wednesday. Do you want to leave a note?' Did Joe want to leave a note? No, he didn't think he did. Married. Of course she'd be married. Married to the upper-class prat, Oliver Frockton. The beautiful, cultured English rose, and the heir-to-a-fortune aristo would be leading a life of laughter, contentment, and sexual perfection. There'd be two beautiful babies by now, and they'd be living on a massive country estate, laughingly called a farm, surrounded by a thousand acres of malt barley. She drove a Mercedes-Benz estate car, wore a cashmere twin-set and pearls, and still spoke with perfect English diction.

He returned dejectedly to Belsize Park. Anna was lost for ever, his son was ensconced in a boarding school miles away, his lab was becoming a bolt-hole from his profession, and his only meaningful relationship was secret shenanigans with his cousin's wife. There must be something more between now and death. He'd just lit a joint and poured a scotch when the doorbell rang. It was Nola. He wasn't in the mood for her, but he didn't send her away. What else was left in life, and it wouldn't take up much of his time.

'I'm sorry, monkey-man,' she said, 'but this has got to be the last time for us. Felix has wanted us to start a family for ages and I can't hold off any longer. My duty must be done so the IUD comes out on Monday. It must be Felix's kid, Joe. I'm not so much of a bitch to shit on him that much. Anyway, you got more than enough on your plate, haven't you?' As she began to undress, she burst into tears. Joe pulled his shirt over his head, slipped off his shoes, and burst into tears too.

He walked her to the tube, where he kissed her goodbye, and thanked her for making his life worthwhile. He told her Felix was a lucky man, and held her in his arms until, on a whoosh of warm air, the train arrived. She got on, put a finger to her lips, and was fast-throttled out of sight.

As he walked away he felt a chasm open up inside him. Should he end it all under the wheels of the next train? If not, he was doomed to a life of loneliness and unrequited love. He knew then that he had to forge a new life. As John Cleese used to say, 'And now for something completely different.' But what? It was surprisingly his mother who found the answer. 'It's about time you became a proper doctor, our Joe. In my book you're not a proper doctor unless you've got a brass plate and a prescription pad.'

CHAPTER FOURTEEN

Monday, continued . . .

A S THE CLOCK SLOWLY TICKS to the end of the day I'm twitchy, and desperate to get out of the health centre. Novels and folklore always give the impression that elective murderers are cool and calm, straight-faced and suave. I wish I felt like that, but my ribcage has become home to a million butterflies and my hands are shaking. I've several hours to go yet and at this rate I'll end up with complete nervous collapse. *Courage mon brave.* Take yourself in hand. Positive thinking. You have one chance and you mustn't blow it.

I go to the drug cupboard and identify the two commonplace drugs I've selected. I remove one bottle of fast-acting sedative syrup, and another containing the elixir of death, but if you're expecting me to name their generic names think again. I have responsibilities to my profession, you know. I bid my reception team good night, and hear the usual bland farewells.

Two traffic-jammed hours later I arrive at The Old Vicarage, but I've no need to ring the bell. She's out of the front door the minute I pull on the handbrake. Her face smiles her usual warmth and welcome, and her arms lock around my neck. She doesn't seem to notice the strange look in my eyes that says 'adulterer', or 'murderer in preparation', but there must be one. I stare at her with a strange sort of masochism, willing her to discover a tic, or a hangdog expression, that reveals my guilt, but thankfully she seems blind to my altered state.

We relax on the sofa in the drawing room. She pours me a glass of red, and lays her hand on my thigh, but our intimacy is ruined by Queenie's busy little body bustling in to tell us that our grub's up in the kitchen. 'Fresh caught salmon,' she announces. 'Some pal of yer Dad's sent it down from Scotland and there's a lovely apple crumble for afters. I'll take 'is up on a tray. Then I'll be off.' We then have a detailed update on Gordon's progress. We had one the minute I arrived but she seems to have forgotten. I'm delighted to hear (again) that he's coping like a trooper and getting back to normal at the rate of knots. How nautical. Soon he'll be sailing away to the permanent land of nod.

Half an hour later, when Anna and I have eaten, and we're about to watch a repeat episode of *Inspector Morse*, there's a violent clanging of the servant summoner bell. Anna runs upstairs. The news is that Gordon's feeling strong enough to come down. Bollocks! I wanted him in bed. We take an arm each, and as we slowly descend the stairs all of our faces are showing some degree of distaste. I must admit my strong GP's stomach lurches dangerously near the edge. We help the stinking old colonial to a large, comfortable armchair in the drawing room, where he collapses wearily, hunched up like a living version of Uncle Bulgaria. Cushions are packed behind him, a footstool is placed beneath his sheepskin slippers, and, despite the delicious warmness of the night, a tartan rug is wrapped around his knees. Our evening is spent politely listening to his boring and bigoted lament for the demise of the Empire, and the breakdown of the old order, but my staying power quickly evaporates. I excuse myself to smoke a small Havana and enjoy the mild night air on the terrace.

'Are you OK?' Anna asks, coming up behind me and leaning her head on my back.

I turn round and take her in my arms. 'I forgive you,' I say.

'Forgive me for what?'

'I forgive you for loving such a selfish and stupid sad bastard.'

'Forgive me in bed,' she says, leading me back to the house, but sadly, despite her obvious desire and expectation, there'll be no chance tonight. She's going to fall into a deep induced sleep while I get on with the business.

The grandfather clock strikes ten with Regency resonance, and it's a joy to my ears. 'Gordon,' I say. 'Would you like a small nightcap before you retire? I believe that's your normal routine?' He mumbles some sort of upper-crust guttural, that I think means, 'Yes please. How kind of you,' and requests his usual – a double slug of Glenmorange, mixed with hot water, brown sugar and a smidge of cinnamon and cloves. So far so good. Everything's going according to plan and I move to the kitchen with the sedating medication in my pocket. A steely reserve has replaced my nerves, and I'm focussed, calm and determined.

I prepare Gordon's concoction and pour Anna a small G and T, carefully adding the dosage to each glass. Water will do for me. Razor-sharp brain required tonight. I carry the nightcaps ceremoniously back to the drawing room on a tray, smiling and attempting mateyness, but we all sit in a strained, polite silence, while glasses are raised to lips. 'Is it all right, Gordon?' I ask.

'Acceptable. Acceptable,' he mumbles. I watch both Gordon and Anna anxiously to ensure that they both down the complete contents of their glasses. Once mission is accomplished I get up, yawn theatrically, and mention my early start in the morning. Anna and I push and pull Gordon up the stairs, and, although he's observed getting into bed, that's as far as our interest goes. I guide a rapidly wavering wife into the Tapestry Room where she plumps down heavily on the four-poster; its drapes still depicting Anglo-Saxon peasants hey-nonnying with lambs and sheaves of corn. I help her to undress, guide her under the duvet and lay her on her side. 'Sleep, my darling, sleep,' I beg her. As if obeying, she sighs, closes her eyes and breathes deeply. I don't get into bed beside her as I have something else to do, but I reach beneath the duvet and splay my fingers on her naked abdomen. 'I love you, Annie,' I whisper. 'Thank you for coming back to me. Thank you for our life, and the children you gave me. You're my moon, and my stars, and the centre of my universe. You're wholly without sin and nothing was your fault.'

April 1987: Joe was now Dr Joe Fortune, Member of the Royal College of General Practitioner's, and working as a single-handed GP in Ravens Hill, a crumbling, but potentially expansible practice, not far from his old London habitat. He'd at last completed a long evening surgery, and although he was tired, the ambience of April felt kind and easeful. The nights were getting lighter, and as strong evening sunlight fell through a high stained-glass window, red spots of light danced around the room. He heard a door bang, and there were bold, firm footsteps on the stairs. It was Lesley, humping in the usual heavy shopping bags.

She'd come into his life quite by accident. He'd been queuing in the deli to buy pastrami, and the girl being served in front of him was thirty pence short. He tapped her on the shoulder and handed her a fifty pence piece. She smiled her thanks. A nice Jewish girl, with clean hair and good teeth. They shook hands. Members of the same club. Politeness and niceties, and of course he wouldn't hear of her paying back the money. Five minutes later they were sitting in the Dun Cow, he with a large scotch, and she with a Dubonnet and lemonade. Now, six months later, they had a strict routine. She'd come to the flat above the surgery on Friday evenings, and prepare traditional *Shabbat*. After they'd eaten they would go to bed for condommed and unremarkable intercourse (once before midnight, and once on Saturday morning). If the local on-call rota didn't claim him, he'd rise late. Lesley would clean up the flat (her choice not his), and then they would take in a movie, or an exhibition, and eat out. Then it was back to bed for a repeat performance. After the Sunday morning gymnastics he'd bid her farewell and drive down to Oxford to spend the afternoon with Danny. The rest of the week they were incommunicado. This little arrangement suited him very well, and although Lesley was no more exciting than a waxwork he couldn't be bothered to look for any greater stimulation. He had no idea how the arrangement suited her, because he'd never asked.

He tidied his desk and was ready to call it a day, but he was in no hurry to get upstairs. Then the phone on his desk rang. 'Dr Fortune,' his receptionist said, 'I've really got to go now, but there's someone here to see you. A social worker.' He didn't want to see a social worker, or anyone else. Discussing the sad, hopeless lives of his patients was always stressful, and certainly didn't bring out the best in him at the end of a tiring week.

'Tell her I've gone,' he said, but the door opened and the social worker walked in. She closed the door quietly behind her. Always quiet. Yes. Always gentle and quiet.

'Hallo, Joe.'

In the space of two seconds he saw her, recognised her, and wished it wasn't her. She still occupied a space inside his head, but it was a special compartment he only chose to revisit when the mood was right, and that was usually in bed. Either with an old velvet monkey for company, or as a mind game to his bland connections with Lesley. As a real person she didn't exist for him any more. Her smell and feel and touch had become vanquished to a collection of amorphous, sensual memories, but he remembered the sound of her voice. There'd been no change. The familiar resonance and perfect shape of the words. Could his heart and head and turning stomach really cope with the reality?

She was wearing tight blue jeans tucked into black leather motorcycle boots, a loose white blouse and a long camel coat. Her hair still hung past her elbows, but was now fashionably cut in layered curls, like lion's mane. If anything she was even more beautiful, but he was struck completely dumb. 'Hallo, Joe?' she said again. 'It's me. Anna.' Oh, Anna, he thought, what do I look like to you? The Joe you remember was a brave young cannibal, with a taut, lean body, and long, thick black hair. Now I'm getting on for forty, and how I've changed. The man you see now is greying and balding. Corpulence has appeared over my waistband, and I'm peering at you through large tortoiseshell glasses. You remember the man I used to be. Not the man I am now.

'Anna,' he croaked out of his tight throat. 'How are you, Anna? Hasn't it been a long time? It's very nice to see you again. What are you doing in Ravens Hill?' The passionate ex-lover was reduced to the standard small talk of a stranger, but what else was there? It had been nearly eight years.

One might expect that in true Hollywood tradition they would collapse sobbing into each other's arms, but they were far from that point. Real life is rarely like Hollywood. She took the chair where his patients sat, and they cross-talked in the manner of a standard consultation. 'Shortly after I left you I married Oliver Frockton, and we settled at Carrickmore, his grandmother's old estate in Southern Ireland. I never loved him – not in the way I was supposed to – but it was a *fait accompli*. We were together for nearly three years, but childless. We parted and got divorced with no animosity. Just a mistake we both conceded. I completed my state registration in Belfast and worked in geriatrics. Then I decided to train as a social worker. I started my first job in this borough a couple of weeks ago, and what a lovely surprise it was to discover you were here. I made some enquiries, and found out you're single now, so I just called to say hallo. Thought you might fancy a drink for old times' sake.'

'Why did you leave me, Anna?'

'Only because of Daniel. It was nothing to do with not loving you. How could I have wrecked the life of an innocent child? If that had happened *your* life would have been wrecked as well, wouldn't it? When I first went to Belfast I met someone from the old days in Oxford, and she told me that you and Urshie had stayed together and moved to London. It gave me some comfort to know that our sacrifice meant stability for one very special little boy.'

Joe then laughed with hollow cynicism, and told her his salient facts. His broken heart at losing her, the poor attempt at patching up with Urshie for Daniel's sake, but eventual divorce. That he'd never stopped loving her for a single minute.

'How *is* Daniel?' she asked.

'In his third year at The Unicorn in Oxford, and doing very well actually.'

'The Unicorn!' she exclaimed. 'Hey. I'm an old Unicorn.'

'Well, I never knew that. I bet he'd love to swap stories with you. He's very happy there. In fact he's just an amazing child all round. You've just said you left me to protect him, but he went to hell and back all the same. Urshie eventually turned the tables on me. She took up with Isaiah Goodman, the heart surgeon, and wrenched Danny away from me.

Then she just as callously abandoned him. Pissed off to South Africa last year when Goodman retired. Best favour she did both of us.'

Joe passed her the framed photograph he kept on his desk. The little curly haired boy she'd seen in a mist was now nearly twelve, sturdy and tall, and the double of his father. 'Oh, Joe, what a lovely boy. Do you miss him terribly?'

'I go down to Oxford to see him most Sundays. It's a long round trip but I've got a zippy sports car.'

'Yes, I know. You're known by Social Services as rocket man.'

Over their heads there was a sound of footsteps moving about. Once or twice she looked up, but he gave no explanation. He reached into a desk drawer, produced a bottle of Bushmills whiskey and poured two small glasses. 'Anna, our love was so precious, and our parting was so painful. I've never recovered.'

'Neither have I,' she said, 'but please don't make me turn it all up. I just can't. It hurts too much. I'm here for good if you want me, but don't ever try to turn the key and expect everything to come tumbling out of the cupboard.' But turning the key was exactly what Joe wanted to do. Each of them speaking in turn. Each answering the other's questions, and building up a picture like a flight of stairs. Climbing up and up until they reached the top and the whole story was told.

'Did you ever get a letter I sent you?' he asked.

She shook her head. 'No. Did you write to me?'

'Crappy attempt at a love letter. You didn't miss much, but it was a last ditch stand to try and get you back. I poured my heart out, and begged you to come back. I would have left Urshie, you know. I'd have never let you down.'

'Must have got lost in the post,' she said.

'Yes,' he agreed, 'must have got lost in the post.'

No, Joe thought. Not lost in the post. Lost to the rubbish bin at The Old Vicarage with all the other garbage.

For what it was worth, that was the completion of their love affair's post-mortem, and they never again revisited the days following that muddled, clouded time.

'Anna, you're still the beautiful girl I remember, but I've changed, haven't I?' He indicated his expanded girth, and his receding hairline.

'Maybe,' she conceded, 'but I've changed too. I'm not selfish and greedy any more.'

'You were never selfish and greedy,' he objected. 'You were always so kind, and gentle and loving. Anna, you were perfect.'

'No I wasn't.' She held up her hand to tell him that was as far as the conversation went. She got up, moved round the desk, and looked down at him sitting in his swivel chair. She removed his glasses, their faces moved together and their lips touched. Suddenly the door opened, and a smiling Jewish girlfriend burst into the room, wearing yellow rubber gloves and a plastic apron. She stood transfixed for a few seconds and, with a little mew of horror, turned on her heels.

'Is that your girlfriend?' Anna asked, pressing his face to her cleavage.

'My cleaner,' he mumbled into her soft cushions, 'but she fancies me.'

Heavy footsteps were then heard thumping down the stairs, and the front door banged with resonance. 'Looks like you'll be looking for a new one,' she said.

'A new cleaner or someone who fancies me?'

'That *was* your girlfriend, wasn't it?'

'Like George Washington, I cannot tell a lie, but nothing serious. No love or emotion.'

'Then I'd rather not go upstairs. It's not jealousy, but we need neutral ground. How's about we go down to the Cotswolds? Then you can still see Daniel on Sunday.'

'I can't see him this weekend. He's off to a swimming gala in Somerset.'

'Then how do you fancy a weekend in Walberswick? My father's bank own a cottage they send their stressed execs to. Just happens I've got the key. Can we go there now, Joe? I mean right now. No packing, no nothing. Just lock the door, get in the car and go.'

Where the hell was Walberswick? Joe grabbed his toothbrush and locked the surgery. Two hours later the Austin Healey was zooming down the long, straight heath road that led to the isolated East Anglian coastal resort. Here was to be found a hidden paradise where seabirds swooped, the wind sang in the reeds, and foamy waves crashed onto a long expanse of fine, creamy sands.

That night, under a full moon and a star spangled sky, they took a walk down to the seashore, putting a little more meat on the bones of their wilderness years. Shortly before

Anna's marriage her mother had been admitted to a sanatorium for alcohol problems. After a month she discharged herself and completely disappeared. Nothing was heard of her again, and Anna didn't wish to elaborate why no-one had bothered to look for her. The following year, at her marital home in Ireland, her beloved Hugo had committed suicide; a victim of severe depression and drug addiction. 'It was a desperate and sad time for me,' she said, 'but Oliver was such a support. My father found it impossible to discuss – you know – stiff upper lip and all that. As you know he'd written him off as hopeless anyway. I was completely alone in my grief, but dear Oliver gave me so much love and strength. Our marriage was a failure, but our friendship and love for each other still endures.'

Joe then looked her full in the eyes, her face blue-grey in the moonlight. 'Anna, that night just before we parted. That awful, confused night at the Vicarage. You talked in a muddle, but you were trying to tell me about you and Hugo, weren't you? You must know that I know, and that I can live with it.' She started to say something, to either explain or deny it, but Joe held his finger over her mouth. 'It's all right,' he said. 'I understand everything. It was love . . .'

'Yes, it was.'

She then suddenly knelt down on the sands. 'Kneel down with me,' she ordered. He knelt. 'Say after me, 'I will always remember and love those whose lives were taken before they began.''

Joe knelt. 'I will always remember and love those whose lives were taken before they began,' Joe repeated. They rose to their feet. Hugo's death, and his part in her life, were now to be another one of her many closed books.

'And how are things between you and your father?' he asked. 'There was so much hatred around, so much angst. Have things improved with the years?'

'I suppose you could say we've both called a truce. He's not an easy man, Joe, but I'm sure he'll be pleased for us, because there *is* going to be an us, isn't there.'

'There isn't *going* to be, Anna' he said. 'There already is. You said you can't talk of our past, so let's just think about our future. There's nothing in it yet, only what we're going to make of it together.'

When Joe preceded her into the small bedroom of the cottage he paused. 'Do you mind if I don't put on the light?' he said. He was suddenly humiliated to be showing her such a changed body. Too many take-aways, too many heavy meals in restaurants to pass the time, too many drinks, not enough exercise. Thick flesh had replaced his sinewy limbs, and round folds covered what used to be his flat, hard-muscled belly. 'Sorry, Annie. Just a bit ashamed. My body's not what you remember.' They stood in the dark, unspeaking, aware only of their body shapes and silhouetted faces in the light of the hazy night sky.

She reached out her hand and began to stroke the folds around his waist. 'Don't be silly. You're lovely. You're you. You're still the same, Joe, but you're the Joe of today. What we had before was a long time ago. We left that couple behind in the past. It won't be easy for me either. Oliver and me were . . . Well, as you might have gathered the romantic side of our marriage didn't work out, but I didn't have any affairs. All I ever wanted was you, anyway. There hasn't been anyone since. Not one. No one at all. Sad nun that I am.'

'I wish I could say the same,' said Joe, 'but I've got to tell the truth. I've had a fair few affairs and even some one-night stands, but you're the only woman I've ever made love to. Let's try to remember our first time. That warm summer morning in Oxford, coming off night duty.'

They slowly undressed and got into bed, but when he leaned over to caress her she drew in her breath, and held him back. 'I'm afraid, Joe. Not frigid. Just afraid. I still want you as much as I ever did, but I think I need a bit more time.'

Joe sent his rising passion away by thinking about trains, and boats, and planes, and bank statements, and snow, and children's ear infections. When she fell asleep he rose from the bed to close a rattling window. A salty wind was blowing and he could see the reed beds swishing. Thin clouds raced across the moon, and shadows darted like witches on brooms, but he felt no spooks or spirits of uncertainty. No bats or black dogs. Tonight his life had been restored. Forever after he'd be swallowed up in her long smooth arms, the sound of her voice, her love for him and the love-making that was to come. She was right; they just needed time. Time spent circling round each other, like two goldfish in a bowl. Seeing the other coming, passing close and only allowing their bodies to tentatively touch until confidence returned.

The next day was clear and sunny, and they drove to Shingle Street; a long stone-banked stretch of coastline that was an even emptier place than Walberswick. The only other person in view was a lone man with a small dog at heel, trawling for hidden treasure with a metal detector. Clasping hands they made slow progress along the shore, shouting to each other above the sound of crashing waves. They stopped to throw stones into the sea and stood to watch its manifesting power. Its surface heaved in a mass of marbled and mottled grey. Diamond-bright hexagons appeared and vanished. It sucked in its breath, threw itself up and bragged its strength. Its force became positive, moving with an intense and purposeful anger, until its fury peaked. When it crashed its white foamy release there was calm. A peace. A momentary pause.

They hadn't noticed that the sky was becoming filled with black clouds. The sparkling on the sea disappeared, and the light changed to a sullen purple edged with luminous yellow. Heavy penny-sized raindrops started to fall. Out at sea thunder boomed like war-guns, and silver forks of lightning cracked on the horizon. They were enveloped in a vortex of friction. 'Quick. The Martello Tower,' she cried.

A shaky wooden drawbridge led to a heavy oak door. As they shut it behind them it creaked and groaned. One would have expected the long-abandoned Napoleonic stone tower to be damp and cold, but it was filled with a warm, solid air that smelled of tar, oil, and rancid fish. The floor was covered with piles of greasy chains, tangled nets, and small, rusty items of sailing ephemera. They leaned against the bare, circular walls, breathless from their sudden sprint. Above their heads, through the high, slitted windows a furious storm sky glowered to create a safe haven.

Joe wanted it to be slow and lasting but he knew it wouldn't be. A white blouse fluttered like an item on a clothes-line, the clink of a belt buckle, the sound of zips releasing, scrambling hands, wet untargeted kissing. They stumbled down together onto the floor, feeling hard, painful obstructions, but knowing that any pause to investigate would destroy the momentum. This would be a clumsy, uncoordinated performance, and their restricted limbs became confused. Who wanted what, and who was putting what where? But the muddled journey had been started and they were travelling too fast. He knew he was leaving her behind, and as he greedily circled his wings to his own dark and agonising place, his head was filled with the whistles and bangs of Thor. But he heard her voice calling above the thunder, the brass studs of her motorcycle boots dug painfully into his calves and her nails scratched his back.

Hard breathing and silence is the reward of passion, but their moment of descending peace was disturbed. The door flew open, and a wet, excited Jack Russell appeared, but his yapping was instantly silenced by the sight of them. The dog's owner then appeared at the door, briefly gaped, and turned abruptly on his heels.

Three months later Joe found himself as a house guest at The Old Vicarage, being introduced to his future father-in-law for the first time. Gordon proffered a long, firm handshake and a welcoming smile. 'Joe. Excellent to meet you at last. I've got a lot to thank you for. Doesn't she look radiant? It's the second time around for both of you, I gather, but I'm overjoyed that Anna's found happiness again. Heartiest congratulations.'

Gordon Morton Moore was an imposing man in an old English actor sort of way; clean-shaven and immaculate in the essential Simpsons weekend uniform of beige slacks, cream shirt, and a paisley cravat. He was friendly, hospitable, free-smiling and open. What a nice man he seemed.

A couple of weeks later he hosted a formal engagement party for them. Outside caterers, silver-service waitresses, champagne and witty speeches. A very smart county-set dinner party, full of people they would never meet again, including – not surprisingly – a bossy, power dressed siren who knew exactly where everything was kept in the kitchen. Apparently a very famous FT hack who spent the entire evening billing and cooing all over Gordon, and broadcasting what a brilliant shot/scubadiver/golfer/skier he was. Joe found he was suddenly a smart, middle class professional man, wearing a black dinner jacket, and his opinion sought on every minor malady the assembled company was suffering from.

Danny attended as a very special guest and sat at the table between Joe and Anna, enthralled with the ambience and enjoying the embraces and affection of his future stepmother. He never left their sides that night and walked with them down to the fish pool to view the dancing swerves of the koi carp; their flashes of gold and orange illuminated by floodlight. He clasped Anna's hand. 'I'm ever so glad you're getting married to my dad,' he said. 'He needs someone to tell him when to get his hair cut and when his shoes needs cleaning.'

'Oh, Danny,' Anna said, hugging him. 'I do hope I have a little boy like you one day. As a matter of fact (and she put her finger to her lips) this is a really big secret between you, me and Daddy. You're going to have a baby brother or sister after Christmas, but it really is our big secret. Not even Grandpapa Gordon knows yet.'

Danny spat on his palm. 'Old Unicorns stick together so mum's the word,' he said, giggling at his pun, but he suddenly threw his arms around Anna's waist, and buried his head deep in her belly. 'Is there really a baby inside you? Can it kick my hand?'

'No, darling,' Anna said. 'It's too small yet, but as soon as it can you'll be the first to feel it scoring goals for Tottenham.'

'The baby won't be a Jewish baby,' Joe told him. 'Anna isn't a Jew and she doesn't want to convert. You and I will be the only true Jews, but he or she will be just as loved and cherished within our family.'

Danny then turned to Anna, biting his lip, and shyly pulling out his words. 'Anna. If you're going to be my stepmother, and we're going to be a family, can I call you Mum? I'd really like to. Then me and my baby brother or sister will have the same mum.'

'Are you sure your real mother won't mind?'

'I don't care if she does mind. She lives in South Africa and I only see her in the school holidays. I have to go over there, because she says I've got to, but I don't want to go. She isn't like a real mummy. Not like you are.'

Both Joe and Anna turned their heads away, hiding the tears that suddenly stung their eyes.

That night diaries were studied. The wedding was duly arranged for six weeks time at the Oxford Register Office, and the reception would be held at Joe's beloved *Alma Mater*, Oriel College. Gordon had been most encouraging and enthusiastic. 'I'll come up to town and meet you at Claridge's next week, Joe. Cross the Ts and dot the Is regarding the wedding. Boys night out, eh? Perhaps sort out some sort of wedding present.'

The only wedding present Joe was offered was £50,000 to fuck off out of it.

The joyful wedding reception spilled out onto the lawns in front of the Senior Common Room, and Joe's family were awesomely impressed by Anna's father, the millionaire, the close friend of the prime minister, and recently knighted for services to charity. He spoke to them with condescending *noblesse oblige*, but in their eyes he was 'a lovely man, and a real toff'. After barely half an hour, though, he had to excuse himself as he had a plane to catch to Amsterdam. 'So sorry,' he announced to the humble crowd. 'Top level muster. You know how it is?' Oh, yes. Of course. Everyone knew exactly how it was, didn't they?

Joe's treasured wedding photograph was taken long after he'd left. The proud Israeli and his Venus are raising entwined glasses, accompanied by Danny, his mother, his father, Auntie Hilda and Uncle Harry, Felix and Nola, Jack and Naomi and Melvin and Rump-Hole, with Mitte and

Patte seated on small gilt chairs to honour their senior status and ageing bones. A laughing inebriated line-up showing off the outrageous hats, very serious gold (depicting the rising fortunes of the family) and the full clown slap. He, himself was dressed in a loose white collarless shirt that fell to his thighs, a silver sequined waistcoat, black trousers cuffed at the ankle and his sockless feet in North African leather moccasins. In order to especially irritate his father-in-law, he'd also worn a black *kippah* disc on his head. Anna wore a full bride's veil and a white kaftan, proudly displaying the gentle bulge of the twins.

Mazeltov!

CHAPTER FIFTEEN

Monday, continued . . .

S O. HERE WE GO. The moment you've all been waiting for. Anna is lying deep and peaceful in her induced sleep, so I undress and slip my clean *thobe* over my head. I'm now dressed the part, but my body has suddenly become alien to me and a strange sort of paralysis is affecting my skin. I scratch my head, but my skull feels numb. I'm neither of this world nor out of it. I feel as if I'm in a dream, but I have no intention of baulking at my opportunity. Having planned this operation down to the last detail, every stage direction must be carried out to the letter. I pad down the stairs, but I can't feel the carpet beneath my bare soles. I enter the drawing room to collect the silver bon-bon dish that will act as my ceremonial kidney bowl. I tip out the sugared almonds onto the closed lid of the grand piano, and the sound of crashing boulders reverberates around the room. I catch my breath with fear, but all restores to silence. I remount the stairs, holding the tools of my trade, and bravely sally forth. In three minutes time Gordon Morton Moore, bastard of this parish, will be stone cold dead. May he rest in turbulence.

CHAPTER SIXTEEN

Tuesday

6.00 a.m.

I EMERGE INTO THE GHOSTLY LIGHT of early dawn, bathed in sweat. Anna lies beside me, as still as an effigy in the church next door, the duvet obscuring her face. I won't wake her to say goodbye. Indeed, she's likely to sleep on until Queenie takes in Gordon's breakfast tray and discovers his corpse lying peacefully . . .

There'll be a serious period of panic and Dr Gibson will be telephoned. There'll be the usual declarations that dying in one's sleep is a perfect death, and Anna will ring me in a state of shock. Andrew Gibson will have a record of three recent professional medical attendances to Gordon for dizzy spells and collapse (Friday's attempt, Saturday's actual and the district nurse on Monday) and his recently prescribed medication for seriously high blood pressure. It will be presumed that the sudden death is due to a standard cardiovascular accident (CVA/stroke), and no suspicious circumstances will be considered in a man of such advanced age and poor state of health. Dr Gibson will sign Part One of the death certificate, and Gordon's body will be removed by an undertaker to a chapel of rest. A doctor from a different practice will be summoned to doubly confirm the death and, after examining the relevant notes, agree the cause. Once satisfied he/she will sign Part Two of the death certificate as per routine procedure. However, until the undertaker pumps

Gordon full of embalming fluid I won't be a contented man. I rise, wash and dress, but before I leave I restore the bon-bon dish and its contents to the grand piano.

At 9.00 a.m. I am behind my desk, ready for another routine day at Ravens Hill. My first patient is Joanie Bayliss. Yes, folks. It's the same Joanie Bayliss; the icon of my adolescence. Joanie's problem, apart from the eight stone she needs to lose, is the presence of her alcoholic slob of a husband. A woman trapped in a vicious circle of drunken beatings and deep, resigned misery. But she is, admirably, a keen member of The Ravens Hill Fringe Therapy Club; this having been set up by the partners in support and co-operation with the practice's social worker. So many of our patients are suffering the sort of problems the socio-medical team can do nothing for, and thus a range of bizarre 'therapies' are on offer. The hope is that the participants gain some sort of benefit – placebo or otherwise – and whilst I fully support, and recommend alternative medicine, such as acupuncture and homeopathy, I find some of the oddities on offer completely cuckoo.

For the last six weeks Joanie has been attending a weekly colour analysis class in an effort to understand herself.

"Allo, Joe,' she says, crashing down on the chair. 'Saw your kids the other night. They're a couple of live wires all right.'

'Yes. They duly reported back. Thanks for giving me a good press. They were suitably amazed that I ever had a morsel of human attraction. Now, my dear, what can I do for you?'

'I've got a problem with this colour malarkey, Joe,' she says. 'That Candice woman told me I'm blue. I thought she meant I've got the blues and all that stuff, but she said blue is a subterranean hiding, like what we do when we're under the water. Not being able to breathe, like.'

'Have you had any problems with your breathing, Joanie?'

'Not apart from a good old fag 'ack in the morning. That Candice said I must sit in the lotus and 'um it all out.'

'Did it have any effect?'

'Nar. Couldn't even get down on the floor. Then last week that Immelda tells me I'm green. I thought she meant the jealous colour like, but she says it means innocence and freshness, so she said I've got to go all girly again and do these little dances like I'm a fairy in a green wood. Fat chance of that.'

'I get the picture,' I say, 'but what really is the problem?'

'Well,' she sighs. 'Last night this Sharif tells me I'm yellow. What I thought was the coward colour like, but 'e says I'm 'iding a warm sunny nature. I 'ave a natural inner glow that needs to be revealed and I ought to sit in the lotus and smile.'

I shake my head. 'I'm not sure I'm grasping the gist of all this.'

'Neither am I, Joe. That's why I'm 'ere. It's all a load of bollocks.'

I can hardly agree with her, can I? Dr Fortune's low opinion of the Fringe Therapy Club will be all over the manor by teatime, doing my street cred no good at all. I thus choose my words with care. 'Look, it's obviously not doing you any good, is it? How's about you give something else a go?'

'Whatever you suggest. Sunita from the Bingo does that blindfold ballet stuff, but that's not me either, is it? What else is going on?'

I reach into my drawer to consult an ever-changing list. 'There's a new class starting next week that sounds just the ticket. An End-Of-The-Pier Comedy workshop. Could be a laugh (and could seriously do Joanie some good).'

'Go on, then. Put my name down.' She heaves herself to her feet. 'Thanks, duck. You're a bloody good'un. Ta-ta. Remember me to your mum and dad.'

Just as she leaves the room the phone rings. It's Anna! There's a shake and a tremble in her voice. 'Oh, Joe, I've got terrible news.'

I commiserate and comfort her. I promise I'll be back down to Monks Bottom as soon as possible. I say I'm so *very, very* sorry. I admit things have sometimes been quite difficult between her father and myself, but nevertheless I'm devastated. Dr Gibson has been informed and he's on his way. I say a very tender goodbye to her but when I replace the receiver my reaction is dramatic and unexpected. I call for an emergency cup of tea, and then collapse shakily onto my desk with head in hands. My receptionist arrives with the tea and is seriously alarmed by the sight of me, so she shoots off to find someone medically qualified. My practice nurse answers the call and the two of them raise me to my feet and steer me to an open window for deep breaths of fresh air.

The word spreads and the rest of the staff immediately rally round, thinking it's a classic case of grief, but I can't tell them it's something completely different, can I? My partners get out their diaries and start to reorganise surgeries, imagining that I'll want to assume the role of grieving son-in-law and supportive husband (half right). I'm to leave after lunch. I'm to take two or three days off to organise things and hold the fort. My partners are good kind people but I somehow suspect they're delighted to see the back of me for a few days.

Having just spoken to Joe, Anna stands mesmerised, numb and disbelieving. The news of her father's death, although only ten minutes old, has passed in both a flash of compressed time and a long, slow, contemplative tableau. Queenie had tiptoed into his room as usual with the morning tea tray, but within seconds her horrified screaming rent the air. She collapsed sobbing into Anna's arms and for a few gasping and gulping moments was unable to convey the devastating news that she'd found him stone cold dead in bed. Anna can't possibly explain why this joyous news caused her to sink down onto her knees and sob intensely too. At last. At last. The padlocks were released and the chains fell to the floor. For the first time in her life she was free. When she spoke to Dr Gibson she was controlled and sensible, but she felt as if she was someone else, and she was talking about someone else's drama.

Cyril is summoned and is quietly supportive to both her and Queenie. 'I'll stay and see 'im taken safely away,' declares Queenie, through a vale of tears. 'It's the least I can do. Ten years come Christmas I've been 'appy to see 'im right. He was a wonderful old gentleman.'

After Dr Gibson has left, Anna phones the undertakers and they arrive within the hour. Once they've heaved and trollied the corpse downstairs the three mourners line up on the drive to watch the shiny black Bedford van disappearing out of sight. One actress daughter, doing sober-faced and devastated, one genuinely heartbroken housekeeper and one kind, supportive gardener, whose delight, Anna suspects, is just as great as her own. 'Take Queenie home, Cyril,' she says. 'Give her a drop of brandy and make her rest up. I'll make sure Joe comes across to check her over later. We'll talk again tomorrow.' The two of them amble off slowly.

Anna waits a few minutes and then walks to the top of the drive goes through the big iron gates and turns into the churchyard. A hole will be dug there shortly to accommodate the remains of Sir Gordon Morton Moore, but it's not his future resting place that she seeks to examine. She's come to talk to Hugo. She sinks to her knees in front of the heavy marble headstone with the plain gold lettering. Lain at its foot are the sun-wilted bunch of flowers she picked for him on Sunday night.

'Dear Hugo. You were as much a victim as I. Today I need to share my elation with you, because it must be your elation too. My poor brother, so beaten and cowed and demoralised. Do you remember how we longed for him to die? After we'd made our forbidden love we would sit up and face each other. We would lock our legs together in a mirror image of Buddha, your chin resting on my shoulder, my chin resting on yours. We would talk and talk it through. "You see, Annie," you used to say. "I know these things. I've read everything I can about it. It's all to do with power. He's really a howling coward so he has to force his domination on the weak. He's sick. Sick in the head and in the soul. What we do isn't sick. It's because we love each other and need each other."

'Every time the hate came out a little more. Our lost childhoods analysed. We built a bonfire of our loathing, and hoisted Papa on top to be burned like a guy. Knifed in the heart. Sprayed with burning oil. Poisoned to writhe in agony. Beaten to a pulp. Held over a wall and a red-hot poker rammed up his arse. Do you remember we reenacted *Repulsion?* I bludgeoned him on the head with a candlestick and I slashed him with a razor. But our forever favourite was castration, wasn't it? That was the best one. Listening to his agonised screams and begging us to have mercy on him. Mercy? Oh, please! We put his legs in stirrups and we did each tiny cut slowly with a Stanley knife. We dabbed his gaping wounds with battery acid, and threw both testicles to the sparrow hawks that circled the meadow. And what of Mummy, Hugo? I've hidden her away, refused to think about what she did. It wasn't what she did, but what she didn't do. She turned her back and drowned in a vat of alcohol. She knew, but she let it go on. How could a mother do that? Was it fear of Papa? Rape and beatings? But she knew what torture our lives were, and she did nothing.

'I can't remember when it started, Hugo. Probably long before I was old enough to have memories, but the first time I really recall was when we were on holiday at the villa near Frejus. I was seven. You and me had had a lovely day in the swimming pool, and we were sitting on my bed together, looking at some French story-books. There was one about a funny little lady, dressed in green, called Beccasine. There was one about a boy called Tin-Tin who had adventures with a little white dog, and another about a funny little Gaul in Roman times called Asterix. We couldn't read the French words, but we liked the pictures and made up our own stories. Papa came in. He told you it was time to go to sleep, and sent you to your own room. When it got dark he came back to me.

'Even when I was seven I thought it must be wrong, but how could it be wrong when Papa said it was all right, and grown-ups are always right, aren't they? It only ever happened in the pitch-black dark, so we never saw each other. He said kind words with a gentle voice. Slow, coaxing words and he gave me lots of kisses. It was the only time I can ever remember him being nice to me. "It's our little secret, Anna." What he did was horrible, but Papa said it was what all daddies did to their little girls if they loved them, but it had to be our secret. I could feel Papa's hair tickling me and the smell of grease and lavender and tobacco. His fingers where his fingers shouldn't be. A hard, warm thing like a baby's arm pushed into my little hand. Heavy breathing and groaning and moving. His voice always told me that I was a good girl, and he loved me. I would lie there, rigid with terror, having to bear the pain. In daylight it was as if all the terrible things that happened had never happened. He was a different father, and I was a different daughter, and we lived on a planet a million miles from the one in the pitch black dark. But I was obscenely robbed. My childhood stolen from me by an evil bastard who dared to pose as my parent.

'It was our horrible secret until I was thirteen. One day his fingers touched blood and he never came back. You told me what you'd read about monsters like Papa, didn't you? You said my body had grown up and men like Papa could only get excitement by overpowering an innocent child. Men like Papa thought that all grown-up women were tainted tarts, and now I had grown up I was a tainted tart too. You told me I wasn't dirty. You told me I was beautiful. You saved me, Hugo, but there was something else that saved me, and I only realised it long after I'd grown up. When you're a child, and even at thirteen you're still a child, you don't know anything about the world of reason and analysis. Things just happen to you. Of course you're damaged, and of course the filth saturates you, and of course you hold hatred in your heart, but you have no strengths or ability to change the situation. You're overpowered because adults are still the controllers, the perpetrators, the rulers. You can be shouted at and manipulated and defiled and abused, and there is nothing – nothing – you can do about it. That was my saving grace. I could do nothing to stop it, and by that token I am exonerated. I was, and I am, innocent.

'And then in the midst of the other hatreds – the beatings and the sarcasm and neglect – we found the pleasure of each other. The time twixt innocence and maturity when you begin to have the strength to put away childish things. We became each other's loving secret; our drug, our free cocaine, our LSD, our inhaled or injected narcotic. You obsessed me in my youth, but eventually our time was over. We grew up and moved on and I gave all my love to Joe. The body I gave him had surged into a woman with curves, and melon breasts and soft flesh on my limbs. This woman had no part of the abused child and the incestuous sister. Dear Hugo. I have found it in my heart to forgive you for Joanna's death, and I still love you. Your addictions were only the answer to your own damage and you paid with your life.'

She rises from her knees and walks back to the house.

After I have finished morning surgery, I have another long and loving conversation with Anna. She sounds very much more together and practical. Andrew Gibson has declared the cause of death to be CVA, and has duly signed Part One. Hooray! The undertakers have collected the body. Hooray with knobs on! I phone the twins to give them the sad news that their grandpapa has passed away, and although they make appropriate noises of sympathy we quickly run out of sorrowful things to say. 'Please phone your mother and be very sensitive,' I say. 'She's had a huge shock.' They say they will, but more important things spring to mind. Like 'are we going to inherit pots of money?' The answer is yes (and it's a very big yes) but it's a secondary perk of my done deed.

My practice manager then appears at the door in a sweet and tender mode for her grieving senior partner. 'How are you feeling, Joe?' she asks. 'I can pop out and get you some lunch if you're up to it.' Can it really be lunchtime? I'm suddenly very hungry and she goes to Giovanni's New York Diner for a double ciabatta of pastrami and salad, with Philly and avocado, embellished with mayo. I also order a square of their lovely gooey, fudge brownie, and a carton of *latte*. Why not? I'm fully recovered from my wobbly patch. I'm suddenly so happy I want to jump on my desk and do a little dance, but I must stay in character a bit longer.

While I'm eating I'm compelled to phone Anna to find out what's going on. Her mobile's turned off and although I ring ten times on the landline, there's no reply. She can't have gone out, can she? Where are the Croftens? After lunch I pick up my medical bag and prepare to leave. A sea of genuinely concerned faces smiles at me with sympathy and understanding. Reassurances that I'm to take off as much time as need be to 'sort things out'. Universal and heartfelt messages are sent to Anna from those who've known her, and loved her, for so many years.

I turn the Discovery into The Old Vicarage, but there are no running steps on the gravel and no hair in my face. I have to look for her. She's sitting down by the fish pool, hugging her knees in contemplation, but when she sees me she gets up and walks slowly towards me, her face serene and holding a Mona Lisa smile. Our embrace is long, loving and tender, with no words of remorse to acknowledge the situation. 'Any news of Part Two?' I ask tentatively.

'No. It's just routine, isn't it? Come and sit with me in the kitchen. I'm star dazed. The Croftens are at home so we're on our own, thank God. Let's have a cup of tea and you can help me fall to earth.'

We sit simply together at the kitchen table, with a large pot of tea and a plate of Queenie's home-made rock cakes, but the atmosphere is curiously loaded. 'You always hated him, didn't you?' she says.

'Do I have to admit to hate?'

'Not if you don't want to, but something happened. I know it did. Tell me. Nothing matters any more.'

'Do you remember, when we first got back together I asked you if you'd ever received a letter from me when we broke up in '79?'

'I remember you asking me.'

'It all started with that letter. I brought it down here myself, hoping to find you. I had Daniel with me. I'd grieved so much for you, I was wrecked. I looked like a tramp. There was an old gardener here; a ghastly old codger with a dripping nose. He said you were ill and that you'd been taken to Switzerland to recover. I gave him the letter and he promised to give it to your father. It was supposed to be sent on to you, but of course it wasn't. It was a begging letter. The one and only love letter I've ever written. I poured my heart out in a pathetic attempt to get you back. It was my last chance. I found out later that your father opened it, and read it, and decided in his wisdom that a bit of rough trade like me would never be allowed to breathe on you. None of it would have happened if you'd got the letter, would it? You'd have come back to me.'

Anna covers my hand with hers. 'I wish I could say yes,' she says, 'but at the time things just seemed so final, so hopeless. I was crushed – completely overruled. I was only just nineteen, Joe. Practically the same age as Sophie, with none of the freedom and confidence that girls like her know these days. All I made of it was that Urshie must have loved you and if I'd taken you away Daniel would have been a bone between two rabid dogs. I was afraid of ruining his life. I had no right to you and I had to leave. There was so much else as well. So much you don't know.'

'Anna,' I say. 'I *do* know. He told me.'

'He told you what?'

'About your abortion. He told me, Annie. Just before we got married.'

'What abortion?'

She's staring at me, her face half a smile and half a glare. I take her hand and kiss her palm. 'My love, it's OK. That night I met your father at Claridge's. He told me he knew I was the man who brought the letter. He had me taped on CCTV and he recognised me. Who could mistake my Israeli features? Of course he deduced I must have been responsible for the mess you were in. He called me a dirty, fortune hunting bastard. A Jew boy without a pot to piss in. He offered me 50,000 quid to dump you.'

She shakes her head from side to side. 'What a bastard.'

'And he told me about the abortion. But I never blamed you. I know things must have seemed irreparable and impossible, but I've always blamed *him*. If you'd got the letter you wouldn't have done it, would you? Tell me. Really, it's OK. I understand.'

'I've never had an abortion,' she says, unemotionally. 'It's all nonsense.'

'Anna,' I say. 'There won't be a row. I just had to tell you that I know, and it's all part of our past. It was why they sent you to Switzerland, wasn't it? To hide you away and get you sorted.'

She's angry. She's agitated. She gets up and moves about old-movie style, jerking her body with fast movements. She touches walls, she touches surfaces, she picks up a tea cloth and swipes it on the sink. She turns on a tap and turns it off, she touches the kettle, she touches the teapot. She comes up to me and shoves me in the shoulder so hard my chair nearly tips back. She yells at me with fury. She's never shouted at me, or been violent in any way, and I'm terrified.

'I have *never* had an abortion, Joe! Either your child or anyone else's. It's a lie. A filthy lie. Oh, for God's sake, you've got to believe me. How could you ever have thought I'd have got rid of our child?'

Her face is flushed, her eyes are shimmering and she looks the most beautiful I've ever seen her. She takes a little gold Rockingham cup from the dresser and hurls it against the wall. She picks up another one and hurls it at me, but fortunately it misses and lands on the flag-stoned floor. It crashes in tandem with her sobbing, and she runs from the room. I know I should run after her, but I don't. I must let her be. She'll calm down and come to terms with things. She'll be able to accept my forgiveness and admit her denial. I have to give her time.

Anna thinks about Joanna so many times a day, when her head is free. Perhaps when she's preparing vegetables, or stuck in a traffic jam, or just dropping off to sleep. Sometimes she drifts off into a reverie and Joe asks her what she's dreaming about. She just smiles and says she's tired. Joanna would be twenty-six now – a little younger than the age Anna married her father. Would she be quiet and reticent like herself, friendly and loving like Daniel, or would she be bold and fearless like Joe and the twins. Would she have long flowing hair down her back? Would it be like her own straight silky blonde or Joe's coal black curls. She wonders if she'd wear blue jeans and motorcycle boots. Would she make love in a Martello Tower? When she was born Anna showed her a photograph of Joe with the queen, to make sure she knew what her daddy looked like. The same photograph that still sits on the bedside table at Sunny Lea, with the wisps of her hair taped inside. The handful of earth she took from her grave lies hidden inside a wooden box at the back of her underwear drawer. She is always with them, as they breathe and hold each other in the night. 'Joanna, your daddy didn't know about you. Is the time now right for me to tell him?'

Anna's fury becalms. She moves her limbs, and turns her neck. The chains have gone and already she feels a stretching freedom. No weights to carry. Her life is now her own.

I remain seated at the kitchen table, drumming my fingers and feeling a ticklish sort of shaking in my thighs. Well, have I got away with it or not? I stuff a fourth rock cake in my mouth for the want of something to do. Cigar? Drink? Spliff? No – not even my usual anxiety props will be of any help.

Why doesn't the bloody phone ring? I want to hear the respectful voice of the undertaker wanting to discuss funeral arrangements. I want to hear from Andrew Gibson that the death certificate is ready for collection. We may even have a little chat and discuss our proposed job swap, but all I can do is sit and wait and worry. I can hardly ring the undertaker myself enquiring about the state of a corpse. 'Hi, this is Dr Joe Fortune speaking. Just enquiring after my father-in-law, Sir Gordon Morton Moore. Is everything all right?' Why should everything *not* be all right? Just the routine death of a sick, old man. The body should now be spread-eagled on a trolley. Both parts of the magical death certificate would be signed, and placed indifferently in a clean white envelope. The undertaker would be getting to work with pumps and tubing and buckets. Perhaps chatting idly to a colleague about cricket scores, or contemplating the progress of his onions and delphiniums. His afternoon's work would be just one more wrinkled and decrepit old has-been that he's been emptying and repacking over his career? My heart pounds and vomit rises in my throat. Fuck, why are my hands shaking. Ring, phone, ring.

Anna comes into the kitchen. She's walks tall, with a strong, positive grace. She's changed her clothes, brushed her hair and remade her face. 'I'm sorry,' she says, sliding her arms around my shoulders. 'I'm all on edge today.'

'Me too,' I say.

'Thanks for turning down the fifty grand.'

'S'alright, lady,' I say with my mock Humphrey Bogart.

'He was even more evil than I gave him credit for. And ...'
She looks at me sadly. Her eyes are soft, her face is straight and
I know she's telling the truth. 'The abortion, Joe. *It was a lie.*
Truly. After I left you on that awful day I went straight to The
Hartington to get examined. They patched me up and sedated
me and kept me in all night. The next day I was discharged
and I planned to come back here, take what money I could
find and just disappear to Hugo in the States. But it all went
wrong. They'd come back early from Scotland, so I was
trapped. He went through my bag, found the hospital bill and
thought I'd had . . . but I hadn't. He confronted me. I tried to
deny it, but he wouldn't believe me. That's the truth.'

I find it difficult to speak and to find the words that will
reassure her. To concede that I know she's telling the truth,
but I don't want to. My daily thoughts have always been for
my lost child. The block of pain I've carried around has been
there so long it's like a hump on my back. Now I have to
unstrap it. Cast it loose. Abandon it. Send it away and forget
about it. I don't think I can do it. I don't think I want to do it. I
want to keep the memory of the child who has become so
real to me.

'Have you spent the last twenty years thinking about our
child that never was?' she asks.

'Yes,' I say. 'Everyday. It became a habit. A way of life.
Like a little ghost that always sat on my shoulder.'

'Me too,' she says.

'What do you mean?'

'I mean I always wished we'd had a third child.'

306

'Not too late, you know. Chances are we can still get another one in.'

'No, Joe. Dan's baby's on the way, and in the fullness of time the twins will oblige. We'll be on our own soon. Just us. That'll do for me. But do you know what I'd really like to do when we've got the funeral out of the way? I'd like to take you to Carrickmore.' She eases herself onto my knee. She's crying softly but she takes my face in her hands. 'Now kiss me, rough trade.'

The phone starts ringing but it takes us several seconds to untangle ourselves. It's Andrew Gibson. 'Hi, Joe. Just to let you know that the bloods from yesterday showed the old chap was really hitting the juice, so we can close the book. Familiar pattern of CVA. The death cert's ready for collection at the surgery. Give me a ring when things are back to normal. I'd like to talk some more about that job swap.'

I replace the receiver. My legs then buckle and I sink down onto my knees, moaning like a storm wind.

'Oh, for God's sake, Joe,' Anna shrieks. 'What's the matter?'

I kiss the flagstones like a Muslim worshipper and begin to laugh. I then turn over to sit on my butt with the biggest, stupidest smile of delight. 'I am so fucking happy,' I say, wiping tears of blessed relief from my face.

The doorbell jangles. Complaining voices and banging. 'Where the hell is everyone?' Sophie and Josh. Huge bunch of flowers for Anna. Cigar for me. We get the message. I find a bottle of champagne in the fridge. Pop goes the cork. After some merry small talk, and plans to go out later and eat at the

307

Lebanese restaurant in Henley, we raise our flutes in a toast to no one. Cheers. An unspoken admittance that Gordon Morton Moore won't be missed for one second by any of us.

* * *

So here we are. Bedtime, and journey's end. Joe and Anna sink gratefully down into the four-poster, inebriated and breathing garlic fire. It's been a long, eventful day, but they embrace, kiss, and begin to slither their way into making gentle, but life-confirming love. The silence is a rare and precious thing. All the ghosts and spirits and crones of the jostling crowd have had their marching orders and have filed off in an orderly line. The black wings have flown away and the black paws have padded off to find pastures new. No chains and padlocks remain. Now they are free; free to find a perfect version of their own peculiar freedom, and they will, dear friend. Rest assured, they will.

Let us leave them quietly or they might hear us. At last they've got The Crowded Bed to themselves.

www.transita.co.uk

transita

To find out more about Mary Cavanagh and other
Transita authors and their books, visit the website for:

- News of author events and forthcoming titles

- Exclusive features and interviews with authors

- Free extras from the books

- Special offers and discounts

- The lively Transita chat group